WHEN YOU FIND ME

WHEN YOU FIND ME

P. J. Vernon

CROOKED LANE

NEW YORK

Published in the United States by Crooked Lane Books, an imprint of The Quick Brown Fox & Company LLC.

Crooked Lane Books and its logo are trademarks of The Quick Brown Fox & Company LLC.

Library of Congress Catalog-in-Publication data available upon request.

ISBN (hardcover): 978-1-68331-749-4
ISBN (ePub): 978-1-68331-750-0
ISBN (ePDF): 978-1-68331-751-7

Cover design by Erin Seaward-Hiatt
Book design by Jennifer Canzone

Printed in the United States.

www.crookedlanebooks.com

Crooked Lane Books
34 West 27th St., 10th Floor
New York, NY 10001

First Edition: October 2018

10 9 8 7 6 5 4 3 2 1

For Barry.
Never meant to be has never been so much.

1

Gray

I wasn't in the right headspace for home. I wasn't in the right headspace for most things, but certainly not for that house—Piper Point. Not for Mamma's company. Not for what I'd distanced myself from.

The turbulent flight from D.C. had left my nerves rattled, and the insides of my cheeks still stuck to my teeth. The faint scent of gasoline touched nearly everything in that claustrophobic cabin. I'd reminded myself the smell was normal, but I still drowned in thoughts of flammable jet fuel.

You're so given to scaring, Gray. Mamma's words played on a loop in my mind the entire trip.

The drive from Charleston to Elizabeth, South Carolina, clocked in at half an hour, give or take. The closer our rental car drew to home, the tighter my chest knotted.

My phone read three thirty in the afternoon. "Plenty of time to make the Christmas Eve service," I announced to my husband. I didn't believe in God, but Mamma could be insufferable. When it came to forcing me into a church, she became divinely so.

"And for you to take a nap," Paul replied, eyes on the road, undoubtedly confident that his displeasure for my drinking had registered. I turned to the steepled skyline streaming by in fits and starts.

I'd gotten a head start at the bar across from our gate at Reagan National. A nine ounce pour of buttery chardonnay to take the edge off the plane ride. That's how I'd sold the first one to Paul.

Now he fumbled with his phone, one thumb dancing across the screen while he white-knuckled the steering wheel with his free hand. What was so important that he needed to text and drive? Who was so important?

I considered asking him—coming right out and asking—but he assumed I was drunk. When I drank, I forfeited credibility with Paul. Even if I pressed him, he wouldn't feel compelled to answer me. Not truthfully.

Instead, I prepared myself to see Mamma like a prodigal daughter sneaking home after a party. But I was twenty-nine.

My Kate Spade purse open between my knees, I unzipped the clear bag for liquids that I'd tucked inside it for the flight. Perfume, eye drops, two single-serve bottles of white wine—I hovered so Paul wouldn't see them—and a travel-sized container of peppermint mouthwash.

I gargled the mouthwash and spit into an empty water bottle. I didn't need to swallow everything with a measurable proof. Three mists of perfume to my neckline. Three was one too many, but I was trading Mamma's disdain for a simple crinkled nose. Wincing, I sprayed once in my mouth. Metallic flavors stuck to my tongue like bitter glue.

"You smell fresh," Paul said, returning his phone to his pocket and noting my wedding ring. "Have your ring cleaned while we're in town. Heart disease fundraiser's next week."

I turned my ring with my thumb. Three carats of cushion-cut diamond. Flawless. Near-colorless. Only perfection for me, he'd said when he proposed.

"No white Christmas this year," Paul added. "Not like D.C."

"No," I muttered.

He took the exit for Elizabeth, and the pines and low palmetto trees gave way to a quaint town, an unsubtle mix of colonial and Low Country. Only the presence of a downtown Dairy Queen kept Elizabeth from camera-readiness in a Civil War film.

A Dairy Queen and a billboard. The picture caught my eye, stuck to the board in fraying paper sheets, and panic bloomed, wrapping my fingers and toes in tingles. A handsome man with coifed hair and a distinctive Roman nose. His smile, jarring. My cousin, Matthew King. Attorney.

As a sour taste joined the lingering perfume on my tongue, I scolded myself for not recalling that the dated billboard stood there. For not remembering that Matthew's face would greet me when we turned into town. As the image shrunk in the rearview mirror, I softened my grip on the door handle and exhaled a long, staggered breath.

We cut a left down Main Street, passing Mamma's church, Blessed Lamb Baptist. Then civilization vanished again into bare tobacco fields beneath ash skies. Atalaya Drive was a bumpy road. Not gravel, but not exactly paved, either. Like the rest of South Carolina, it wasn't sure what it wanted to be. Short trees and tall grass to one side, saltwater marshes on the other.

From Atalaya Drive, you could see Piper Point for nearly a mile before arriving. Beneath an overcast sky, the house sat like a rotting log concealing secrets beneath its moist belly. A malignant

3

tumor latched onto the surrounding marsh-side bluff. The King family home. My family home.

Named for the sandpipers and killdeer that flitted about the property, Piper Point was a white antebellum with a double wraparound porch. Six Corinthian columns supported a steep roof dotted with half as many dormers. The Christmas candles in each window did little to lessen its long shadow. They turned the home into a twisted jack-o'-lantern. Ready to swallow me whole. Ancient oaks wept Spanish moss, and the palm fronds kept their green well into winter. The whole scene could be picturesque, and growing up, it mostly was. I'd etched it into my memory that way on purpose. But I'd put more than simple distance between myself and Piper Point.

Skidding against gravel, Paul braked halfway round Piper Point's circle drive. He parked behind Charlotte's Mercedes SUV. My sister had driven in from Raleigh. She'd done well for herself after the divorce, and I was happy for her.

Before I managed to step out of our car, the front door opened, and a rail-thin woman no older than thirty walked towards us. The new housekeeper Mamma had gone on about.

"Hello, Gray. Paul." Her smile lit up an otherwise mousey face. "I'm Cora. I'm your mother's new live-in."

I nodded a hello as she stepped to the rear of the car where Paul hoisted our bags onto the driveway. The fact that Cora was a white woman relieved me. I know it did the same for Paul. Mamma had no concern for optics. *The blacks* in town loved her, she repeated fondly. Too often.

Mamma had little to worry about in Elizabeth, but Paul and I were different. We lived in D.C., where optics were all that counted, and even more so with Paul's political future. The wooden steps up the front porch creaked beneath my ballerina flats.

Since Daddy passed, Mamma had ignored much of the home's upkeep. A bizarre oversight for a woman preoccupied with appearance. And the closer one got to Piper Point, the more apparent the neglect became. White siding peeled like curling fingernails. One upstairs window wouldn't close and another had been painted shut forever. Snaking vines withered into stringy skeletons rather than grow lush.

Crossing the threshold, the air inside struck me first. It was the same stale air my family had breathed for two centuries. So stagnant mosquitoes could breed in it.

In the foyer, sliding parlor doors cordoned off the joint dining room and salon to my left and the library on my right. Ahead, the staircase climbed to a second story with slouching steps, plateauing in a landing halfway up.

"I'll take your things to Gray's room," Cora announced.

"I'll help you," Paul replied, refusing to hand over our rollers. "This isn't *Downton Abbey*. Despite what Joanna thinks." What people thought mattered quite a bit to Paul. In that way, he wasn't so different from Mamma. And they got along well. Well enough for the occasional, "Be kind to your mom, Gray," to fly from Paul's lips.

The only family he had left, an invalid mother, recognized his face less and less over time. I guessed Mamma took on an outsized importance to him because of it. Sometimes at my expense. But even he'd been unusually eager to get me out of the city. The suspicion I held over his phone extended to this, too.

"Where's Mamma?" I asked Cora as she started up the groaning stairs behind Paul.

"In the kitchen," she answered. "Making your favorite, if I'm not mistaken. Banana pudding. Charlotte's out back with the twins."

They abandoned me in the foyer. Clutching my handbag and the wine nestled inside it, I made for the kitchen. As I passed the polished stairs, I caught my reflection in the mirror on the landing. The swollen knot in my chest pulled tighter.

At least ten feet tall, the enormous piece of glass was set into the wall, stretching up from the baseboard. Crown moldings—*prewar*, Daddy called them—framed the immense mirror. In Manhattan, prewar meant before World War II. In South Carolina, we had longer memories. Daddy had the mirror taken down and stored in the cellar decades ago when it first broke, but Mamma must've set it back into the wall at some point, strangely unrestored. A single crack cut diagonally from one side to the other in a near-perfect line. It gave the appearance of a guillotine. Top and bottom blades meeting like clenched teeth.

A tingle crossed the nape of my neck.

Moving to the kitchen, the sound of a wooden spoon beating a bowl greeted me. Mamma could never be idle when guests arrived. The moment she'd heard our car pull around, she'd likely sprinted to the pantry, squawking at Cora that she planned to make banana pudding. My favorite.

"Hummingbird." She smiled as I stepped onto the tiled floor. "If I had known you'd be here so soon, I would've had this pudding done an hour ago," she lied.

Mamma had aged well. She'd let her hair fade to a sophisticated silver which she styled meticulously. Her breath was always scented spearmint with whispers of cigarette. A string of pearls hung in a graceful knot from her neck, no matter the outfit. An iridescent hangman's noose.

"How was your trip?" Her drawl had thickened with time.

"It was okay. Bumpy."

She sat the bowl on the counter and paced towards me. "It'll be so wonderful to have you and Paul and Charlotte and the kids together at church." Mamma's way of decreeing we would each be attending the Christmas Eve service, even though I'd already planned on it.

She squeezed me in an embrace that grew tighter the older she got. She never hugged me so close when I lived at Piper Point.

"There's alcohol on your breath, Gray." The hug vanished as she recoiled. "I can smell it through the perfume you've splashed all over yourself."

I stood silently as my face flushed. Very rarely did I resent Mamma for telling the truth. She'd had a difficult relationship with it my whole life. But the instant honesty became convenient, she wielded it like a dagger.

"Paul's spoken to me more than once about your drinking. You think you can hide it by swimming in fragrance? You smell like a drunk who got hold of too much cologne."

I cleared my throat in an attempt to stifle embarrassment. At once, I was a child again—a bad girl—the tips of my ears burning after being caught misbehaving. "I don't like flying. I drink when I'm nervous."

"Save the perfume next time." She pursed her lips, scowling. "And have a cup of coffee. Jesus might've spent time with drunks, but I'd rather not bring one to church."

Itching to change the subject, I looked over her shoulder, outside. "Cora said Charlotte's out back?"

"She is. Brush your teeth before you kiss those twins."

Mamma's voice and its distinct edge dwindled as I spied the door to the cellar. I locked my knees and whitened my knuckles around the strap of my handbag.

Perhaps it was being a little day drunk or maybe just the feeling of being home again—choking me with invisible hands—but for an instant, I was nine years old. Standing before the cellar door while Matthew loomed behind. His belt buckle pressing into the back of my skull. He turned the brass handle and pushed the door open. A lurching groan like a foundering ship followed a wave of cold air. Moist and musty.

I shook my head and the cruel memory away. But the ground still rocked and swayed beneath my feet.

Go on down, Gray. Go see where the Devil lives.

2

Gray

Spots danced before my eyes. I'd arrived only moments ago, and I already craved fresh air. *Mamma said Charlotte's out back*. Clasping my throat, I made my way to her.

Dead ferns in porcelain planters and one Christmas tree, very much still alive, stood in the conservatory off the kitchen. Passing through, I stumbled out of the French doors and onto the patio. The brick courtyard beyond had been better maintained than the rest of the house. I guess Mamma kept a landscaper on payroll.

Taking deep breaths, I passed the babbling fountain that served as the garden's centerpiece. A stone angel with lichen-covered wings spit an arc of icy water.

At high tide, the water's edge stopped twenty yards or so from here. But now, only saw grass and festering mud surrounded Piper Point's naked dock. Charlotte tossed a foam football with her children, Joseph and David, in the crabgrass a safe distance from the marsh.

She spotted me approaching.

"Gray," she shouted, waving both arms. "Merry Christmas!"

"Charlotte," I said, taking my sister by the hands as I reached her. I seemed to find a mooring again, and my anxiety uncoiled a little. "Look at you. You look lovely." I was thin, but Charlotte was thinner. She'd always been bony, and the divorce hadn't helped.

A couple sharp "Aunt Grays" sounded as my nephews latched onto me, a four-year-old on each leg. Runny noses and two shaggy mops of soft hair. I gave one a shoulder squeeze and the other a head pat. I couldn't distinguish between the boys and had given up trying.

"I missed you," one said.

"Me too," said the other, coughing from the sprint over. "Christmas is tomorrow, and Mom told Santa to bring presents here instead of our house."

"I'm sure she did, and I'm certain Santa will. I missed you guys." A pang of guilt shot through me as I avoided naming them. "So much."

Charlotte retrieved the football and tossed it towards the courtyard, sending them both chasing after it.

"You can't tell them apart, can you?" Charlotte asked. From her tone, I was unsure if she was genuinely offended.

"You know that's not true."

She deftly changed topics. "Have you seen old Hattie? I can't believe she's still alive."

Hattie the Cattie. The sharp guilt from not naming the twins blossomed into something worse. I'd forgotten about Hattie.

"Queen of the Lost Cats of Piper Point," I added. She'd be an astounding twenty years old now. "Where is she?"

"Funny she's the only one that stuck around." Charlotte motioned behind my left shoulder. "Maybe she's the monster that killed all her brothers and sisters that year."

I turned, and sure enough, the cat crept through the grass,

cautiously headed my way. A tangled mess of mottled black and white fur, she stalked as though unsure if I was still an ally. Hardly the monster Charlotte joked she was.

"Don't bring her in the house." she chuckled, but she wasn't kidding. "The boys are just as allergic as I am."

Though survival was never guaranteed for yard cats, Hattie had been the only one of her unnamed mother's litter to make it. In fact, every kitten *but* Hattie had vanished the year I turned nine. The mamma cat, too. And the shrill cries of the tomcats went silent shortly after, like something had chased them all off or killed them or both.

After outlasting the others, Hattie—as I came to call her—deserved a little pampering. I made a habit of stealing her away to my bedroom. But whenever she'd been inside, Charlotte's eyes started watering and her throat tightened. She hated the two of us for it.

The mottled cat threaded herself through my legs in a figure eight. I stroked her back. In an instant, Hattie transformed from lingering ghost to companion.

"I'm still your friend," I whispered, running my nails down her knotty spine.

Charlotte sighed impatiently. "We'd better get ready for church." She started for the house, but paused. "You doing alright these days, Gray?" The earnestness of her question startled me. But she'd been here for a day already. Plenty of time to fill with talk from Mamma.

"Of course, I'm okay," I answered, standing up and forcing a grin. "I'm gonna walk out on the dock, and then I'll be in for a bath and a change."

Charlotte crinkled her nose. "That stinking thing? Low tide's grown nothing but smellier."

I smiled at her again as she collected her boys and made for the house. When they'd vanished inside, I turned back to the marshes. Charlotte was right. They stank like briny vomit.

Dusk settled over Piper Point, and the planks groaned as if in pain as I walked to the end of the dock. To each side, swarms of frail sand crabs darted across pocked mud. People said you could sail all the way to New York City without ever venturing out to sea via the Intracoastal Waterway, of which our marsh was an extension. I didn't know if that was true. I'd never bothered to check.

Hattie had followed me to the water before stopping at the shoreline. Now she cried, calling me back to the safety of land. As a rising moon tugged on the tide, the slopping murk began its creep back towards the house. Barnacled pylons shouldering the dock's final planks stood in lapping seawater again. Gulls cried in shrill squawks, and the salt in the air did little to mask the stench of rot. Useless, like my perfume.

*　*　*

My bedroom hadn't changed a lick.

Mamma called it the Yellow Room. She'd had the walls painted a calming canary and strewn yolk-colored pillows everywhere. Charlotte had the Red Room, done accordingly in hues of scarlets. The Green and Blue Rooms were for guests—Cora took the colorless carriage house.

Mamma's preoccupation with colored bedrooms stemmed from Daddy's failed presidential bid. She'd never live in the White House, so she'd done her best to replicate what parts of it she could at Piper Point.

Daddy had flamed out early in the Republican primaries, failing to clench even a third of South Carolina's vote. If he couldn't win his home state, there'd been no point pressing on. It was a spectacular failure, and he had only himself to blame. Himself and a tape recorder.

I sat my handbag on my white wicker dresser—a juvenile piece I'd always resented. I don't know how it survived the transition into the Yellow Room, but my dislike probably played a role in its sticking around. Like the mirror on the stair landing.

Paul lay on the bed, legs crossed over one another, eyes on his phone. He was so guarded around it. He kept it far from my fingers, and it bothered me. Was he still messaging work? If he was so afraid he'd miss something important, why would he drag me back here in the first place?

"You haven't been home in a long time, Gray," Paul had told me weeks earlier. "Show up, hug your mother, strike it off the to-do list for another decade."

I'd pushed back. "If this is about your run, you know Mamma will be supportive. She'll use her contacts whether we show up this Christmas or not."

Fingers skittering across the screen of his phone, he'd not answered me. He'd already made his mind, and his silence told me negotiation wasn't an option. And here we are.

I slid out of my blouse. I didn't realize he'd gotten up until his hands were on my shoulders.

"I want to fuck," he whispered in my ear. My skin raised in chilled goose bumps. Not in an erotic way. Between the flight and the wine I'd gulped to white-knuckle my way through it, my temples throbbed. I didn't want to be touched. And definitely not in front of my dresser mirror.

Paul didn't seem to want a reply. He'd already undone my pants and pulled them to my ankles. I didn't stop him, didn't say no. My thoughts anchored to the two servings of room-temp white wine in my bag. Paul's horniness, the only thing standing between me and my next drink.

With a burst of hot breath on the back of my neck, he came quickly.

"I can always tell when you've been drinking," he said as he pulled his slacks back up. "You get dehydrated, and it's like sandpaper down there."

My cheeks flamed. His remark—the truth in it—pricked my heart like a hot needle. He was right. It was biological. I'd had too much to drink. I'd grown dehydrated.

Stinging comments from Paul used to be infrequent, but each new instance seemed to embolden him. He tested me that way. Pushing me towards some threshold, wearing me down, then moving the invisible line back to push me all over again. There was a time when I'd have erupted in anger, when I'd have demanded an apology at the very least, but probably much more. Now, his digs lingered in my mind like stale cigarette smoke.

I used to care about things. All sorts of things. Now everything was muted. Static-filled. I still walked amongst sharp blades and needle-like hazards, but their edges had been dulled. It was a broken way of seeing the world. A dangerous one.

I collected my purse and stepped out of my pants in silence. In my old bathroom, I twisted the top off one tiny wine bottle, turned it up, and shoved it in the back of a cluttered drawer. Then repeated the process with the other. When I finished, I caught my breath. I kneaded and dug at my chest as though trying to crawl inside myself.

The bath water poured piping hot from the faucet. Mamma may have let some things fall through the cracks, but the water heater wasn't one of them.

When did it become worth it? When did Paul, the life he

offered—and its distance from here—become worth it? The acidity of cheap wine tickled the back of my throat, reminding me that it wasn't worth it, but my priorities necessitated it anyways.

My priorities. Now there was something to scoff at. I really did used to care about things. The sick, homeless people at the AIDS shelter I volunteered for. Tossed from their families like subhuman garbage. But empathy was replaced by guilt as I'd catch myself watching the clock. While dying people described what life was like *before*, I'd zone out and count the minutes till I could go home and uncork a sweaty bottle of chilled chardonnay.

The bathwater fizzed as it mixed with flecks of old soap stuck to the sides of the claw-foot tub. The hot water swallowed my body, and my mind stilled as Paul washed off me.

3

Annie

The buzz-sawing songs of the cicadas outside break in rhythmic waves. The kitchen windows, glass bubbled from the passage of too much time, do little to stifle the sound. It's oppressive. Like Paul.

What does Paul think my death will look like? How will he ultimately choose to do it? Will it be painless? Will it come to me in my sleep in the form of a heavy pillow sunk over my face? Only enough time to *start* to panic before cold darkness swallows me up?

Or will he make it hurt? Draw it out. Will he want me to know he's had the last word, after all? That he's won. Will he get off on the fear in my eyes? Know I've seen the hate swirling in his? He came to Elizabeth to find me. Dragged his wife with him, too. I won't let him win.

When I think about him, and who he really is, it tears me up inside. He gnaws at me like a rat chewing through concrete. Oh yes, rats can chew through concrete. If they're hungry enough. Desperate enough.

I open a kitchen drawer. A rolling pin. A potato masher. A

cheese grater. No. These won't do. I close the drawer, careful to shut it quietly.

I spy the knife block out of the corner of my eye. A butcher's knife? A meat cleaver? Honestly, how cliché. Gauche, even. Unlike women more suspicious than myself, I don't carry mace. I should but I don't, and now here I am. Searching for self-defense.

I need delicate. The paring knife. That's delicate. Like me.

A blade no longer than a couple inches. But there are plenty of important things just a couple inches beneath the surface.

4

Nina

Winters in Elizabeth rarely grew cold enough to kill the crickets. They chirped their singsongs from the sullen palmettos in front of Auntie Tilda's place.

Auntie's mailbox was a rusted-out mess. I made a mental note to buy a new one the next time I drove to Dale's Hardware. It'd only been a few days since I last opened it, but it was stuffed like a turkey with letters.

The world had a lot to say to a dying woman.

I started back up the overgrown yard stones to the house. Another note to myself: ask James next door if he'd mow again this weekend. The gutters that ran the length of her tin roof were swollen with pine needles. Maybe James had a ladder to spare, too.

I tugged hard on the front door before it gave. The wood framing buttressing the rickety home had shrunk since summer. Inside, red carpet covered the living room. The last time anyone updated the place, red had been a trendy choice. A tattered recliner, Auntie's favorite in better times, sat before a TV box. A floral-patterned couch pushed against the room's long wall. Above it hung a photo of Barack Obama. She'd been so proud to vote for him. "I never thought I'd live to see it," she'd told me through tears.

In the kitchen, I rifled through her mail. Plenty of bills, but since I'd taken to coming over, the number of past-dues had dwindled. Coupons for the Dairy Queen—I stuck those in my jeans pocket. Two Christmas cards from my cousins.

I paused with disbelieving eyes. And one from Joanna King.

A holly green envelope with a return address label stuck to the corner. The only residence on Atalaya Drive. An embossed "K" in fancy font. I sat the others on the table. I very much wanted to know what Mrs. King had to say to Tilda Palmer.

"Nina," Auntie called from her bedroom down the hall. Her voice strained. My wristwatch indicated it was time.

"Coming, Auntie," I shouted, pacing to the fridge. The card from the Kings would have to wait.

I'd gone through the fridge days earlier for spoiled foods, but I hadn't wiped the shelves yet. A fresh box of baking soda fended off the smell until I found more time. The bottle of liquid morphine sat in the butter drawer.

The police officer in me had scratched a tiny pen mark to indicate the level since I last poured from it. James might be good for mowing, maybe ladders, but I didn't trust him around Auntie's painkillers.

In Auntie's room, a glass hutch displayed dolls and crystal trinkets she'd collected over the latter part of her life, but her brass bed had been replaced with the one hospice provided. I pressed the side button to raise her upright.

Sick as she was, Tilda Palmer wore her lined face proudly: crow's feet by her eyes from years of laughter and the wrinkled brow of a woman who'd handled more than most. A pile of gray hair sat clipped into a bun atop her head. "I'll keep my hair, if you don't mind," she'd said sternly to the doctor.

A fiber-optic Christmas tree a bit taller than a toaster sat on the side table. It threw a spectrum of colors across the darkened room as it changed shades to a motor's hum.

"Nina." Auntie smiled. "Anything nice in the mail today?"

"Some Christmas cards. Here, drink up." I held the measuring cap of morphine to her cracked lips. I intended to fetch Vaseline for those next.

"Who from?" she asked after swallowing.

"Auntie Linda's kids. Also, Terrance and Valerie."

"Nobody else?"

Did she expect a card from somebody else? Certainly, not from the Kings.

I took a deep breath. I wanted to lie but couldn't bring myself to. "Joanna King sent one."

Auntie cleared her throat with a raspy cough. "Bring it here, would you?"

"Sure." I walked back to the kitchen table where I'd left the heap of envelopes and plucked out the green one. Auntie started to tear at it, but her eyelids sagged as the morphine kicked in. I opened it for her, and a paper check flitted out, landing on her lap. Written sharply across the payment line were the words "One thousand dollars." Swooping, elegant cursive said the check was for something Joanna King called "Severance."

True, Tilda Palmer had worked at Piper Point for decades. It might as well have been the Big House, the way they treated her. For years, she watched over Gray and Charlotte. Cooking meals for that family. But after everything that had happened, she was supposed to be done with the Kings.

I was only nine or ten years old when news of Auntie's secret recording broke. Joanna's late husband, Congressman Seamus King, had been knee-deep in Kentucky bourbon after a bruising campaign day. Auntie had tucked a tape recorder in her pocket and made for Piper Point's library, Seamus King's dinner tray in hand. The whole country heard what Seamus had screamed at her, but I remembered what she told me perfectly.

"Don't you ever let someone speak to you like that. Ever," she'd said, trembling. "If you stand for nothing, you'll fall for anything."

She told me it'd only been a single instance, but I never believed her. If it'd been the first time he'd gone off on her like *that*, she wouldn't have kept a tape recorder in the pocket of her frock. Auntie had been careful about it. Smart. But why the check?

My cheeks grew hot, and I arched my brow. "How long have you been taking money from them?"

"Don't mind my matters." Auntie's voice was tinged with stubbornness. Cancer wouldn't wipe that out till the very end. "Sign my name to the back of that check," she whispered. "Sign it over to yourself, you hear me? I don't have much, but it's what I can do for you."

I stuffed the check in my pocket with the coupons. I had no more plans to argue with a dying woman than I had to cash a check from the Kings.

"You take that check, Nina." Her eyes closed as she drifted.

I gave her hand a squeeze. "Merry Christmas, Auntie."

In the spare bedroom, I unfolded the check and sat it on the nightstand next to my badge. "Elizabeth County Sheriff's Office" arched across the top of the faux gold shield. "Detective Nina Palmer" written below that.

All my things, still unpacked. I'd been checking in on Auntie for weeks, but now that the pain had moved to her bones, it needed squashing more frequently. Bigger bottles with higher doses. I'd sat next to her when the Charleston oncologist laid the facts out bare.

"The incidence and mortality rates of pancreatic adenocarcinoma are roughly the same," he'd said, glasses resting on his nose.

"And what the hell does that mean?" Auntie asked, eyes narrowed.

"It means just about everyone who gets it passes away," I told her.

The next words out of Auntie's mouth came quickly. "No chemo. I'm not going through all that mess just to die a week later than if I hadn't."

I didn't blame her. Neither did the doctor.

But when it became clear that nobody else planned to help, I'd moved into Auntie's spare room. When the funeral finally rolled around, they'd be bickering over whose flowers sat closest to a dead woman. The one they couldn't be bothered with when she wasn't so . . . dead.

I owed Auntie Tilda. She looked out for me, more or less raised me even when Mom—forever preoccupied with her *next* husband—was still alive. Now that Tilda was on her way out, helping her was the least I could do.

After pulling on a pair of sweats, I tied my hair back. My stomach growled, and I thought of the fast-food coupon in my pants' pocket. But the more dusk settled, the more unappealing driving anywhere became.

On the twin bed, I flipped my laptop open across my stomach. I began to type "Netflix" into the web browser but paused. Instead, I opened Wikipedia to polish my memory.

I searched for Congressman Seamus King, scrolling past his biography, his early work for the family business—Charleston shipping. His career in politics. I stopped at the heading labeled "Domestic Staff Controversy."

Auntie's check from Joanna King seemed to scream from its new home on the nightstand. The word "severance" had a very real meaning, but it'd been twenty years since Auntie had set foot in that home. At least, I assumed it had been.

Why the hell would Joanna King still be cutting her checks? If not because of a controversy dead for decades, then what else might be worth the trouble and the money?

5

Gray

The pews at Blessed Lamb Baptist could straighten out a spine before the collection plate made a single round. No cushion. Just hard benches to go with all the Good News.

We sang "O Come Let Us Adore Him" as the offering plate zigzagged its way through the pews collecting crinkled bills and loose change. And Mamma's check, folded in reverse so the amount showed.

A rotund Pastor Calcutt stood as we took our seats. "Welcome all, and Merry Christmas Eve," he said, tufts of white hair clinging to his lightbulb-shaped head.

Charles Calcutt had been our pastor ever since I could remember and the principal of Elizabeth Baptist School. He'd been forced to resign from the latter position when his affair with my English teacher, Mrs. Grant, came to light.

Mamma had phoned to tell me he'd confessed before the congregation. I'd been away at college. Pastor Calcutt begged forgiveness for his transgressions and, in the spirit of Christ's love, was forgiven. As for Mrs. Grant, her husband promptly divorced her, and she fled town. I'm not sure what happened to her.

At the time, the notion that their two fates could be so

different, so unfair, had angered me, as though the plot from *The Scarlet Letter* had found a small nook in modern society in which it could unfold again. But that was a different time. Paul was charming then, and I was deeply in love. Surviving, or perhaps even thriving, in the world had seemed doable. A fate like Mrs. Grant's felt distant. Impossible.

Pastor Calcutt went on, "Such joyous singing. The Lord's heard us, and he's smiling, I guarantee it. Before we get down to business, let's greet one another. Turn to the folks on your left and right and shake their hands. Wander around a bit. Fellowship!"

Hymnal notes rang from the choir piano as chatter and laughter filled the vaulted sanctuary. I turned to Paul as he leaned down to whisper in my ear.

"I love you, Gray Godfrey," he said. "Don't you ever forget it."

I quickly turned to my right and then my left, wondering for whose benefit he'd spoken. It could only be for Charlotte, who sat on my other side, since it sure as hell wasn't for me.

"Charlotte! Gray!" A voice rang from somewhere amongst the milling suits and doily-collared dresses. Frances Miles shouldered her way through the crowd. From the looks of it, she still baked herself in tanning beds, and blonde extensions did their best to snuff out whatever dark roots the bleach failed to touch. "I can't believe it! Both of you together." She beamed. "Merry Christmas Eve!"

I didn't recall her twang being so sharp.

"Merry Christmas," Charlotte and I replied together.

Frances Miles had been a childhood friend to both of us. I didn't like her now and I wasn't even sure I'd liked her back then, but friendships in small towns were like family. You often couldn't choose them.

"Charlotte, I'm so sorry about Will." She frowned. "I saw your status change on Facebook. I thought about calling."

"Frances, you remember Paul?" I intervened on Charlotte's behalf. Paul extended his hand past me, shaking hers.

"Why of course I remember Paul," she replied. "Even if I didn't, I'd have television to remind me." There was a note of envy in her voice that I doubted she meant anyone to hear.

"Y'all are coming to Ruby's tonight, aren't you?" she asked, fingering a glittering tennis bracelet around her wrist.

Ruby's sat on a corner a few blocks west of downtown. The pub was half bar, half dance club, and one-hundred-percent high school reunion. Especially on the nights before Thanksgiving and Christmas.

"We've had a long day of traveling," Paul answered for me.

"Y'all have to come," Frances pressed. "Everyone's going to be there. All the out-of-towners." She looked past me and Paul. "What do you say, Charlotte? You deserve a drink after Will's mess."

Charlotte shifted her weight from one heel to the other. That was twice in a minute's time she'd heard her ex-husband's name. I felt for her, but I felt for myself more. A few drinks would ease my headache, and Mamma had no doubt locked the wine cabinet before I'd even taken off from Reagan National.

"Maybe we should go, Charlotte," I said. "Blow off some steam and see everyone?"

Frances' bloodred lips split into a smile from one ear to the other. Paul's face remained flat as a sidewalk.

Between his constant watching and the liquor store closing for Christmas, there'd be no way to snag a stowaway bottle anytime soon. I'd suffer one evening at Ruby's for a stiff drink or two. Funny how I'd spent so many underage years trying to get inside Ruby's, and now it was nothing but a means to an end. A bitter pill.

"Are you sure that's such a great idea?" Paul asked. The correct answer was obviously *no*.

I swallowed hard and summoned a younger Gray to plead my case. The Gray who was the life of the party back when drinking was something I did for fun. With other people.

I nudged Paul. "Nonsense. I haven't seen my friends in so long. Let's go. We'll stay for an hour. That's all."

He remained silent.

I locked eyes with Charlotte, straining to keep desperation from trickling into my voice. "It'll be fun. Frances is right. You deserve some fun."

Her eyes cut to Paul's for a moment. They didn't think I noticed, but I did. She seemed as concerned as him. Seemed she'd spoken to Mamma about me, after all.

Paul wasn't happy, but the hopeful politician inside him knew better than to show it. Manipulation was never a one-way street. "One hour," he said, relenting. "And I'm coming with you."

"Of course you are, love," I replied. Frances gave Charlotte and I both unwelcome hugs and darted back to her pew, victorious.

The piano cut off as Pastor Calcutt stood, and we rejoined Mamma and the twins. As the good pastor went on about Bethlehem and its bright star, the dull pain tugging at my temples loosened a bit. I'd have a drink soon and knowing so stilled my roiling head.

*　　*　　*

As soon as our rental car doors slammed shut, Paul didn't mince words. "One drink, Gray." His tone cut like a knife. "You've been drinking all day."

I ignored him. Instead, I began to think through all the ways my one drink might turn into four. Four was my goal for the evening. Four would unwind the knot in my chest and get me to sleep after.

I'd make my first drink—the one Paul would see—into a double. That'd get me halfway there. He'd believe one trip to the restroom. There'd be time for a shot of something on the way. Ruby's would be crowded enough for him not to see.

Should I get bourbon? No, vodka. Better stick with clear liquor. Gin would be more festive. Gin tasted like Christmas.

If Paul went to the restroom, which he rarely did, that'd be winning the lottery. I could replace my drink with a second double and sip it down to the level he last saw. If he didn't, I'd have to figure out something else.

His sandpaper comment from earlier, the latest in an endless parade of digs, replayed in my head. I'd get drunk tonight. I'd get drunk and that would be my revenge for his biting words. The thought was warped. Skewed like my priorities. But I no longer lent a voice to the part of me that said so.

Mamma's face had burned, too, when we'd announced our plans. As she'd tucked her crocodile clutch under her arm to hold onto the twins, she'd turned to me and spoke low. "You watch yourself tonight, Gray. You hear?"

* * *

People packed the parking lot of Ruby's, everyone sipping from glass bottles and solo cups under neon lights. Cigarette smoke and lime wedges. Shouting and laughing and backslapping. Covered awnings kept most of the rain off, but the slick asphalt shined in all the wet. Charlotte's SUV pulled up next to our rental.

Everyone in Elizabeth aged eighteen to fifty seemed to be there. Pockets of older folks, too. A radical departure from the Georgetown pub scene Paul and I knew. The look on Charlotte's face as we made our way to the front door told me it was different than the places she frequented in Raleigh. We'd both spent years away from Elizabeth, but Ruby's was like riding a bicycle. Step inside, and it all comes rushing back. And that's exactly what happened.

Frances found us as soon as we stepped into the crowded bar. "Girls!"

She spilled her drink as she hugged me. Cranberry and vodka. I could smell it.

"What are y'all drinking?" she asked.

"Water," Paul said. "How about you, Gray? Water?"

"I'll have a gin and tonic," I shouted. In bars, I deliberately raised the volume of my voice. It would give Paul doubt I'd heard anything he said, were it convenient not to. Ruby's or the Ritz Carlton, the rules of the game never changed.

I turned to Charlotte. "How about you, sister? What'll it be?"

"The same."

"You got it, guys," Frances replied, looking at her own drink. "I'm due for a refill, too."

As she started off, I pushed past Paul and whispered in her ear. "Make mine a double," before adding, "for the holidays." She winked and made for the bar.

Despite the heels, I couldn't see the counter past the crowd. On the one hand, that'd make things easier when it came to my own refills. On the other, I couldn't tell how long the line was. How long until Frances' return.

I clutched the strap of my handbag. The dance floor the next room over pulsed with bass from bad speakers. Even if I could hear over the music, it certainly didn't help my pounding head.

"Gray King," a man called from behind. I recognized the husky drawl almost at once.

"Jacob Wilcox," I answered, turning. "And it's Godfrey. Gray Godfrey."

Jacob looked the same. Curled brown locks always a week late for a cut. His square jaw a week late for a shave. He hugged me. Tight. My thoughts went to Paul's eyes, undoubtedly fixated on this interaction. The fluttering in my chest dissolved into something else.

"Hey, Charlotte." Jacob smiled. She nodded.

"I'm Paul." My husband thrust his hand between Jacob and myself. "Paul Godfrey."

"Nice to meet you, Paul." Jacob shook his hand.

The discomfort of my situation sank in, and a lump built in the back of my throat. My husband and Jacob Wilcox stood nearly shoulder to shoulder. I wanted to vanish into thin air. Where the hell was Frances with my drink?

"And you two went to school together?" A simple question, but it flew from Paul's mouth like an accusation. In this case, his suspicion was on point.

I'd never told Paul about Jacob because Jacob was no ex-boyfriend. What I also didn't tell him was that Jacob and I were friends with benefits before either of us knew there was a name for what we did together.

Jacob flashed a toothy, white smile. "Yeah, we went to school together."

"Jacob Wilcox!" Frances cried like she didn't see him all the time.

She returned with our drinks not a moment too soon. She hadn't the slightest sense of balance, so I grabbed mine fast. Should she spill any of it, there'd be no easy replacement. The liquor sloshing in my cup smelled like pungent pine. Frances winked again. Either she'd done well or the bartender had an extremely loose pour. Merry Christmas, I told myself as I took a gulp. My earlier buzz crawled out from under my headache. I warmed up again as my cheeks flushed. I'd get what I needed from tonight and make it through to the other side.

"I have to be honest, Paul," Jacob chuckled between swigs of Corona Light, "I know exactly who you are."

"Is that so?" Paul didn't appear amused. His patience with Ruby's had disappeared somewhere between stepping out of the car and Frances greeting us.

"I see you on Fox News every so often. Saw you on *Sean Hannity* a couple weeks back. Talking about solar-powered sky-scrapers or something."

Paul nodded. "I'm a lobbyist for a clean energy think tank, Cooper and Waters. Maybe you've heard of us?"

"Can't tell you I have, but I will say you put up a good fight for a liberal," Jacob replied, speaking out the side of his turned-up beer. He wiped his mouth and added, "Still think Hannity shut you down."

"I'll take that as a compliment." Paul retrieved his phone from his pocket, shutting down the conversation.

That damned phone again. I took in a mouthful of gin, already feeling more talkative. "You know, Paul's running for congress next year. Like Daddy." Men in my life followed the same ambitious pattern. The differences from one to the next, Daddy to Paul were almost entirely superficial. Another swallow.

"Paul!" Charlotte's mouth hung open. "You didn't tell me. That's wonderful news. We need more environmental lawmak-ers. No matter what Mamma says."

Paul slipped his phone back into his slacks. "We're trying to keep it mostly under wraps until the party's finished vetting other potential candidates, but Gray's right."

"Congratulations," Frances added, no doubt hoping to punctuate the topic and move on.

As I tipped my cup, Charlotte mentioned something about leaving early, "gotta kiss the kiddos before Santa comes" is all I caught before ice hit my upper lip. I'd finished my drink. I glanced around the circle. Paul's demeanor lifted as he went on about his work. Everyone else's eyes were on him as he practiced a stump speech. Between that and Charlotte's goodbyes, no one noticed I'd finished. Folding my hands behind my back, I concealed the empty cup.

"I'm going to use the ladies room," I said aloud.

Only Frances heard. Probably anxious to leave a conversation she found dull. "You want me to come with?"

"No, no. I'll just be a minute." I caught myself speaking loudly, not meaning to this time. My buzz returned strong right off the bat. I might not even need four, but I'd try my best.

"I'll catch you two in the morning," Charlotte said, interrupting Paul and slinging her purse over her shoulder. "Lovely seeing you again, Frances. Jacob."

A rushed hug goodbye from Charlotte. After she vanished, I began shouldering my way past an assortment of people. Some I vaguely recognized, others I didn't. I spoke with no one. My small frame fit perfectly between two men standing at the counter.

"Can I get you something?" The bartender asked, pouring a line of shots.

"Tanqueray and tonic," I answered. "A double."

"I like the sound of that," one of the men said. A balding guy built like a truck. He could've been overweight or all muscle depending on how you squinted at him. He nodded to the bartender. "Add her in, too. I like a woman who can put down."

You have no idea.

"You got it." The bartender placed an empty shot glass behind the others.

"I'm Jonas," he said, pointing to the shot line, "and that's tequila."

Jackpot.

A moment later, my double gin and tonic sat before me. A shot of swirling gold followed. I salted the back of my hand. "Merry Christmas," I cheered with Jonas. I licked the salt and downed the shot. It took two swallows. Sour acid climbed up my throat between gulps. Still, I managed to keep it all down, and Jonas laughed as I sucked a lime wedge clean.

"You want another one?" His lips split into a hearty smile. I nodded, and we repeated the ritual. This time the shot slid down like fiery butter.

My head swirled. I'd sleep tonight.

I thanked Jonas, politely declined to follow him to a second bar and made for Paul. As I walked, my shoulder jerked backwards. My purse strap had lassoed a stool back. I tugged, but it wouldn't give. I pulled harder. The older woman sitting on it turned to me, scowling as I rocked her seat. Before she could say a word, a hand steadied me.

"Let me get that for you," Jacob said, pulling the strap off the woman's chair.

"Thanks." I smiled and began walking back to the others.

"Hold on, Gray," Jacob said, stopping me with a firm hand on my elbow. "You've hardly spoken one word to me tonight."

"Paul's here," I said, slurring. Mamma's words replayed in my mind. *You watch yourself tonight, Gray. You hear?*

"He doesn't know about us," I added.

Jacob smiled sideways, and his green eyes glistened from drinking. "Us?"

"Our history." I closed my eyes, reopened them. "Or whatever it is."

He talked past me. "You wanna go to the other side? Let's dance. You look like you haven't danced in a while. They even have dancing up there in D.C. with all those stiff suits and cocktail parties?" he joked, infusing faux skepticism into his words.

"What part of 'Paul's here' aren't you understanding?" More slurring. The shots had compounded with the gin which had already met my bathroom wine from earlier.

Jacob didn't stop. "Paul's talking to your sister and Frances. He's having his own good time. Let's skip over to the dance floor."

How many beers had he turned up?

I eyed him head to toe. His white tee shirt looked painted onto the contours of his hard chest, tiny features visible through a sweaty sheen. I remembered what his chest looked like. The warmth against my cheek as I laid my head on it. Paul never allowed me to lie on his chest. Even if he did, there'd be nothing but his new beer gut to look at.

"Okay," I said, taking another swallow. "One dance, and then it's straight back to Paul, you hear?" My own drawl returned the more I drank. My husband detested it.

Jacob took my hand and led me through the crowd onto the darkened dance floor the next room over. A techno remix of "Greensleeves" blasted from the DJ's table, creepy but appropriate for Christmas. The floor teemed with wet bodies. A disco ball turned overhead, spinning flecks of silver light around the room. Everything grew dreamy, almost abstract, the drunk and the darkness working together.

I tried to keep my distance from Jacob, but there were too many people, all twisting their hips and grinding against each other. I had nowhere to stand other than pressed up against him. His hands went to my hips and moved me with him. For a country boy, he could dance. But then we'd always had body chemistry.

I turned to take another gulp. Nothing but ice left.

Jacob took my cup and passed it off to someone. I didn't see who or where. The room spun with the disco ball. If losing my drink didn't bother me then I was good and drunk.

He raised my left hand. "Some rock."

"It's expensive." My words were sloppy.

"I'll bet it is. You're Gray King."

"Godfrey. My name's Godfrey."

The room turned faster. Jacob pulled me tighter against his body. The hard-on under his jeans rubbed against the inside of my thigh. I liked it so I let him keep doing it. Drunk Gray let him keep doing it. He lifted my chin with his hand, pulling me close to kiss my mouth.

"No. Paul's here—"

At least, I think I'd said "no." I don't know if I did or not. If it was aloud or only in my head. His lips cut me off, his ashtray-flavored tongue inside my mouth.

Sinking into the swirling, sparkling dance floor, I closed my eyes and kissed Jacob back. It was deep. The sort of kiss that brought back a life I'd purposely forgotten.

As I pulled away, an icy hand fell on my shoulder. The dream I danced within suddenly felt . . . wrong. Like a painting pulled crooked. The hand squeezed hard like its owner intended to hurt me. To break my collarbone.

I turned to face Paul. My vision blurred, but it was definitely him. His voice sounded muffled in my ears. He screamed, but the louder he did, the more distant his words became, as if we were submerged in water.

Squinting, I could see by the way his lips moved he was saying "fuck" over and over again. As he tugged my arm, I spun on my heels. The jerking sent bolts of pain through my shoulder like electricity. Sharp burning cut through my swirling daze.

My heart beat with the music. "Greensleeves" was a bizarre choice for a club. Even a techno remix. Even if it was Christmas Eve.

6

Nina

A nightmare jolted me awake. Nearly as soon as I sprang up, the memory of it vanished. I couldn't recall the terror of moments earlier. Something about a snake? A nasty, mottled snake coiled in a doorway?

I turned my phone over on the nightstand. Four-thirty AM. *Merry Christmas.*

I splashed my face with sink water, pulled my jeans up, and threw on a knitted cardigan—navy with wide white stripes. I grabbed my badge.

On the way to the living room, I peeked in on Auntie Tilda. She was deep in a morphine slumber, her chest slow to rise and slower to fall. She wouldn't wake for hours.

My stomach growled worse than before I'd fallen asleep. A cheeseburger, some fries, and I'd swing by the station to check on my partner, Sammie. I'd covered for both of us on Thanksgiving, so he was up for the Christmas vigil. But, I could still get a head start on the day-after's paperwork. I'd be back before Auntie woke up.

My patrol car choked for a moment, but cranked. The recession had cut deep into Elizabeth's already starved budgets, and new civil cars were a pipe dream. Recovery hadn't touched this town yet. I didn't flip my headlights on until I'd backed out of Auntie's driveway.

I pressed the radio. "Greensleeves" played. A techno version. I turned the dial until I found a soft rock station. Nothing too crazy.

Ten minutes later, I'd picked up my Dairy Queen combo and radioed Sammie.

"You don't need to come in," he said as soon as he picked up. "It's quieter tonight than most holidays. Clinic's catching most of them. Drunks as usual."

"I'm gonna swing by for a few minutes," I answered.

"What about your aunt?" Sammie paid attention like that.

"She'll be okay for a while. Morphine always does what it says it will. I can't sleep. I'll get a jump on my files so they don't drown me later." I smirked. "I won't even speak to you." I could almost see Sammie's grin on the other end of the radio.

"Better not." He clicked off.

I turned down Main Street and hung a right at Marion Ave. Twinkling Christmas wreaths hung from cast iron street lamps. Floodlights kept the single-story sheriff's office lit up almost as well as daylight did. SHERIFF JIM F. BURTON III in gold lettering.

Braking out front, I snatched my greasy paper bag from the passenger seat and threw my book bag over my shoulder.

"We can't keep you away, can we?" The officer at the front desk joked as I passed through the revolving doors into the station.

"You know you can't." The irony of his statement wasn't lost on me. There were only a handful of detective positions in Elizabeth. And there were more than a handful of good old boys who did their damnedest to keep me away. Me and Sammie both.

A room of cubicles waited for me as I turned the corner. The lamps in Sammie's were on, but I'd promised not to talk to him. At least not until I finished my sandwich.

My computer came alive as I toggled the mouse. I took as big a bite as I could manage, my stomach feeling better already.

"You're gonna hate this, Nina." Sammie smiled wide as he poked his head into my cubicle.

"Jesus, Sammie, can I finish my burger?"

"And where the hell's *my* burger?"

"What am I gonna hate? And there isn't one," I replied, taking a second bite.

"Ya know, carbs don't scare all gay men shitless." He patted his belly. "If you can believe it, we don't all decorate—"

"I've seen your apartment, Sammie. It's a pigsty. Now what am I gonna hate?"

"Guess who took the Whitman case?"

Greg Whitman, the owner of Whitman Autos, had been pulled over for speeding a week ago. Not surprising considering he kept an inventory of German sports cars. The sort only a few folks in Elizabeth could afford. But doing sixty in a thirty-five turned into the lesser charge when the patrolman spotted the coke baggie. Blow was supposed to make folks think fast on their feet, but Greg must not have had much to work with.

"A public defender, I'm guessing?" Mr. Whitman was up to his chin in debt. I'd had his finances pulled myself.

Sammie stepped into my space. He was younger than me by a couple years. The sort of sharp-jawed guy who'd wanted to be a cop his whole life. Not a lot of book sense, but street smart where it counted.

"Yep. A public defender," he answered, running his hand through his sandy hair. "Guess who took it from him? Matthew."

Matthew King had a knack for spotting slipups in the process. They sometimes seemed to materialize from nowhere for his clients. Mouth full of bacon and beef, I scoffed. "Figures."

"You wanna bet Matthew starts puttering around town in a spanking-new Porsche?"

"Not even if I was a betting woman," I replied. "It won't matter. The arrest was clean. The case is solid."

"Just thought you'd like to know." Sammie flashed a grin and turned to walk away.

"Oh, and by the way, Sam, Merry Christmas," I shouted to the back of his head.

"Merry Christmas, Nina," he called.

An hour later, I gathered my things. My eyelids had grown heavy in the time I'd been at my desk. It was why I did twilight paperwork—the closest to meditation I'd ever get. Book bag back on my shoulders, I made for the front door.

"Nina," Sammie shouted from behind. I turned to face him jogging my way. "Your Aunt gonna be okay for another hour or two?"

I knotted my brow. "Should be. Why?"

"Trucker called in an abandoned vehicle on his way up to North Carolina. Thought you might wanna check it out with me."

"What makes you think that? Tow it, and I'll give it a look tomorrow." I started to turn towards the door.

"It's a rental. Parked in the emergency lane, passenger door open marsh-side."

My eyes narrowed. "Okay . . ."

"The rental company operates a twenty-four-hour line. Gave them a call. They matched the vehicle to a Paul Godfrey who'd taken possession of it at the Charleston airport."

A name I didn't recognize at first. *At first.*

"As in Paul Godfrey, the environmentalist?"

"Yep. Paul Godfrey, the environmentalist," he replied. "Paul Godfrey who married Gray King."

*　*　*

The morning sun had just started to pierce the pine trees off Paul Revere Highway as I pulled up. A lonesome road with a fitting name. The sort of desolate stretch one could picture its name-sake galloping down.

Sammie's car cut through the gravel behind mine. We'd driven separately so I could go straight to Auntie's after. I eyed the black Lincoln sedan parked haphazardly as I approached the driver's side door. Aside from the fact that it had been abandoned on the highway shoulder, passenger door swung out, there wasn't anything grossly strange about the car. No scratches. Windows intact.

Driver's side unlocked, too. I tugged the door open. It smelled like a rental. Not exactly *new car*, but not *my car*, either.

Sammie appeared beside me. "Anything unusual?"

"Aside from the fact that it's here, no." The car was clean as a coat of paint. "Keys seem to be gone."

"Should we phone the Kings?" Sammie asked.

"Not yet," I said.

"But how can we be certain the driver's okay?" he asked. "It's possible no report means nobody left to report it. Car door left opened and—"

"Wouldn't the family notify us if someone was unaccounted for?" A guilty edge crept into my voice.

Sammie sighed. My reasoning seemed to leave him unsatisfied. "You want me to attach a twenty-four-hour removal notice?"

Something stirred deep inside me. The whole thing could be innocuous, but just enough was off-kilter, just enough wasn't right. Folks left cars behind when they partied, and the night before had been a party night for a lot of folks. But they left them at bars. At houses. At restaurants. Not in emergency lanes. Not on Paul Revere Highway.

"No. Get a tow up here. Take it to the impound lot," I instructed. "It's a hazard in the highway shoulder. Let's let the Kings—or Paul Godfrey—come find it."

7

Gray

Piper Point's stagnant air greeted me when I awoke in the Yellow Room. My room.

There are a few precious seconds after you wake up from a night of hard drinking when you're at peace. A temporal comfort doled out by the universe to remind you how you *could* feel in the morning—if you'd made better decisions.

Then it's gone. Torn from you. And the world you were at peace with, for the briefest of moments, shatters.

Cotton mouth.

A drill bored into my temples. With every grinding turn, a memory burned into sharp focus. Staggered images bled into the space behind my eyes.

The flight. My filthy ring. Mamma's church. Ruby's. Jacob.

My heart plummeted, and my stomach tied itself in knots. Shameful knots.

Jacob. I kissed him. Or he kissed me. I didn't know which.

Paul!

I turned to an empty spot beside me in the bed.

As I sat up, the world spun. Sweat beaded on my forehead. Liquor wafted off my wet skin. I wore a silk negligee that clung to my body like sweet-smelling paste. A wave of queasiness rippled through my insides, and I sprang for the toilet.

A dry heave at first. Followed by bits of salad that I'd had at the airport, all I'd eaten yesterday. As I retched, drops of yolk-colored bile dripped into the basin.

Footsteps. Paul maybe? The door to the bathroom creaked as it moved. I wiped my chin, mouth filled with acrid spit, and braced for a confrontation. When nothing happened, I turned around. No one stood behind me.

The door had been pulled closed, not opened. Probably Mamma, then.

Christmas. It was Christmas morning. She probably didn't want Charlotte's twins to hear me retching while they opened gifts. Mamma wouldn't try to comfort me. No glass of iced water or damp cloth for my forehead. No, I should be kept away from the family. Hidden behind a shut door because I might ruin fucking Christmas.

I splashed ice-cold water on my face, stuck my mouth under the faucet and gulped until I couldn't swallow another drop. Eyes down, I made for the hand towel. I didn't want to see my face. Not yet. I wasn't ready for that.

I ran hot water in the tub, turning the brass lever to send it piping up the shower head. Stripped naked, I stood beneath the stream. Tendrils of steam rose off it, misting the room in foggy wet. The heat stung my skin, splotching it red. I didn't care. I needed to sweat out the booze. Still drunk, the room swirled around me.

Kneading shampoo into my scalp, I ran through last night in my mind. Each time Jacob's face flashed before me, my stomach twisted again. I'd kissed him in a crowded bar. With Charlotte and Paul and everyone else there.

My arms ached as I washed. How had they gotten so sore? And the pitch soil packed deep under my nailbeds? But then I'd woken up with dirt-caked nails on a handful of occasions before, after my worst binges. I struggled to collect my thoughts.

I didn't remember the ride home, but if I'd made it home, then Paul or Charlotte must have brought me here. I didn't put myself in a nightgown. When I drank into that kind of stupor, I fell asleep in whatever I wore. Paul must have dressed me. Which meant he hadn't been mad enough not to care.

A sliver of hope. There'd be apologies, of course. To Charlotte. To Mamma. Paul, most of all. But he knew I'd been drinking all day. He'd said so himself countless times. I'd screwed up, but the nightie meant he must be approaching the situation with some compassion.

I finished scrubbing my body. Washing my face. Rinsing my hair. As I toweled off, I glanced at the mirror. Clouded with fog, I saw only a pink blur. I still wasn't ready to look at myself.

I'd dress well this morning. Something smart. Something that would work against the picture of me they'd expect to stumble down the staircase. A fresh silk blouse tied off with a bow around my neck. I'd do my makeup. I'd steady one hand with the other to do it just right.

As I unzipped my suitcase on the hunt for my cosmetics bag, something was missing. Where were my clothes from last night? The laundry bag tucked into my roller was still neatly folded. I scanned the Yellow Room. My slacks and blouse were nowhere. I reminded myself to ask Paul. If he'd thrown them in the laundry room, there was a chance Mamma would find them, soiled in ways I didn't want to think about. I headed back into the bathroom.

Now was the time to look. I pressed my palm against the fogged mirror and swept it sideways, clearing a spot of glass. Condensation ran down its surface like tears.

Saline drops had soothed my bloodshot eyes. Heavy bags hung under them, but cold cream had helped. After I finished with makeup, I pinched my cheeks to redden them and found my ring sitting alone on the wicker dresser. Paul must've taken it off as he tucked me in. I slipped the diamond on my finger.

A couple sharp squeals from downstairs caught my attention. Joseph and David.

My hands trembled. The drunkenness had worn off, and the way my hangover washed over me, I knew it would be a bad one. Category five—I'd taken to describing them as though they were hurricanes. It would last awhile, maybe even a couple days if I didn't drink or take something soon.

More giggles from downstairs. Mamma's high voice, too, feigning excitement along with the children and likely wishing I wouldn't come down. But I would, and I'd be pleasant to be around.

The pine floors groaned as I crept down the empty hallway. Not to the stairs, but to Mamma's bedroom. She might've locked up the liquor, but I had no intention of facing them—facing Paul—without help. Her door stood ajar. I opened it and slipped past her four-post, floral bed. The walls had been painted on all sides with a mural. Garden scenes mostly. Gracefully meandering peacocks. I made for the bathroom. Pausing, I waited to hear Mamma again. To make sure she was still downstairs with everyone else. A woman laughed, but it could've been Charlotte. It pealed once more. No, definitely Mamma's dramatic cackle.

I opened her medicine cabinet and found a whole row of vitamins and oils and minerals. Another shelf of cholesterol medicines.

A beta-blocker for her heart. Bottles of antidepressants left over from our try-before-you-buy family doctor, Mary-Ann Conner.

Mary-Ann Conner. Her name in print froze me. I'd once stood in this bathroom with the woman when I was very young. As a child, the circumstances had been confusing. I only remembered pulling my skirt back up to my waist, returning Dr. Conner's plastic container to her. Filled with vinegary urine.

I shook my head. Jackhammers tore into my skull. No, Mary-Ann's prescribed antidepressants wouldn't do. They wouldn't help *now*.

As I rifled through the containers, a bottle peeked out from the back, a label warning for drowsiness and a caution against driving. Diazepam, 10 milligrams per tablet. *Valium.* The bottle was half full. The label said ninety tablets and had been dispensed a year ago. Around the time Daddy passed away. If they'd been in the cabinet for so long, that meant Mamma didn't use them regularly. And that she wouldn't miss a few, either.

I gulped down three and stuck a handful in my pocket. As I shut the medicine cabinet, Mamma's face appeared in the glass, and I nearly screamed.

"What are you doing, Gray?"

"I have a headache."

"That's no surprise," she replied, arms crossed. She eyed me up and down. "At least you've put yourself together. Best you can."

She'd noticed that much. I tugged at my bow and brushed the sides of my slacks.

"Is everyone downstairs already?" My voice caught on my throat.

She paced to her vanity and began to retouch her own makeup. "The boys got up early. They've nearly torn through all their presents. There's still a few under the tree with your name on them, though." A pleasant accent punctuated the last sentence like she expected me to be happy to open gifts. Like I was a child, too.

I dug my nails into my palms.

"And Paul? How's Paul this morning?" I clenched my teeth waiting for the answer. Mamma and Paul often whispered behind my back. He treated her like the mother neither of us ever had. Whatever *had* happened, Paul had probably briefed her by now.

She ignored me. "Cora's put out a proper breakfast, and there's plenty of coffee. Get on downstairs."

I did my best not to face the cracked landing mirror as I made my way down the steps. The last thing I needed was to catch another glimpse of my face.

Downstairs, the twins chased each other from one room to the next mimicking airplane noises and gunfire as they clung to new toys. Johnny Cash's "Silent Night" crackled from a record player in the salon. The smell of bacon and coffee filled the whole of downstairs.

I walked into the kitchen. The griddle sizzled as Cora worked to keep every inch of counter covered with hot food.

"Merry Christmas," she offered cheerily as I passed behind her.

Charlotte sat on the cushioned window bench in the breakfast nook. We locked eyes. Hers were heavy with bags, too. She hadn't bothered with makeup but then she didn't have anything to compensate for.

I turned to the French press by the toaster oven. Some coffee would help keep my mind sharp once the pills kicked in.

Paul wasn't around, and my anxiety dissolved. I felt an inch better about things. He'd probably needed space to calm down from last night. He might be out back. Or perhaps watching TV in the den. With Joseph and David running amok, he might've been chased there. Paul didn't care for children.

As I stirred my coffee, Charlotte walked up from behind, and my shoulders jumped. "Gray, I need to speak to you," she whispered in my ear.

"Of course," I answered, tapping my spoon on the cup's rim. She spoke softer. "In the library."

My pulse spiked. Even the pills couldn't stop it. Thank god, I'd found some. I took a sip of coffee, bitter and strong. "Okay."

In the library, oak shelves covered three of the room's four walls each lined with elegant books, occasionally interrupted with a marble bookend of some sort. Heavy drapes were pulled to the sides of tall windows.

Charlotte slid the parlor doors closed, shutting the room off from the rest of Piper Point. "Paul didn't come home."

Her words struck me like a hammer.

She paused. Either letting them sink deep or waiting for a reaction. I wasn't sure which. How could Paul not have come home? Hadn't he dressed me for bed?

She folded her arms, worry painted on her face. "Do you remember last night?"

The question shook me. I had to tell the truth. "No. Not much."

"You kissed—"

"No!" I yelped before lowering my voice. "No, I remember *that*. Just not much after. And wait. How did you know? You left Ruby's before?"

Her brow knotted, eyes glistened. "Paul called me on his way home. He was heartbroken. Sobbing. Told me what happened."

A sense of dread began to gnaw away at my insides.

"I tried to wait up, but I fell asleep. When the kids woke me up early this morning, I looked out my window. My car's the only one in the driveway."

The dread latched onto my ribs, pulling them inwards, pressing hard on my lungs.

"No car?" I finally managed to say something. Useless, but it was something. I picked at a tiny sliver of skin at the corner of my thumbnail.

"I went to your room to see if you made it home alright. I heard you throwing up, and I shut the door so Mamma wouldn't hear. Paul brought you here, and then . . . left, I guess?"

"Does Mamma know?" Another useless question.

Charlotte looked uneasy. "I had to ask her if she'd seen him. Heard from him."

I tore the piece of skin off. Blood pooled in a crescent. I shoved my hand into my pocket to wipe the blood on the inside fabric. My fingers brushed past more pills.

"I don't know," I whispered. It was all I could say or think. *I don't know.* Welling tears stung my eyes.

"It was quite a night," she said, pulling me close. She diluted the anxiety in her voice. "I'm sure he just checked into an interstate motel for a good night's sleep. One with no arguing. He'll be back. If we haven't heard from him by the time lunch is done, we'll start making calls. I'll speak with Cora, too."

"Okay," I answered, coughing.

"To tell you the truth, I'm a little relieved," she said before casting her eyes to the floor.

"Relieved?" I wiped my own. "Why?"

She hesitated. "Paul sounded so upset, and you had a lot to drink. I was afraid he might . . ."

"Hurt me?"

"I'm just paranoid, that's all. It's not helping and it was obviously off base." She offered a tiny smile and pulled me in for a second hug. "But he never has, right? Hurt you?"

"No," I answered. "Of course not."

"Of course not. Now go up and get your phone. Make sure it's not on silent." She kissed my cheek and slid the creaking doors back open.

My phone! It should've been the first thing I thought to look at. I raced to my bedroom, buoyed by a sense of hope.

But there'd been no missed calls.

And by lunch, there was still no Paul.

8

Nina

Half way through Christmas Day, the Kings—or Paul Godfrey—still hadn't reported their rental missing. Or reported anything else that might account for it. If a trucker hadn't spotted it, it'd still be sitting on the highway. Bizarrely unmissed by its renters.

Auntie stirred beneath her snow-white blankets. She'd wake soon. I'd sat next to her bedside since returning from Paul Revere Highway, the morphine ready to go the moment she could swallow it. I hated this stretch of time more than anything. The few seconds after she woke but before I got the meds in her—those seconds lasted years.

I knew the abandoned rental and Auntie's "severance" pay weren't overtly connected. Only related. Like kin. Related just enough to leave me with questions. And every second that ticked by without a call from the Kings fed my questions like fuel to a fire. *So odd.* Why *did* Joanna King write checks—large checks—to Auntie Tilda?

Auntie had been clear the discussion was off the table. I'd respect that, but there were two other ways I could answer this question—and both turned my stomach sour. I could use my badge to pull Tilda's accounts without any sort of legal reason—a fireable offense for which there'd be a record—or I could become executer of her will. Except, she likely didn't have a will and certainly, no executer if she did. I could spare her the trouble and apply for the job myself at the probate court. The vacancy and my reputation would land me the gig, no question.

But no matter which I chose, I'd be giving Auntie the runaround.

She stirred, moaning.

"Here you are," I whispered, rushing the measuring cap to her lips. They hardly moved. I watched her throat like a hawk till she swallowed.

Another pained groan, the sort that stabbed my heart, and she went still again.

As the drug coursed through her body, I relaxed back into my chair. On my phone, I thumbed through recent news articles written about or by Mr. Godfrey. Judging by the op-eds he penned for sites like *Politico* and the *Huffington Post*, he seemed mighty important.

If they didn't call soon, I'd have to phone them. No other choice. I chased the thought away. Surely, they'd call. Who the hell loses a rental car and doesn't care one way or the other?

Sammie made it seem as though I had some ulterior motive for not reaching out to them immediately, but I didn't. I'd checked that the Kings hadn't reported anything and kept Sheriff Burton posted. There'd been no questions from any of them. The car wasn't stolen. There was no harm in letting them come to me.

I circled back to the check instead.

I'd visit the probate court and apply to be executer in person. No reason to bother Auntie Tilda with any more of the

Kings' mess. Lord knew she'd seen more than her fair share of it already. If she died never hearing the names of anyone in that family again, I'd be content. The same went for me, too.

I'd been on the receiving end of a poverty scholarship thanks to that family. They called it something different though, a term with less sting to it. An academic advancement award, I think. But a poverty scholarship's what it was.

Only two high schools had served Elizabeth County since the nineteen sixties. The public one—Pickens High. And the private school racial integration had spurred the creation of—Elizabeth Baptist. I entered freshman year as an Elizabeth Baptist School Lion—named after the Lion of Judah.

Most folks in the county couldn't afford private school no matter what color they were, so Pickens High had a healthy mix of students. Elizabeth Baptist was a different story, and the handful of awards they doled out each year helped mitigate their white problem. But for those few *lucky* students given one? Loneliness was an understatement, especially at a school like that.

Adding to the isolation was the knowledge of where the money had come from. I knew it'd been Auntie Tilda's work at Piper Point, complete with Congressman Seamus King's signature at the bottom so I never forgot where to direct my gratitude.

Indeed, I learned quickly to take nothing for granted and find my seat early. Gray usually walked in right as the bell rung.

At Elizabeth Baptist, Christ was lord. But for the four years I attended, a queen reigned, too. Or a king rather. Gray King. She wasn't a mean girl by any stretch, though there was no question her father and her family's money placed her squarely atop the totem pole, just as my lack of both dictated my own station.

She was every bit what a Low Country girl should be: Demure, polite, a touch enigmatic. I'd be lying to myself if I didn't admit how easy it was to get caught up in her, in the cult of personality that surrounded such a pretty King.

We wore the same uniform. Pressed khaki skirts and white polos. She wore it better somehow, or at least I convinced myself she did. She took her assigned seat directly in front of mine.

"It's freezing in here," Gray announced to no one as she rubbed her goose-bumped arms. That day I wore a knitted sweater over my polo. The room might've been cold to Gray, but I was warm. In fact, I'd planned to remove my sweater anyhow. I didn't think twice and tapped Gray's shoulder. She turned.

"You want my sweater?" I asked.

She hesitated, her face devoid of emotion. At once, I grew painfully aware of my mistake. I knew what was running through her head. She was desperately searching for a reason to turn down my sweater. She'd have accepted it quickly from her friend Frances. Or even the guy always buzzing around her like a bee—Jacob Wilcox.

She didn't want to wear a sweater from *me*, and I knew exactly why.

"No thanks," she finally replied, half smiling. "I'm not that cold."

It was a lie. She meant she wasn't cold enough to wear *my* sweater.

Years later, I learned the term *microaggression*. They formed the basis of an entire lecture topic at the police academy. Casual offenses, they were usually trivial, ignorable even. But they were deeply anchored in racism.

I said nothing. Class went on, but the comment lingered at the front of my mind. Later, when I shut my locker door, Gray stood waiting. My heart jumped.

"Can I talk to you?" she asked. Her voice had an earnestness I didn't often hear at this school. I nodded.

"I wanted to say I'm sorry," she told me. "I'm sorry for not taking your sweater." She went on, "To tell you the truth, it ate me up inside. All class long. I had to confront something ugly inside me. Something that pushed me to turn down your sweater."

Her honesty floored me. As my face flushed, I clutched my books to combat the awkwardness. "It's okay," I replied, discomfort creeping into my voice.

"It's not okay," she said. "And I know that it isn't. Pretending otherwise won't make me any better." She smiled at me once more. "Lacrosse tryouts are in a couple weeks. Think about giving it a shot, alright?"

"Sure," I replied. She turned back down the hallway beneath a fluttering school banner strung from the drop ceiling.

Frances had been stalking like a lioness a few yards back during our conversation. When Gray disappeared, she pounced. "School doesn't provide equipment, and it's expensive," she'd said through a meaningless smile. "Team's okay the way it looks now. Nothing personal."

By junior year, I'd made captain of the varsity team. If I recalled correctly, Frances hadn't made the cut. She'd been relegated to another year on JV.

In a big way, I was grateful for my time in the lion's den. High school taught me all about microaggressions, but Gray showed a stunning level of self-awareness. The sort that spoke of potential. A potential to overcome, and one I suspected she hadn't lived up to. Frances Miles was no mystery. She was a bitch, plain and simple.

I cut my teeth on courage. I thought of Auntie Tilda's proverb again. "If you stand for nothing, you'll fall for anything."

But this time, the responsibility to confront was mine. This time, I'd have to go to the Kings. I needed to inquire about the abandoned rental, but on a deeper level, something about making contact with the family exhilarated me. I hadn't seen Gray in so long, and the rental suggested she'd come home. What kind of woman was she now? The one I caught a glimpse of outside my locker? Or maybe she'd become more like her mother over time. Entitled bordering on petulant.

Maybe Auntie's checks would come up, maybe they wouldn't, but I liked the idea of sharing a room with the Kings. With the women who held those answers.

9

Gray

Hours since lunch, and still no word from Paul. The closer evening drew, the more my palms itched. The taste of grapey fermentation, whispers of cool white wine, rose in the back of my throat. My body anticipated a drink my mind knew wasn't coming.

"Where could he be?" I asked my sister. My voice cracked as I paced back and forth in my stale bedroom. It still smelled of sweet liquor. A queasy cotton-candy stench. Charlotte sat on my unmade bed.

"There's the Ramada on Keebler Street." She thumbed through her phone, jotting down numbers on a notepad. "And the Days Inn by the Greyhound stop." She paused. "You don't think he'd—"

"He'd never take a bus," I said. "He'd fly, and I've checked our accounts twice now. He hasn't booked anything."

She knotted her brow. "You're sure you checked all the accounts? He doesn't have, I don't know, another one?"

"What's that supposed to mean? Like a secret bank account?" My words caught on my throat again.

"Men hide things from their wives all the time. Will certainly hid a lot from me."

There was no way Paul had secret accounts. A corner of me wished he did. Then I wouldn't be so certain none of his cards had been used since 11:07 PM. Excruciatingly certain.

"No, that's crazy. Not Paul. Paul and I don't keep secrets." The statement soured in my mouth. My thoughts went to his phone. To the way he always kept it out of reach. And I hid my drinking from Paul. I wasn't always great at it, but I tried my best. "Besides," I added, "he insisted on merging all our accounts after we got engaged."

Charlotte froze. "All your accounts?"

"Well, yeah. We were going to be husband and wife. It made perfect sense."

"Even the trust from Daddy?"

"All of them." I hadn't shared her concern, but the look she wore made me wish I had. But we were married. What's his was mine and mine was his. The same vows everyone else took. No caveats. Whatever a financial planner had said shrunk in comparison to the idea of keeping things from one another—at least in the beginning. I didn't want to be like Mamma. I'd wanted a marriage built on truth, on disclosure.

And Paul was successful in his own right. When he landed the lobbying job with Cooper and Waters, our future seemed real. Our place in Georgetown, a pristine empty canvas on which the two of us could paint a life together. Far from Elizabeth. Far from Piper Point. The signs—the slippage—were obvious now, but back then they were normal, routine. Even endearing.

I'd have a few too many glasses of wine while cooking dinner. I'd hiccup, and Paul would say, "You're cute when you're buzzed, Rosy Cheeks. You looked sun-kissed."

I'd pick out a dress for a night out, and Paul would point to another. "But this one's such a stunner." He took an interest in me, in my appearance. But glasses of wine with dinner grew into bottles by myself, and soon, kindly worded suggestions became instructions. Non-negotiable.

Charlotte's chiding refocused me.

"You know what Daddy told us, Gray," she replied. "What if Will had access to my trust? He'd have made off with half of it." She turned back to her notepad. "Never mind. That's a discussion for another day. I'm jaded on men, anyways." She began to dial one of the motel numbers she'd scrawled down. But if Paul stormed off to some highway hotel, why had his cards gone unused since? Sure, he carried cash, enough for a room for a few nights, but not so much as to book a flight with it. Could you even book a flight with cash these days?

Then there was his luggage. A topic Charlotte had delicately avoided. His black roller sat in the bedroom's far corner collecting a sheen of fuzzy dust. Mocking me. Why would he have left his luggage?

He hadn't used the cards. He didn't have the cash to fly out. But he had to be in Elizabeth. He had to be somewhere cooling his heels after what I'd done. The last phrase echoed inside my mind over and over. *After what I'd done.*

The pills from earlier had worn off, and my heart was beating faster. I itched for a drink. My armpits dampened, and more sweat beaded on my brow. I fished another two of the Valium out of my pocket and swallowed them with spit.

"Gray." Charlotte caught me as she hung up with the motel. "What are you taking?"

"Nothing." I adjusted my answer. "Something for my headache." She didn't seem to buy it, but I didn't care. "Did Cora hear anything last night?"

"No. Didn't see any lights in the driveway, either. Have you called his work? Maybe Cooper and Waters has heard from him? I can't picture him without his phone in hand. Surely he's emailed or texted or something."

"I thought about it," I replied, "but Paul would be furious if I bothered work with something like this, something that's my fault." Given the circumstances, I knew how foolish my answer would sound to Charlotte, but it was the truth. And that made me feel even more foolish. Tears gathered in the corner of my eyes again.

"Okay. It's okay." She could see my struggle and pulled me next to her on the bed. "I know this isn't easy. You made a mistake. Everyone makes mistakes. Paul makes mistakes, too. Hell, he's in the process of making one right now." She placed her arm behind my back and rubbed.

"What if," I spoke in staggered heaves now, "what if something happened to him?"

"You shut up, Gray." She gave my elbow a squeeze. "You had a fight. He took off to chill out. *That's* what happened, do you hear?"

"But his luggage?" I asked, desperate to believe her.

"Means he didn't think this through. That he won't be gone long. Besides, I didn't dress you for bed, so Paul must've. He must've come home before leaving again."

I nodded vacantly. I still hadn't found my clothes from last night.

My door creaked open, and I jumped. Mamma stood on the other side, her lips tightly pursed. Not in a spiteful way but worried.

"The police just called." Her tone sharpened. "They've found Paul's rental abandoned by the highway."

Paul's rental? Abandoned? The statement weighed a metric ton, and Mamma dropped it directly onto my head. I stopped breathing. A sinking feeling swallowed me and any consolation Charlotte had offered. *Police?*

"There are detectives on the way here now to speak with us." Her pale eyes locked onto mine. Unable to hold back, I sprang to the bathroom and vomited again.

* * *

Night fell over Piper Point. Pealing thunder announced the steady rain that followed. It nearly drowned out the doorbell when it rang.

"Hello, Gray." Nina Palmer smiled as she stepped into the foyer. A stout blond man whom she introduced as Sammie walked in behind her. She seemed uncomfortable to be here. I didn't blame her after what had happened with Miss Tilda. I never forgave Daddy for that night in the library.

Despite her unease, she was every bit as I'd remembered, though it had been a decade or longer since I'd seen her. Her cheekbones were high. Her face, sharp almost like a bird of prey. It didn't surprise me she'd chosen a career in law enforcement. She'd been tenacious her whole life, like her aunt.

The grandfather clock that loomed in the corner by the door chimed for seven o'clock in the evening. Still no word from Paul. The dread that had latched onto my chest hadn't left. I breathed, but the way it tightened, I wasn't sure how much longer I'd be able to.

"Please, have a seat in here," Mamma instructed as she motioned to the salon. We took our places on opposite couches. Charlotte and myself on one. Nina and Sammie on the other. Mamma dragged a Queen Anne chair from the hearth and took her seat between all of us. "Cora's put some coffee on. She'll be here any minute with it."

"Thank you, Mrs. King," the man named Sammie replied.

The rain fell in heavy sheets. The clock's second-hand ticked by, extending the time Paul had been gone tick by tick. And now there were police at Piper Point. What if Paul really *was* gone? *If he is*, another thought tickled, *do I want him found?* Guilt squashed the sentiment, and the room smelled like wine that wasn't there.

"I want to start by apologizing," Nina began, shifting in her seat. "I know this is an unpleasant situation, and a visit from us doesn't help."

Her eyes shot to mine as I bit my bottom lip. It had begun trembling.

She went on, "I also must say, I'm perplexed we had to call. We found the vehicle early this morning."

Mamma spoke up, "We assumed he'd taken it. Paul, that is."

"We've been phoning hotels all afternoon trying to track him down," Charlotte added, taking my hand. Nina arched her brow.

"So this is more than a missing car," Nina stated. I knew what her next words were going to be. I braced myself. "Mr. Godfrey is also missing?"

"Not missing," I corrected. "We just can't account for him at the moment. I understand that could be misconstrued as missing, but really. We had an argument last night."

Nina stopped me. "If you don't mind?" She pulled a tiny recorder from her book bag, switched it on, and sat it on the coffee table.

"Another Palmer with a tape recorder," Mamma whispered. She couldn't help herself. If Nina heard, she maintained a strong poker face and didn't respond.

"You were saying you had an argument?"

As I scratched my throat, my jaw tensed, craving for a drink. "Yes, there was a misunderstanding at the bar last night. Ruby's. He got angry with me."

"Angry?" Nina leaned forward. "About what?"

"Jealous, actually. He was jealous of a guy at the bar. Jacob Wilcox. You remember him?" I strained a smile.

Nina's face remained devoid. "I know him. What happened next?"

"I don't know." I picked at the fresh wound in the corner of my thumbnail. "I don't recall. I was intoxicated."

"Lord, Gray. Really?" Mamma scoffed. Charlotte gave her a stern look, and Mamma rolled her eyes.

"Even if the details are fuzzy," Nina asked, "was there a confrontation? Anything to suggest one might've gone down?"

I scoured my memories, but the further back I traveled, the tighter the invisible fists beating my temples pounded. The dance floor, Jacob, Paul. "I can't say if there was or not."

"And then you left?"

"I don't know—"

"And now your husband is gone?"

"I guess—"

"And how much did you have to drink?"

Three. Say three. Three could account for embarrassing behavior but didn't sound quite like binge drinking. I looked down to my lap, then back at Nina. I wouldn't lie. At least, not this time. Not if the truth was what I needed. "I can't say for sure. I'd had some earlier on the plane. The bartender had a loose pour at Ruby's, too. At least six or seven." *Ten? Eleven?* Even now, I couldn't *not* lie.

I girded for Nina's judgement, but she moved on, "An abandoned vehicle paired with an unaccounted-for person is a serious matter. And you've had no luck tracking down anything? A reservation? Even a gas station purchase?"

"No," Charlotte answered for me. "But he did call on the way home, upset. So, we know he brought Gray here."

"Upset with regards to the argument? Jacob?"

"Yes," Charlotte said.

"I see. And his luggage?"

"Still here," Charlotte replied. "Upstairs in Gray's room."

My mind felt submerged. Soaked and waterlogged and not working when I needed it to most. The lights in the room stretched into long rays. I'd only taken two pills, at least, I thought I'd only taken two. I ripped more skin from my nail bed.

"Where did you find the car?" Mamma asked, stiffening her spine against the upholstered chair.

"Paul Revere Highway. An empty stretch, but not a bad walk from here," Sammie answered, brushing his pants with his palms.

"I don't want to alarm the family, especially you, Gray," Nina began, "but I'd like to consider this a missing persons case. Only as a precaution, and just for the time being."

A missing persons case? Jesus.

Eyes wide as saucers, Mamma looked aghast. "Why on Earth would this be a missing persons case?"

"Because, Mamma, a person is missing," Charlotte retorted.

"It's just a precaution, Mrs. King." Nina looked at me. "It'll get the ball rolling on protocols. Put ears to the ground. Notify police in D.C. to look out for him, too. I'm sure this will turn into nothing, but the formality increases the likelihood it turns into nothing sooner."

"But he's hardly been gone a day. Not even twenty-four hours," Mamma argued. She appeared unimpressed with Nina's reasoning. "Isn't there an elapsed time to be reached before a person can be called missing? Legally speaking?"

"No," Nina answered. "A common misconception, but no. To the contrary, when circumstances prove unusual—like an abandoned rental car, for example—we encourage friends and family to file the report quickly."

Despite the panic pulling my chest into a Gordian knot, Nina's response struck me as odd. She and Sammie had discovered the car early this morning. "Why are we only learning this now?" I asked.

Nina hesitated, seemed unsure for the first time. "I expected a call from you, to be honest."

Whether she intended to or not, she redirected blame to me. If I hadn't drank so much, these questions wouldn't matter. I would've known exactly what happened last night. I'd know where Paul had gone. If I could at least remember the argument we must've had when we returned home, before he stormed off—

The rattling of porcelain scattered my thoughts like cockroaches. Cora sat a coffee cup on the table before me. "Gray, sweetheart," she whispered, leaning down. "Your finger's bleeding."

My thumb. Crimson smeared across the nail as blood oozed from my wound. I stood, thrusting my bleeding hand into my pocket.

"Excuse me, for a moment," I announced and walked through the dining room into the kitchen. As soon as the door shut behind me, I shattered like a hammer taken to glass.

Paul wasn't *missing*. Paul was angry. Paul was jealous. Paul was not . . .

The pendulum in my head swung. I had a handful of pills left, but I had to save them for later tonight. If I took them now, I'd never sleep. Not after this. The thought of not sleeping, of what that'd do to me tomorrow, made me shudder. I began to open cabinets. One after another. Open. Shut. Open. Shut.

When I spied the baking shelf, I froze. Vanilla extract stared from behind a box of cornstarch. I recalled being younger, throwing parties when Mamma and Daddy had gone to the lake house upstate. My friends and I had poured vanilla extract in our diet cokes, and it might as well have been rum. Retrieving the tiny opaque bottle, I read the label. Thirty-five percent ethyl alcohol. I swallowed all of its contents in two gulps before gagging on the brutal bitterness.

When I'd finished, I tossed it in the waste bin beneath the sink and held my mouth under the faucet. The awful taste drowned out whatever buzz the vanilla might have given. Drinking it made me feel silly more than anything.

Voices from the salon carried over the running tap. As everyone went on without me, I bandaged my thumb. When I was finished, I reclaimed my seat next to Charlotte.

Nina looked at me again. Worry etched across her face. "I was telling everyone, I'd like for you to come down to the station first thing in the morning, Gray. Fill out paperwork and give a formal statement. Would you be able to do that?"

Lingering vanilla residue stuck to the inside of my cheeks, and they felt pasty and dry. "Yes."

Charlotte began to speak, but Mamma cut her off. "I'll take

you, Hummingbird." She glanced at my sister. "Those boys have hardly seen their mother as is. Cora will drive us in, won't you dear?"

"Of course, Joanna," Cora replied as she collected our saucers.

* * *

After bidding goodnight to Nina and Sammie through a half-hearted "Merry Christmas," I went up to my room. I locked my door, swallowed the rest of Mamma's Valium, and paced from one wall to another while I waited for them to kick in.

A torrent of rain now lashed against my window, and I recalled Paul's words from the drive in. *No white Christmas this year*, he'd said, eyes on his phone. Who had he always been messaging?

This thing, this *vanishing*, seemed to choke me, pressing on my sternum. Tomorrow the liquor store would reopen.

Minutes marched by, and I grew calmer as the drugs began to slow time. I tried to reason things through the best I could. I'd screwed up. Really screwed up. Enough to send Paul off, but he was no missing person. That was insane. He'd call. Of course, he'd call.

He'll call. My pulse spiked. *My phone!*

I leapt to my nightstand. Why the hell did I keep leaving my phone behind? On today of all days?

I pressed the home button, and the screen lit up. I had a missed call. And a voicemail. Though, the number had been blocked. I couldn't key in my PIN quick enough.

As the message played, my sudden elation deflated. A woman's voice. Not Paul's. And not one I recognized.

"*Hi, Gray,*" she said in the recording. Almost stuttering. "*I'm *sorry for the late call. You don't know me. My name's Annie. I'm calling—*" The woman—Annie—paused. "*I need to talk to you about Paul. I'll be back in touch so keep your phone close.*"

I held my breath.

"*Something else—*" A second, longer hesitation. "*There's something going on here you don't know.*"

10

Gray

No callback number. Nothing. Only the brief voicemail. A handful of words from a stranger. Hushed like she'd held her hand over her mouth while she spoke them.

"Who the hell is Annie?" Mamma asked. She rarely swore. Hearing it shook me.

"I'm not sure. I don't know anyone named Annie." I sat next to her in the rigid backseat of the family Jag on the way to the police station the next morning. The seatbelt pulled tight against my chest and throat.

"Neither do I. Does Paul?"

"I don't think so. I asked the firm to check his contacts."

"They called?" Mamma demanded. Of course, they'd finally called. Nearly two full days of radio silence from Paul might as well be the disappearance of the pope by the way they behaved on the phone.

"Yes, but I didn't tell them anything," I assured her. "I said I misplaced the number for our decorator, Annie, and asked that they check his contacts. Told them undercooked Christmas ham had given Paul food poisoning, and he could barely speak."

"You lie with such ease, Gray," Mamma half whispered, shaking her head. "Hardly have to stop and think about it, do you?"

The question was rhetorical, but who the hell did she think I'd inherited the talent from? Besides, I'd kept the extent of the situation from Paul's bosses for fear of what he might say when he returned. There was still no reason for them to know. Paul was fine. He had to be fine. There wasn't any other way for him to be *except* fine.

Mamma's fear came from a different place. To her, until a thing's been talked about openly, it hasn't yet happened. I turned in time to catch a fleeting glimpse of Matthew's billboard downtown. As far as Mamma was concerned, what he did, what my cousin did, never happened. Her silence had rendered it unmentionable.

She sighed. "That's good. The Palmer woman said not to worry. She said all this is nothing more than a precaution."

"Her name is Nina," I corrected. Mamma's casual slight irked me, and I couldn't stop it from leaking into my voice. "Nina Palmer."

She rifled through her clutch, producing a pack of Virginia Slims. Her sterling lighter sparked alive like an expensive firecracker.

"Jesus, Mamma," I said. "In the car?"

She scoffed. "You're going to speak to me about vices? And don't take the Lord's name in vain. I raised you better than to talk like that. D.C. has been nothing but bad for you. It's a blessing we never moved there years ago."

"Put the window down for Cora's sake, at least." I motioned towards the driver's seat. Cora said nothing as she hung a left onto Marion Avenue. Mamma cracked her window a reluctant sliver.

"None of this makes sense," she said, pulling in a long, glowing drag. "Why would Paul not come home two nights in a row? What happened on Christmas Eve?"

"I told you I don't remember." I tugged at the seatbelt, but the harder I pulled, the less it gave. A constricting safety mechanism.

"This has to stop, Gray." Her eyes remained turned to the window as tendrils of smoke danced around her silver hair. "The drinking has got to stop."

I stifled a chuckle from somewhere deep down. Didn't she realize I knew that? Didn't she know I traced every trouble that found me to drinking? In the rare instances it wasn't the cause, it was always a contributor.

My job at the National Museum of Natural History. I'd studied anthropology in college before dropping out senior year to follow Paul to D.C. It had been a part-time post giving guided tours.

Had been.

My coworker—a geriatric woman who made small talk a difficult chore—had taken a healthy swallow from my water thermos. We used the same brand, and she'd mistaken it for hers. The notion that Vodka could possibly be tasteless was a lie.

"We can't have someone under the influence around children," the chief curator had told me, before leaning in to whisper, "Don't worry, Mr. Godfrey urged discretion, and we intend to leave it alone. But you need to go."

Even when I was careful, when I really tried, drinking caught up to me. Now Paul was missing. Or gone, rather.

Where could he be? I swallowed a knot in the back of my throat. *Is he safe?*

Outside my window, the brick courthouse whirled by. Then

a park with a derelict gazebo followed by a strip of boutiques and specialty shops all trying too hard to be something they weren't. An overcast sky sagged low to the ground. It had rained every night since I'd arrived. Today looked like it would be no different.

The pills had gotten me to sleep last night, but I didn't remember dreaming. When I'd awoken, I was relieved I'd made it to five forty-five AM. But that relief vanished as Paul's absence flooded back into my mind.

Still, I'd greeted the morning with a clear head. I hadn't had a drop of alcohol the day before—if I didn't count the vanilla extract, which I didn't. Mornings without a hangover were usually easy for me. The itching wouldn't show up until the afternoon.

"And this woman. Annie. She didn't leave a number?" Mamma asked.

I shook my head. We'd been through this earlier in the morning. I'd been through it with Charlotte the night before nearly as soon as I'd set my phone down.

Mamma prodded. "You don't think Paul would ever be unfaith—"

"No."

Cora parked the car and picked up a pile of clothes wrapped in plastic from the front passenger seat. "I'll be at the dry cleaners," she announced. "Phone as soon as you're finished, and I'll be back to collect you."

"Thank you, dear," Mamma replied as she stepped out of the car. I followed suit, and together we walked up to the sheriff's office.

"We need to have Cora sign a nondisclosure agreement," she said as she outed her cigarette in the ashtray out front. "I'll have one drafted this afternoon."

Mamma's obsession with privacy was nothing new, but the lengths she'd go to keep secrets always jarred me. Together, we crossed the threshold into the station.

"Have a seat," the receptionist—an officer—told us. We retreated to a row of hard plastic chairs against a far wall.

"Uncomfortable," Mamma said, shifting in her seat.

My pulse raced. No word from Paul for two days, and now I sat in a police station. No matter what Charlotte or Nina or any-one else said, events seemed to be marching closer and closer to some worst-case scenario, one I'd been imagining since Christ-mas morning in the library. It wasn't yet a fleshed-out-nightmare situation, but something more nebulous. A faceless, nameless dread. But so long as the dread wasn't made real, so long as no one spoke it or named it, it lived only in the shadows of my mind—and I intended to keep it there, trapped. I wasn't so dif-ferent from Mamma in that regard.

Nina greeted us. "Gray, Joanna." She held a folder under one arm and wore fitted jeans and a light cardigan. Mamma had insisted the two of us dress up. "Sunday clothes, Gray," she'd said when I first came downstairs in a pair of slacks and a loose button-down blouse. Standing before a casually dressed Nina, I now felt awkward. A trip to the police station isn't an *occasion*, and it was stupid of Mamma to make me change.

"Follow me," Nina instructed. We traced her steps through a maze of cubicles. The space smelled like any other office. Coffee. The hum made by low chatter and typing bounced off thin walls.

We passed officers and admins. Some in blues. Others in plainclothes like Nina. I recognized a handful of faces from school and growing up. Mamma must have as well, from the way she smiled at folks. Sammie walked by on his way to the restroom or the water fountain. It didn't seem like he planned to join us.

Would he be on the far side of some two-way mirror? Was Nina going to play games the way police on TV did? My arms goose-bumped. *I am the last person seen with Paul.*

"In here." Nina motioned to a glassed-in conference room. No two-way mirrors. "We call it the Fish Bowl." She smiled. Three sides looked into the station, one faced the dreary outside. We took our seats around a long, lacquered table.

"Can I get you anything? Coffee? Juice?" she asked, pulling back a roller chair.

"We're fine," Mamma answered. "We just want to get this done and over with."

"I understand," she replied, taking a seat at the table head and opening her folder. She began to pass me printed forms. "I'll need signatures on these papers to file the missing persons case on your behalf."

My palms dampened. Mamma, my sister—they couldn't come up with simple excuses for Paul's vanishing anymore. Now police were involved. A couple pen strokes and everything becomes brutally real. Fingers shaking, I signed them hastily. Nina watched my hands as I scrawled, so I signed faster than I otherwise would've, a series of slapdash lines. Illegible.

"Thank you." She took the papers back. "Now, I'll need to conduct a formal interview. Let's start with the basics. Date and time of last contact, age, height, weight, eye color. That sort of thing."

She noted my answers as I gave them. I couldn't tell her Paul's driver's license number. Who knows that offhand? The questions quickly grew more complex.

What medications does Paul take?

What's Paul's blood type?

Any reason to believe Paul might be at risk of either injury or death?

Under the table, I dug my nails into my thighs.

Nina exhaled as she finished writing down my answers. "This next one's going seem a bit redundant after our conversation last night, but I'll need an official answer."

"Okay . . ."

"What reasons do you, as the reporting person, have to believe Paul is missing?"

"I don't think he's missing," I answered. "We're going through this as a formality. At your suggestion. We had a fight. He took off to cool down." My reasoning rang hollower every time I repeated it. More and more time had passed since I'd first made the assertion.

Nina held that same stout poker face, but she no doubt heard my argument for all its hollowness, too.

"You indicated there had been a fight? Over Jacob Wilcox?"

"Yes."

"Intoxication from alcohol prevented your recollection of events beyond that initial fight?"

"Yes." I avoided Mamma's eyes.

"Has Paul been jealous before?"

"Well, yes. But everyone gets jealous."

She paused for a moment, then continued, "Let me turn the question around: Have you ever been jealous of Paul?"

"I don't understand," I told her. *What do I have to be jealous of Paul for?*

"Have you ever questioned Paul's own fidelity? The way he seemed to have questioned yours?"

This line of inquiry made me itch, and my thoughts darted to his phone. To the way he'd kept its screen obscured. "Why is that important?"

Her face was unchanged. "Sometimes in stressful situations,

people project their own feelings onto others. When someone's hiding something, it's not unusual to accuse loved ones of keeping secrets themselves. Perhaps Paul became accusatory because of his own insecurities?"

I shook my head. "That's crazy. He'd never. Besides, I . . ." I hesitated as Nina leaned forward. "I kissed Jacob. Or at least, he kissed me. I don't remember which."

"Gray!" Mamma's face flushed.

I explained quickly. "Briefly. I tried to stop him. At least, I think I did."

"And Paul saw this?" Nina asked.

"Yes. He did. I'm sure of that much."

"And that's where the memories stop?"

"Yes."

Nina leaned back in her chair.

"There's something else," I dug my phone out from my hand bag. "A voicemail. A woman called me last night, but I didn't have my phone." I placed my cell phone on the table top. Screen up.

"You didn't have your phone, and your husband is missing?" Nina looked incredulous.

My foolishness had caught up to me again, like a razor-toothed trap I'd set, only to forget about and later walk into. "I know it sounds stupid. It is stupid."

She creased her brow. "Who is the woman? What did she say?"

"She said she wanted to talk to me about Paul. She said her name's Annie, and she'd be in touch. No callback number. The caller ID had been blocked, too."

Phone on speaker, I played the cryptic voicemail.

". . . *there's something going on here you don't know,*" the woman whispered as she wrapped up her message. She sounded a touch different now. A dash smug.

Nina spoke, "A woman named Annie calls the day after Paul disappears and indicates a desire to communicate with you. But leaves no number? That's interesting."

"It's absurd is what it is," Mamma added.

"And I'm guessing the name Annie rings no bells?" Nina's tone had changed. Maybe Annie's voicemail would change her approach? Take the glare off me?

"No. And why would she say she wanted to talk and not provide a number? Set her own number to private?" I scoured Nina's face for an explanation.

"Perhaps she's afraid of something, something leading her to hide her contact information. But it's not frightening enough to prevent her from at least attempting to reach out. Or . . ."

"Or?" My eyes widened. I clung to each new word as though they were rungs on a ladder meant to rescue me from drowning.

Nina spoke slowly, "Maybe she's alerting you to her presence. To her existence."

11

Nina

As the interview concluded, I handed off the paperwork to Sammie, who'd popped in to collect it. His timing had been perfect. Sammie had a sixth sense for when he was needed as a foil. To drain whatever tension the Fish Bowl had accumulated.

Joanna King came with her own set of concerns. "You won't disclose the report to anyone, will you? Beyond law enforcement?" she asked as I escorted her and Gray to reception.

"It's standard practice not to comment on any ongoing investigation when asked. But—"

"But someone like Paul," Joanna said, "he's so well known amongst certain people. Important people. And this is a very delicate matter."

Her unusual request stopped me in my tracks, and I did my best to speak clearly. "Mrs. King, alerting the media to Paul's absence might be helpful. At the very least, it'll multiply the pairs of eyes on the lookout for him. If he is engaged in something . . ." I glanced at Gray, "untoward, it might expedite his return to the family."

"Untoward?" Joanna arched her brow. Gray remained silent, fidgeting with the strap of her designer bag.

"If he's in some way involved with this woman, Annie, wider knowledge of his absence might compel him to come home. For someone like him, the media is often the best tool for this."

"But he's not a child. There's no Amber Alert to send down the wire. You don't have to tell anyone on the outside."

The idea of people knowing irked her. I wondered if uncovering Mr. Godfrey's whereabouts was nearly as important to her. Joanna's check to Auntie Tilda rushed to the forefront of my mind.

"Recall, Mrs. King, it wasn't until news of Governor Mark Sanford's absence broke, that he returned from his trip to Argentina," I said.

Joanna shot down the comparison to the disgraced South Carolina politician. "Don't be ridiculous. Paul's not cavorting with some South American mistress."

Dancing around the subject was getting us nowhere. "According to you and your daughter, Paul isn't at risk of injury from any medical condition. The keys had been taken from the abandoned vehicle indicating a desire to maintain access to the car or whatever else he had keys for in his life. And a woman makes her presence known the instant he runs off. After a jealous altercation. I believe it would behoove us to alert news outlets."

Joanna began to speak again, but Gray interrupted. "Do it," she said. "Inform the news."

"Gray, he's preparing a run for office." Joanna struggled to whisper, but her icy eyes remained tightly focused on mine.

Now it made sense. "Mrs. King, until Paul is located, he's not running for anything."

"I said to do it," Gray repeated. "I'm his wife. It's not up to Mamma."

"Thank you." I nodded. "Sammie's uploading your report to all the appropriate databases now. We'll begin monitoring the accounts Paul maintains access to. And, importantly," I paused to lock eyes with Gray, "we need to identify *who* Annie is and *where* Annie is. Whatever her motivation, I suspect she'll reach out again. You need to let me know the moment this happens."

"I understand," Gray replied.

"I'll phone Channel Thirteen and the *Elizabeth Gazette*. Be prepared for questions, phone inquiries, reporters showing up at Piper Point unannounced. Remember, the more information we share, the sooner Paul returns."

"Mrs. King." A baritone voice called from behind me. *Sheriff Burton.*

A moment later my boss stood beside me, uniform diligently pressed. Short and completely bald. Arms gym-thickened to compensate for both.

"I wanted to say hello before y'all left," he drawled. "Give you my personal assurances this matter will be resolved quickly and to your liking. Won't it, Nina?" He managed to patronize me and overpromise in a single breath. A personal best on his part?

"Absolutely," I replied.

"See that you do," Joanna said, added, "The both of you."

The two women smiled—Joanna's faked and Gray's strained—and vanished through the revolving front doors.

I'd yet to fully make up my mind about Auntie Tilda's will, but Joanna King's penchant for secrecy put me over the edge. I'd become executer over my lunch break today.

Intense discretion, my ass.

* * *

Later on, I sat at Auntie Tilda's kitchen table. Jasmine tea in a Disney mug, notepad, and tape recorder in front of me. I rewound the tape and played it back again.

Gray's words came off staggered. She was nervous, which was understandable. But I couldn't help feeling something else was weighing her down, punctuating her sentences with a fear that went beyond Paul's absence. Perhaps the idea of an unfaithful husband burdened her heavier than a missing one.

"Can you list everyone you recall having contact with that evening? Paul, too?" I asked on the tape. *"I'll need to speak with each of them."*

"Yes. Of course," she replied. *"There was Frances Miles—you know her. Obviously, Jacob Wilcox. Oh, a man at the bar I chatted with briefly. Jonas was his name, I think. We took a couple shots together."*

"But no Annie," I'd said.

"No. There may have been an Annie there, but if there was, I don't know her."

I stopped the tape and took a sip of tea. I'd listed Jacob Wilcox, then Frances Miles next. Then Jonas X and Annie X. The list of names on my notepad wasn't long. I needed to speak with Charlotte, too. She could corroborate Gray's intoxication and give me a more reliable timeline than either Gray or her mother.

I fished my phone out of my book bag on the floor. The sooner I contacted each of these people, the better. Charlotte, Frances, and Jacob would be simple enough. It might take a few calls to find this Jonas, but Elizabeth was only so big. Annie, on the other hand, might not be easy.

But I had a feeling she'd make another attempt at contact with Gray. The question was why'd she pause midmessage to abort without leaving a callback number? Even if she wanted to help, perhaps she viewed whatever information she had as dangerous, potentially damaging to the soon-to-be candidate Paul or Gray or both. The King family may no longer be Elizabeth's feudal lords like they once were, but an echo of their influence remained. *If* Annie had ever been in town, Matthew and his damned billboard might've scared her off.

The other possibility was tawdrier. And more believable. Annie was Paul's mistress. The mistress he'd presumably run off with—at least temporarily. And mistresses tended to be territorial. My own mother had played the role more than once herself: The persistent phone calls to the man's home. The hang ups that followed once the wife answered. The calls often continued or intensified when the husband was out of town—sometimes even when he was out of town *with* the mistress. Regardless of the husband's long-term intentions, inevitably the mistress wanted him as her own. And for that to occur, the family must be destroyed. The calls acted like terrorism. They spread insecurity and fear throughout the household, predisposing it to unraveling.

I couldn't help but wonder if this was what Annie intended. If not terrorism, perhaps this was a victory lap?

My phone vibrated. Sheriff Burton's number displayed.

"Sir," I answered. "What's up?"

"Paul Godfrey," he started.

"Right."

"I know I said this earlier, but I want to make sure you get it. Paul's case is priority number one. Folks betting on his election are getting antsy up in the District. Wanna know if they've still got a candidate they can count on."

"Understood."

"I've relaxed your budget. I want this put away fast. I've also phoned Charleston; they're dispatching a forensics team to Paul Revere Highway. I've declared it a pending crime scene till Paul turns up. They'll take care of everything on that front."

I took another sip of tea. Still hot. "Thanks for that, Sheriff. In the meantime, I want to move on my current theory."

"The Governor Sanford hypothesis?" Laughter hid behind his words.

"Correct. Anything that ratchets up the heat on Paul to return to his family gets leaked to the press. We need to pull his finances, everything. Anything potentially embarrassing needs to be identified."

"To use as leverage in a missing persons case?" Burton's promise to Joanna scrolled through my mind: *To your liking.*

Another sip. "We need to smoke Paul out. If he's in Bermuda with a woman named Annie, this is how we do it. Besides, forensics won't be done in a day."

"I'm concerned with how this might look," Burton replied. "Not that I don't buy into your working theory. I'm just worried about how this might come off. Especially . . ."

Returning the mug to the table with a thud, I got ahead of him. "Because of my aunt's past with the family?"

A pause on the other end of the line. Even if he was thinking it, he wasn't ready to go there. Yet. "Mr. Godfrey is a VIP, and you know damn well that family is, too. At least around here. Everything we do is going to be scrutinized. This ain't a John Doe by any stretch."

"Agreed."

Burton hesitated, said, "There's already a snafu in the timeline." Papers rustled. "A delay with regards to a rental car."

"I checked reports, kept you looped in."

"I recall, Nina. But you've got to be careful. Do this really right."

"We're on the same page here, sir." I drew a deep breath. "Look, as far as we know, Paul's run off. And as far as I'm concerned, the less I have to do with the Kings, the better. Believe me. But this is my job, and I'm taking it seriously."

"See that you do." He redirected Joanna's instruction to him to me, verbatim. With a muffled click, he hung up.

I paused as his words replayed in my mind. *Leverage in a missing persons case.* When you said it like that, of course it came off sounding sour. But likely, that's what had happened. Paul had run off with Annie. This was how you brought someone like him back. *You give him something to lose.*

This had nothing to do with damaging the King family. Nothing to do with Joanna's checks to Auntie, either.

I stood and paced to the junk drawer by the fridge. I'd tucked Auntie's last few bank statements in it. Word had spread around town that I stayed here to look after her so the probate office hadn't hesitated to grant me executorship. They happily looked the other way when I forged her signature next to mine. Funny how well "cancer" served as an explanation for nearly anything. After that, the bank hadn't given a second thought to giving me access to her single checking account.

As I expected, Mrs. King's severance check had been the latest in a long line of them. Always issued towards the end of the quarter. Always one thousand dollars.

It read like a payoff. But why? The damage from Auntie's tape had already been done. In a huge, nasty way. The late Seamus King had left the campaign trail in disgrace. It had been bad, but long forgotten. At least, by most folks.

Having something to lose motivates folks to behave unusually. I was counting on the idea to force Paul to surface. But what did Joanna have to lose?

12

Gray

Exactly one television existed at Piper Point. An older model in a wooden box stood in the cramped den off the kitchen. The same green loveseat sat before it, broken in from years of service to Daddy.

At 5:58 PM, I sat there with Charlotte by my side. Mamma hovered behind us. Cora was baking cookies, chocolate chip by the smell, with Joseph and David. We waited for the six o'clock news. For the iron shoe that promised to drop with it.

I'd never needed a drink so badly.

Not once had I been left alone today. There'd been no chance to slip into the liquor store, and I'd taken the rest of the pills I'd pilfered the night before.

"You better call Paul's mother. She's the only living family Paul has, and she deserves to hear this from you. Not the news," Mamma declared.

The grandfather clock in the foyer chimed, cutting her off. *Too late.* The screen turned to Channel Thirteen's logo along with the station's trumpeting soundtrack.

"*Missing,*" a voiceover boldly announced. "*Prominent*

Washington lobbyist Paul Godfrey's whereabouts unknown. This is a special report."

The shot opened to a woman behind a simple news anchor desk. I recognized her face. She cheered for Pickens High, if I remembered correctly.

"Good evening," she began. "I'm Bethany Douglas, and tonight, I come to you with news of a missing persons report. Paul Godfrey, husband of Charleston shipping heiress Gray King Godfrey and Democratic candidate for congress, was reported missing earlier today."

I couldn't see Mamma's grimace, but it was plain in her voice behind me. "The run hadn't been announced. That Palmer woman leaked it."

"It'll put more pressure on Paul," Charlotte said, taking my hand in a tight squeeze. "It was the right thing to do." I clasped hers mostly to stop my own from shaking.

Bethany continued, "Mr. Godfrey was last seen patronizing Ruby's Pub in the early hours of Christmas morning with his wife and several family members."

"Several family members?" Mamma interrupted again. "They make it sound like we were all there. Celebrating Jesus' birth with hard liquor. Channel Thirteen never bothered with facts before, why start now?"

"His vehicle was discovered abandoned on Paul Revere Highway hours later by county law enforcement in a spot not far from the King property. Police are asking anyone with information regarding his whereabouts to phone the sheriff's office tip line immediately."

The screen showed a photo of Paul, smiling in a tuxedo. I recognized it as a shot from the black-tie gala at the Jefferson

Hotel early last spring. Cooper and Waters had just secured the government of Saudi Arabia as a client.

As Bethany went on with details of Paul's looks and stature, my vision blurred, and her words grew distant. I needed something for my crawling anxiety. Anything to stop the skittering up and down my arms and legs.

The telephone in the kitchen rang.

"Here we go," Mamma sighed.

A baking sheet clanged on the counter as Cora left to answer the phone.

My thoughts flew straight to Annie. Was she calling? Did she have Mamma's house number, too? Would she have more to say? If she knew where he was, that was almost worse. That would mean Nina was right, that Paul was involved with her.

"Joanna, telephone," Cora called out. "A reporter from the *Gazette*."

I exhaled. Why did that relieve me? They could be wrong. Nina, Charlotte, Mamma. They could be wrong about an affair or whatever other thoughts they harbored. Maybe Annie had information that would help us find Paul. Innocent information.

"Tell them we have no comment and direct them to Sheriff Burton," Mamma answered. Twenty years later and she still remembered how to handle the press. The bitter taste they'd left in her mouth must have lingered.

The doorbell rang.

"Good lord. Shoo them off, you hear?" she instructed Cora, whose steps dwindled as she made for the front door.

Unattended, the twins entered the den. "Where *is* Uncle Paul?" one asked. Baking cookies had been a futile attempt to draw their attention from the television in the den, but the room breathed tension. Stealing the air from all of us. They'd have sensed it. Children always sensed when things were off. I did when I was young. Though, I'd been too late.

Charlotte released my hand and went to them. "Uncle Paul had some business to do. You know how important he is. Lots of people need his help, and he went to help them." She hugged them both. One stared blankly while the other's face scrunched up. "He'll be back soon."

"But when?" the child asked, scratching his nose. Charlotte shushed him with a kiss to the cheek. Taking each by the hand, she led them out of the room.

Another ring from the telephone. With Cora at the front door, Mamma stood to get it. I pulled my phone from my pocket and entered my PIN. There were two calls I was willing to take: Paul's and "Unknown," in the event Annie reached out again. Instead, only the same thirteen missed calls displayed. All of them from Paul's firm.

"That was Cooper and Waters," Mamma said as she returned, taking Charlotte's vacated seat in the slouching sofa. "They send well-wishes to the family. They also expressed a great amount of worry. They've been trying to reach you, Gray. They feel blindsided by all this."

I returned my phone to my pocket. "And how do they think I feel?"

Mamma appeared startled by my sharp reply. I didn't care. I was blindsided, too. *I'm his wife for Christ's sake. Not a child.* But that's the way everyone thought of me. *Can't be trusted. Can't be left alone.* It was no wonder my thoughts went straight to wine.

I shut my eyes.

My response seemed to register, and she softened her voice. "They've also offered services."

I opened my eyes. "What sort of services?"

She folded her arms. "An investigator. A private one to work alongside the police here."

"They don't trust the police to do their job?" I asked. Did I trust them? I thought of Nina. I trusted her, had no reason not to. Then I remembered my nagging question from the evening before. Why had she delayed contacting us about our lost rental car? If filing a report quickly was so important, why the wait?

"I can't say I blame Paul's firm." Mamma shrugged. "I suggest we take them up on the offer. It'll do no harm to have more folks on the case."

It pained me to admit it, but Mamma was right. It would do no harm. At least none I could think of. "Alright," I relented. "I'll call them back in a moment. I need to collect myself."

The look on Mamma's face, nose slightly upturned, said we both knew exactly what I meant. "I need to take a minute or two to breathe, okay?"

The phone rang again. Cora was free to answer this time. Another reporter with questions for the family.

"I tucked the boys in early," Charlotte said as she returned. "They need a break from all the excitement." She glanced at me for a brief moment. Did she blame me at all for this? I wouldn't fault her if she did. I blamed myself.

Mamma leaned back a bit. "I can't help but wonder . . ." We stayed silent as she pondered her thought aloud. "It might do us good to retain a lawyer. With reporters coming out from the woodwork, and given the details surrounding the disappearance, a family spokesperson might be nice."

My mouth dropped. She couldn't possibly mean—

"Someone local," she went on. "Someone who knows Elizabeth and the people who have roles in these matters. Matthew is—"

"Jesus Christ, Mamma!" Charlotte snapped. "Don't you finish that thought. Even if we did need a lawyer, which we don't, Gray and Paul already have one in D.C. But we'll *never* need *him*."

Him. Matthew.

An invisible band wrapped around my head. It tightened and squeezed as Charlotte and Mamma argued. Two drinks and it'd loosen. Two more drinks than I could get.

Mamma had been campaigning with Daddy in Beaufort. Miss Tilda had caught a nasty stomach bug, and my cousin had stepped up to watch us in a pinch.

I was nine. Four-year-old Charlotte had gone to the playroom at the end of the long hall. Spritely giggles from a cartoon she watched echoed through Piper Point. A home empty of anyone but Charlotte and myself. And Matthew.

He had been my favorite relative. I bickered with the others—the cousins closer to my own age. We all wanted to play with the same dolls at the same times, act out the same characters during make-believe. They weren't fair like Matthew, who was older, more mature at seventeen. They didn't love me like he did, either. In our games, he'd let me be whatever I wanted, play with any toy I cared to. We never fought. Not once.

Eyes to my black polished shoes, white lace folded over their tops, I'd made my way to the playroom to join Charlotte. I was tiny, but the pine planks still groaned under my feet. They groaned heavier as Matthew's steps joined mine not far behind.

"Gray," he whispered. A scratchy whisper. I froze, turned. "Gray," he repeated, nearly caught up to me. "Gray, you're a good girl, aren't you?"

A weird question. But the way he asked it excited me. What was he after? I supposed I was a good girl and told Matthew as much.

"Shame," he replied, shaking his head. "Too bad."

The disappointment on Matthew's face was plain, and I chewed my lip. He wanted to hear something else.

"Why?" I asked. I was a good girl. Or I always tried to be. And Mamma and Miss Tilda always said so. To me, to other folks. But a corner of me thought I didn't have to be. At least not all the time. If being a good girl disappointed Matthew, I could change. Just for a little while.

"Because I know something." He shrugged.

"A secret?" My thumping heart fluttered.

Matthew leaned closer. "Well, yeah. A secret. But I'm worried—"

"Tell me! You have to tell me!"

"But you're a good—"

"Tell me, Matt!" I stomped one foot. He would tell me. I knew he would. He just wanted to watch me squirm a little. He always teased me like that at first, before coming around. Everything with Matthew started off as a trick but never stayed that way. He'd let me in on the secret. Sometimes, *just* me.

He paused, bit his bottom lip. "It ain't pretty. It's not nice, I mean. That's why I asked if you were really a good girl." He knelt. Our eyes met one another's, and the black centers of his grew large.

"What is it?" I searched his silent face.

"I've seen the Devil." His eyes flickered like candle flames. His breathing, heavy.

"The Devil? How do you know?"

"Because, Gray." He hesitated, leaned in closer. The tips of our noses nearly touched. His breath smelled a little like metal. Wet copper or tin. "The Devil lives here. *Inside* Piper Point."

A tingle inched its way up my spine, and my arms goose-bumped. All the way to my bare shoulders beneath the ruffled straps of my blouse. "Where?" I whispered now, too.

"In the cellar. The Devil lives in the cellar."

"He does not!" My voice rose as pictures of cackling demons from Sunday School books formed in my mind. Fire and pitchforks. Even this was little too far for him. He'd be impressed to see he couldn't fool me.

But Matthew's tone remained steady. "He lives inside the furnace. Down in the cellar. I seen him."

Was he tricking me? A knot formed in the pit of my stomach.

Matthew continued, "You wanna see?"

No. I didn't want to see. I didn't want to go down into the cellar, and Mamma said I wasn't allowed to, anyways. Except, a piece of me did. The piece of me that wasn't a good girl. At least, not right now. And if Matthew was lying, I'd show him I didn't buy it. I'd show him I wasn't afraid of breaking the rules, and I wasn't afraid of the cellar. But if he wasn't lying—

"I'll show you." Matthew clasped my hand in his. It was damp; ice-cold and sweaty all at once. I caught the flash of a crocodile grin across his face as he led me down the foyer stairs.

Mamma's sharp drawl pulled me into the present, back into the TV room—the TV that had just told the world Paul was missing.

"Don't you shout at me, Charlotte Belle." Mamma stood to brush the front of her checkered dress. Her cheeks reddened. "I'm only looking out for this family."

"With a suggestion like that, one could be forgiven for thinking otherwise," Charlotte retorted. "Come on, Gray, let's go for a walk before the rain starts up again."

"Yes," I whispered. "A walk might help." She reached down and took my limp hand.

"Gray, are you okay? Your hand," she creased her brow and squinted, "it's so cold."

I nodded dismissively, but Charlotte was right. The tips of my fingers, my toes, all tingled from bloodlessness. Matthew had that effect on me.

13

Nina

Le Beans Coffee Shop stood between a shuttered tailor and an antique chandelier dealer on Edisto Street. Elizabeth had yet to catch the attention of Starbucks so a town local had taken advantage of an unusual vacancy in a crowded market. Like its name, the café came off as contrived. Liberal use of the terms *nondairy, fair trade,* and *locally sourced* made me wonder if the owner knew what the phrases meant. One placard even indicated the coffee beans were *free* trade.

"I'll have a medium house brew," I told an eager barista. The young man wrote my name on a cup and took my cash. I found a seat by a long row of windows. The nasty clouds looming over Elizabeth had parted and sunlight—however brief—swaddled a handful of tables.

I'd asked Charlotte to meet me for a cup of coffee this morning, and she'd obliged. Being present at Ruby's on Christmas Eve made her a priority, and I didn't like the way Joanna had stifled her attempt to bring Gray down to the station yesterday. It was like Joanna didn't trust Charlotte to handle things correctly—*her* version of correctly.

That the truth might not factor prominently in Joanna's decision-making bothered me. The biggest rise I'd gotten out of her hadn't been during Gray's anxiety-ridden interview, it had erupted when I mentioned the press. It was important to cut Joanna out of the conversation when possible.

Halfway through my coffee, I spotted Gray's younger sister coming up the sidewalk. She waved as she stepped through the glass door. I waved back and waited until she returned with her own cup before saying a formal hello.

"Mrs. Barfield, thanks so much for meeting me."

"No problem, Nina. And please, call me Charlotte." She took the seat across from me. "Absolutely anything I can do or say to help."

She sounded genuine. We were off to a good start, then. "I take it all of this has hit the family hard. How are you doing?"

A deep sigh escaped her as she slid her handbag towards the edge of the table. "It's crazy. Things were already so . . . tough. And now this?"

"It's unbelievable," I said, softening my tone and taking a casual sip. "Were things not okay before?"

"It's not important." Charlotte picked at one of her nails. Not obviously manicured, but polished and kept nonetheless. "At least not in this matter."

I leaned closer. "Talk if you'd like to talk. In my experience, even the tiniest details can be important."

She offered a tiny grin, but it appeared to take considerable effort. "I'm sorry. I don't want to make this about me, it's just I've had a lot going on. My divorce was finalized a month ago."

"I'm sorry to hear that."

"Please, don't be." She looked at the ceiling, then down again. "It's the best thing for me and the boys. I'm not sure if you know, but I have twins. Joseph and David." Her eyes lit up as she named them.

"Congratulations," I added, though I didn't recall seeing any children on my visit to Piper Point. Of course, they may have been hidden away in an upstairs room. Kept away from the procedural conversation downstairs.

"In any case, Will was trouble. He was wrong for me, and judging from his texts from a woman named Florencia, I was obviously wrong for him."

"I'm sorry," I said, shaking my head. Privately, I was pleased to hear it. Not pleased that Charlotte had been put through the wringer by a cheating husband, but happy she spoke so freely about it. If I could get the information I needed without pushing, it might keep me in the sister's good graces. I held no illusions when it came to my welcome status at Piper Point.

Charlotte continued, seeming to chuckle in disbelief as she did. "Life's felt like a complete train wreck over the past year. I thought it would be a good idea to come back. Get the boys out of Raleigh and away from painful memories. Give them some room to run."

"Makes sense. It's important to be around family during the holidays."

Her eyes widened, and her shoulders shook in exasperation. "Then this happened. This thing with Paul. I don't know why I ever thought coming back to Elizabeth would solve anything. This town—it seems like shit happens more often here."

"You never could've predicted something like this would occur," I replied.

"You're right about that." She shook her head and took another swallow. I noted her ring finger. Empty save a faint tan line matching her story. "I assume that's what you'd like to talk about. Not my personal catastrophe. Paul and Gray and Christmas Eve, right?"

"Yes." I did my best to smile warmly. "As someone who was there that night, I was hoping you might've come down to the station with Gray and your mother."

Charlotte returned her cup to the table, and her face grew long. "I would've liked to, but Mamma's always vehement when it comes to how things are done. And honestly, I had reservations about leaving the boys alone with all the uncertainty around Paul."

I leaned forward on the table, resting my chin on my hand. "Right. How are they handling things?"

"They seem to be okay. On the surface, they appear oblivious, but I don't buy it. Kids always know more than they let on. I know I did as a child. And Joseph and David are always so watchful. I'm planning on doing something for them later this afternoon. Maybe a movie or a trip into Charleston."

"And how about Gray? How's she holding up?" I asked guiding the conversation back to her sister.

Charlotte cast her eyes to the table and paused. As though taking a moment to decide exactly what to say.

"Not well," she finally answered, meeting my eyes. "But given the circumstances, I'm just happy she's not completely broken, truth be told."

I nodded. "Understandable. I try to empathize, but I can't really know what's going through her mind or how she feels."

"Not only is her husband missing," Charlotte went on, "but she was there and can't remember a damn thing. The helplessness must be excruciating."

"That much to drink, huh?"

Charlotte twisted and crumpled a pink packet of Sweet'N

Low as she answered, dusting a spot on the table white. "Yeah. She'd been drinking all day long. It was the flight. She hates flying."

Her answer came off like an excuse for Gray, but I decided to agree with her. "Lots of people do." I shrugged. "'Five o'clock somewhere' takes on a new meaning in airports."

"Towards the end of the night, before I left, I could see she was . . ." Charlotte hesitated. It seemed difficult to speak of her sister this way. "Plastered. She could barely stand on her own two feet."

"That uncoordinated?" I asked, realizing at once I'd chosen the wrong word.

Charlotte crossed her arms. "I know what you're looking for, Nina. Paul is missing, and his wife was the last person seen with him. You want me to tell you what I saw Gray doing that night. You want me to tell you if she might have had something to do with his disappearance. Look at the wife first. That sort of thing."

No use pretending any longer. "In so many words."

"The answer is no, *detective*," she stated firmly. "Gray was drunk. Incredibly drunk. And if you really want to know what I think, it wasn't Paul I was worried about after he called me on the way home."

"What do you mean?"

"Paul was crying. He was very upset, and I knew Gray was likely passed out in the passenger seat. I was relieved to find her the next day with *only* a hangover."

An interesting point. It wasn't unusual for the successful to be hot-tempered, but did Paul cross a line that night? Maybe a line he'd crossed before that led Charlotte to worry? "I'm sorry for the questions, but I've got to ask. Have you ever known Paul to hurt Gray?"

"No. I haven't personally seen anything to suggest that," she answered. "But there's a first time for everything, and that night might've been it."

"Was Paul also intoxicated?"

"Paul doesn't drink," Charlotte replied with an assuredness I'd expect from a spouse. Not a sister-in-law who lived in a different state.

"What do you think happened that night? Any idea where Paul is?" If Charlotte had a theory, it might provide insight into Gray's relationship with her husband.

She answered quickly, perhaps eager to clear Gray of any wrongdoing. "I think he planned to hurt her. I think he was so upset, so angry, he planned to hurt my sister." She pushed her empty cup away and spoke forcefully. "Then he thought better of it. If word got out he'd laid a hand on his wife, he could kiss a political career goodbye. I think he brought her home and then left for a motel. He didn't trust himself near her so he put real distance between them."

Her reply made perfect sense except for one glaring omission. "And what about the voicemail? The one from the woman calling herself Annie?"

She exhaled, gathering her handbag back to her chest. "I don't know what to think about it. A prank call, maybe?"

"But the timing—"

"Yeah, I know. It's really bizarre she called right after Paul took off." She glanced out the window and then at the watch on her small wrist.

"Really bizarre."

She shifted in her seat, making evident her patience was stretching. "Coincidences do happen, though. All the time."

"One last question, Charlotte. I can't count on Joanna for

straight answers, and your sister seems too broken up to even consider the possibility. Do you think Paul was having an affair? Maybe with this woman, Annie?"

"No," she answered, eyes lingering on mine. "I've never suspected Paul of an affair. And I'd know. I slept next to an adulterer for years."

Charlotte dropped her purse on the table with a heavy thud that screamed our conversation was over.

"Excuse me, detective. Busy day. Kids," she said and exited the café. As the door swung closed behind her, I began processing our discussion. Leaning back in my chair, I folded my arms. I didn't believe Charlotte had been lying about anything she'd said. She never broke eye contact during her answers. Her jawline never even tensed. The only nervous fidgeting came when she discussed the state of her sister, but that simply indicated sincerity. Telling me how drunk Gray had been made her uncomfortable. When it came to her older sister, discussing matters that could be framed as disparaging wasn't easy for her.

Most importantly, I'd verified Gray's condition on the night in question. She'd been too intoxicated to carry out any sort of crime resulting in Paul's disappearance. He weighed twice what she did and had been stone-cold sober. At least according to Charlotte.

Then there's the voicemail. Annie's message. Gray could've called herself from another phone to throw off suspicion. The thought had crossed my mind, but the desperation in Gray's voice—the frantic search for answers in her eyes as she played the message for me? That was real. I didn't believe that she'd called herself to muddy the waters.

Charlotte's theory, too, had some weight to it. A drunk wife was an easy target for a guy like Paul. But he was too smart and had too much on the line to trust himself around her. Instead of striking Gray out of jealousy, he might have extricated himself from the situation. Worried over what he would do if he spent any more time with Gray than he absolutely had to, he might have even left his luggage behind.

It was certainly a possibility.

* * *

Back at the station, Sammie found me at my desk, poring through my interview notes from Gray and Joanna.

"Any luck getting contacts for the other folks at Ruby's?" he asked, pulling up a swivel chair from the next cubicle over.

"I've scheduled sit-downs with Jacob and Frances. We've got a police record for an Elizabeth local named Jonas Hatfield. Disorderly conduct two years ago and public intoxication last spring. I've left him a message to get back in touch."

"And Annie? Whoever the hell she is?"

I sighed. "'Whoever the hell she is' sounds like the right sentiment. No luck. No leads. We just have to hope she reaches out again."

"How'd coffee with the sister go?"

"Okay," I answered. "No new information beyond what Gray and her mother already told us. Charlotte was ashamed to speak about Gray's intoxication, so at least that's verified. Didn't suspect Paul of an affair, either."

"Speaking of," he started, shifting his weight in the squeaking chair, "I've found some unusual stuff on Mr. Godfrey."

"Oh?" I said, meeting his eyes. "What sort of stuff?"

"Well, debts. A startling amount of debt for somebody so well off."

"Sometimes folks who look rich are just MasterCard-rich. Remember Greg Whitman of Whitman Autos," I reminded him.

"I remember," he replied. "Just, given his connection to the King family, it's a bit surprising is all. Extensive debts."

"Go on." I put my interview notes back in a manila folder and pushed it away.

Sammie leaned forward in his chair, elbows resting on his knees. "Well, for starters, he apparently has a bank account Gray ain't privy to."

"Gray gave me a list of their accounts. She was absolutely certain it was exhaustive." Of course, well-executed lies inspire confidence in others. Especially spouses.

"She didn't include it in her disclosure." He pulled a flip pad from his back pocket and began to tick through his notes. "She gave us the joint checking and savings. And the Charleston firm holding her trust. A whopper of a trust, mind you. Three credit cards—all in her name with him listed as an authorized user. Not surprising after seeing his credit score. But she never mentioned Paul's Navy Union account."

"Paul never served. How'd he acquire a servicemember account?"

"His late father was a naval airman. Fought in Korea, I think. That makes Paul eligible for Navy Union banking. That's the account the government garnishes his wages from."

"Wait, Paul's wages are garnished?" I narrowed my eyes.

"Yeah. And he does some accounting sleight-of-hand to keep Gray in the dark. His salary is direct deposited into two accounts. Their joint checking and the credit union account where Uncle Sam takes a slice back for the student loans he defaulted on."

That's unusual. "How and when did he default on student loans?"

"It turns out Paul lived the high life well before he married into the King family. Lavish dinners, three-hundred-dollar bar tabs on a regular basis. Get this, as a law student he shelled out almost two thousand bucks a month in rent. All from student loans he didn't pay back."

"Are you kidding me?"

"That honking diamond Gray sports? Another loan. Sixty thousand dollars borrowed against their D.C. townhome. Possibly fraudulent since only Mrs. Godfrey's name is on the title, and the cash was disbursed into an account she doesn't know exists."

Another thought struck me. "Or does she know it exists? Maybe she lied to us."

"What would her motive be?" Sammie asked.

"What's the single thing the entire family—Paul, Gray, Charlotte, especially Joanna—is preoccupied with more than anything else?"

Sammie thought for a moment, answered, "Appearances."

"If Paul's hiding debt, Gray might not know *or* she might not want *us* to know. She may not have even tipped Paul off that she was onto his money moving. Easiest way to maintain a lie is to tell as few folks as possible."

"Same for a crime." Sammie added.

"Regardless, whether she knowingly or unknowingly bought her own ring, this doesn't make sense. If Paul's hiding debt, why would he run off from a wife who just so happens to be, oh, I don't know, a shipping heiress?"

Sammie ran his hand through his hair. "No idea. Especially since his name is on the trust, too. He's entitled to half of it if they divorce—so long as he doesn't cheat. And half of it ain't nothing to balk at. He gets it all if he outlives Gray."

I thought about that for a moment. South Carolina marriage laws are antiquated, often filled with all kinds of morality clauses. Paul gets half of the trust if they divorced, but if he was unfaithful he'd forfeit the whole thing. If he and Annie were engaged in an affair, he'd be under intense pressure not to let Gray find out.

Pressure Annie might not feel so much. Or care about.

Sammie interrupted my thoughts. "Other things don't add up, too."

"What other things?"

"Well, his debts are bad, but they look paltry compared to the King trust. I don't understand why they don't just pay them off in one lump sum from his wife's inheritance?"

Sammie asked a perfectly normal question, but somebody ambitious like Paul Godfrey didn't operate under the same paradigm as normal folks. The more he gained, the more he had to lose. And the more one had to lose, the more warped his priorities became.

I offered an explanation. "If he rented a posh apartment as a broke law student, then Paul cares about appearances quite a bit. He didn't rack up those bar tabs drinking by himself. Bills like that come from buying rounds. And people buy rounds when they're flush with cash or want to *look* like they're flush with cash. Combine that with an upcoming run for office, and you've got somebody who would do everything he could to keep debts hidden. Perhaps even from his own wife."

"You mention the run for office," Sammie replied. "Don't political parties vet potential candidates? Especially for defaulting on something like a student loan? Hell, if that's not showing disregard for government, I don't know what is."

I chewed on the cap of my pen. "The run hadn't been announced, but you're right. They would've requested financial disclosures from him. Or at least they would have very soon. If Paul was cheating on Gray, he'd be under severe pressure to keep it quiet. And if he planned to run for congress, he'd be under as much pressure to settle his debts."

"None of it makes sense. His disappearing or running off or whatever. There's no narrative to any of it." Sammie was right about that, too.

"None of it makes sense *if* Paul ran off."

"And if he didn't?"

"Then he's missing for some other reason, and we need to know who stands to benefit from his absence."

14

Gray

Rain pelted the window like bullets. Hard and fast. It turned out the afternoon's sunshine had been nothing but a spiteful trick. The night-light in my bedroom threw exaggerated shadows against the walls, sharp and violent.

Three days now. Three days without a drop to drink, and the third night was always fucking hell.

My sheets, soaked in sweat, twisted tighter around my legs as I turned from one side to the other over and over again. My phone sat facedown on the nightstand. I couldn't bring myself to look at it. I had no interest in knowing how little sleep remained for claiming. Assuming I even could.

It had never been this bad before. Of course, there'd been the sleepless nights. But having Paul next to me had always provided an inch of comfort. That tiny comfort would have been like oxygen to the drowning woman I'd become.

Now he was gone. Maybe even missing, whatever that meant. The renewed separation anxiety compounded my withdrawal, and my heart pounded away erratically in my chest. Sometimes it beat too slow, sometimes far too fast. Never like it should.

And there was no way to stave it off. I'd stolen away to Mamma's bathroom again only to find the Valium removed from her cabinet. I should've grabbed more than a handful that first day. I was always so impulsive. Never thinking down the road. Never beyond the immediacy of the present.

I'd confirmed the wine cabinet had been locked. The same with the liquor in the dining room buffet. The police had the rental, and town was too distant to walk. No one, not Mamma, not Cora, not even Charlotte would lend me a car. I'd run out of fresh excuses to be dropped off in town alone.

All day, the calls had been relentless. Vapid messages from everyone that wasn't Paul or Annie. Friends of ours in D.C. sending me their thoughts and prayers. I could hear the hesitation tainting each well-intended message, the inevitable pause before reminding me to stay strong. Not to let the "circumstances of life" get to me. I was unsure whether this referred to the affair they suspected Paul of having or my drinking. It became harder to distinguish the two. To pull them apart and keep them in separate boxes in my mind was impossible. Maybe I wasn't as great at compartmentalizing as I thought.

Nothing more from Annie.

Paul's Annie. That's how I'd started to think of her.

How long had it been going on? My memories of Paul hunched over his phone became more detailed. Now, when I recalled each instance of peculiar secrecy, I plainly saw the screen of his device. Now it read "Annie."

Perhaps I'd die tonight. A heart attack or cardiac arrest or whatever happened to the hearts of drunks. I'd read online withdrawals from certain drugs, even the most dangerous ones like heroin, were almost never fatal. But drink? You can seize up and die. The culmination of *delirium tremens*. DTs. The worst sort of shakes.

I'd used the threat of a seizure once as leverage in an argument with Paul. He'd come home from an overnight trip in Toronto to find me waking up from a particularly hard binge the day before. Whenever he left for business, I tended to overdo it even for me, but I usually managed to clean myself—and the house—up before he returned. This time had been different. I'd been caught off guard.

Purpled splotches of dried cabernet spattered the kitchen sink, slung across the counter, and pooled in places on the floor like a sweet-smelling murder scene. A cadre of fruit flies danced on the rim of a half-emptied wineglass. A take-out box of Pad Thai spilled out onto the kitchen table, leaving greasy imprints from a late night binge.

The waking pain was unbearable. Too severe to drive or walk to the liquor store. Too severe to do anything but drink. I could drink it away if only he'd bring me something.

"Do you want me to die, Paul?" I'd half screamed, half cried when he confronted me in our darkened bedroom. Coffered ceilings and fermented air. "The store is just around the corner. One bottle of wine."

"Look at yourself," he'd said, disgusted. He'd held the back of his hand to his nose as if the sight of me might make him vomit. "You've done nothing but drink since I left."

"Please," I begged, my dry eyes stinging with fresh tears. "One bottle. If I can just get to sleep tonight, tomorrow I can start clean, I promise. I can't start over like this. I can't."

His brow remained creased, but he relaxed his hands and knelt by our bed.

"One bottle of wine." I coughed, running quaking fingers through my knotted hair. "If I have a seizure, I could die."

"Jesus Christ, Gray," Paul whispered, stroking my wet cheek with the back of his hand. "What the hell is wrong with you? What are you running away from?"

I began to shake all over. Maybe from my hangover, maybe from fear, probably an unhealthy mixture of both—but I didn't answer his question.

He stood, collecting his car keys off the dresser. "One bottle," he relented. "You're not going to the hospital, I promise," he said with a small smile. I strained to take it for genuine caring, but I knew that the thought of an emergency room visit—and the publicity it'd invite—had been the real motivator.

As he left our home for the liquor store, I lay back on my satin pillow. The shaking stopped. My body still ached and an invisible vise tightened around my skull, but the trembling had vanished in an instant.

The answer to his question had been simple. Perhaps the most obvious thing in my life. Myself. I was running away from myself.

*　　*　　*

When I opened my eyes, I only heard stillness. I wiped my sticking eyelids and daylight broke through. My cheeks stung. They felt creased from lying motionless across crinkled sheets for hours. *Hours.*

I'd slept! I sprang for my phone. Ten fifteen AM. I didn't care what time I'd finally drifted off. It no longer mattered. It could've been three in the morning, and I'd have still slept for seven whole hours.

And then I saw the missed call. "Unknown" at 4:28 AM. And the voicemail.

Annie.

Scrambling, I input my PIN and held my breath as I waited for the message to start. Should I be happy? Or terrified? She'd finally reached out again like she said she would. But why call so early? Here I was sleeping away while vital information waited in my phone's mailbox.

Her voice was a near whisper. Lower than last time. *"Hello, Gray. It's me. It's Annie. I'm sorry to call at such a crazy hour, but I still want to talk to you about Paul. If it's possible, I'd like to meet with you."*

My heart pounded in my chest as adrenaline bolted outwards through my arms and legs. Annie wanted to meet me.

"Some place private. What I have to say is very . . ." she hesitated, *"sensitive."*

I wasn't sure what to think of that. Sensitive meant risky for Paul. But if taking unnecessary risks on Paul's behalf was something this woman was worried over, that likely meant Paul was okay.

Annie continued, *"The bistro on Oleander Avenue. The Italian place. Meet me there this afternoon at one thirty. Come alone. Don't notify anyone. Not your family and certainly not the police."* Her voice lowered even further. I could barely make out what she said next. *"This is incredibly sensitive, Gray. No one can know, or everything could be ruined. Paul's future bid. Everything."* The message ended with a click as Annie hung up.

Annie was in Elizabeth, and I was going to meet her. My worst fears began to erode as I reasoned through her message. She wasn't his mistress. She wasn't *Paul's Annie.* If she was, she'd have no reason to meet with me. And if she was afraid of harming Paul with whatever information she had, then Paul had to be alive. At least for now.

She knew about his planned run for congress. Maybe she worked at Cooper and Waters, too? What sort of information could Annie have? Worry over my last question disappeared in the wake of intense relief.

I leapt to my suitcase, next to Paul's, still unpacked from my flight days earlier. So much had happened since then, but there wasn't time to dwell. I had to get dressed and ready. And then I had to find a way to get to the restaurant on Oleander Avenue.

* * *

"I don't like the idea of this," Charlotte announced as she slid my cell phone back across the kitchen counter. She'd just finished listening to Annie's voicemail. I picked it up and returned it to my bag next to my laptop.

"I haven't had a drop to drink in four days now. *Four days*. And you know it's true. You've been with me every second of each one."

"It's not that," she said, picking at her nails. "It's not *just* that."

"Then what is it?" I asked, lowering my voice. Mamma's footsteps echoed upstairs, and if she heard us arguing and became involved, my plan was shot. "You heard her. She has important information regarding Paul, and she told me to tell no one. To come alone. I wouldn't have said a word to you if I didn't need—"

"Didn't need a car?" Charlotte crossed her arms.

"You know that's not what I meant," I replied, folding my own.

"It's exactly what you meant. You ticked through a list of all the people at Piper Point with available cars and decided I'm the weakest link. The one who'd bend under pressure."

"That's not it at all, Charlotte, I—"

"Take a cab," she said tersely, casting her gaze over my shoulder to avoid mine.

I strained to whisper now. With Mamma around, this couldn't turn into a debate. It was far too important. "A taxi will leave a record and a witness, and you heard her yourself: The information she has could cost Paul the election."

"Paul seems to be doing a fine job of sinking his own chances with this mess." Her eyes darted to the television in the den, and I was certain Bethany's news report was replaying in her mind.

"Charlotte." My eyes widened. "I need information. Any information. Annie has some, and she's willing to share it with me. I have to play by her rules. I'm struggling here, I really am. I haven't had an ounce to drink. At a time like this—"

"The chance, you mean."

I knotted my brow. "What?"

"You haven't had the *chance* to drink at a time like this," she sighed.

My phone indicated it was half past noon already. Time slipped away with every moment we wasted talking in circles. "A few hours. I need it for a few hours."

"I'll drop you off a couple blocks away. You can walk."

Why wasn't Charlotte understanding? When her relationship with Will was collapsing, she'd called me almost daily, and unless I was worried about slurring, I always answered. I was a sounding board for her anger. But then again, was I really? How often had my drinking sent Charlotte's needs to voicemail? More than I cared to remember. Did she resent me for it now?

I tried my best to remain calm, but desperation edged its way into my voice. "She said to tell *no one*. Not the detective. Not my family. What if she sees me get out of the car with you in it?

We have no idea where she'll be coming from or if she'll even be on time. I can't risk it. You heard Annie's first voicemail. Something frightened her from leaving her contact information. I'm lucky she reached out again. If we spook her now, what will I have? What will I do then?"

Charlotte unclenched her jaw and exhaled. She was starting to come around. I always knew when I'd begun to gain ground with her. "I said it wasn't *just* that. The car, I mean."

"What else?" I asked.

She appeared uneasy, shifting her weight from one heel to the other and back again. "I understand this woman claims to have sensitive information, but Nina explicitly said to notify her the moment Annie made contact again. Spooked or not, she predicted this would happen. I don't like the idea of keeping this from her. She knows more about handling these things than you and I. She's a detective for Christ's sake."

I hadn't made up my mind on how much I trusted Nina yet. How could I when she'd delayed on coming to us over the rental? And with her family's history with ours. Besides, I wasn't going to keep her out. I just wanted to talk to Annie before she did. I didn't know *who* the woman was, and I didn't know *what* she knew. Both things I'd prefer to learn before Nina.

"We can't tell her just yet," I answered. "Not until after I've met Annie. I need to put a face to her name. I need to speak with her. To hear what she has to tell me." Tears gathered in the corner of my eyes.

I pressed on. "I've had nothing to cling to these past few days. No information, no means of understanding why Paul took off. Sure, there was the fight at the bar over Jacob, but this is something else. To vanish, to risk complications with work and his congressional bid? Something happened to him. We have problems, but this woman has answers I need before I can even think about Paul and me."

"I know, but what you said isn't true." Her eyes at last returned to mine.

"What do you mean?"

"That you've had nothing to cling to," she replied. "That's not true. You've had me, Gray. You've had your sister."

I forced a grin. Maybe she wasn't resentful. "Then don't take that away from me. A few hours, Charlotte. A few hours and its right back home. Back to Piper Point."

"Okay," Charlotte finally relented. The worry deep in her eyes overshadowed the tiny smile she sported. "A few hours, and Mamma can't know. I'll think of some way to hide it from her."

15

Nina

"I've got Ms. Miles waiting for you in the Fish Bowl," the officer at reception informed me.

"Thank you," I answered, hanging up my desk phone. I took a deep breath before gathering my files and heading to the glassed-in conference room for the second time in the Godfrey-King case. This could go any number of ways, but fun wasn't one of them.

"Hello, Ms. Miles." I smiled as the door clicked shut behind me.

"Nina," Frances said through a pearly grin. She sported a white sundress covered in a pattern of stitched crimson poinsettias. Cocking her head to one side like a playful kitten, she added, "And please, call me Frances. We're old friends, after all."

"Sure," I replied. "Frances."

She may have changed a thing or two over the years, but the look she wore remained the same. Vapid. Filled with superiority. Even seated, she somehow managed to look down on me.

"It's just awful what happened. With Paul Godfrey, that is. It's been all over the news the past few days. Gray must be a wreck. I've left a few voicemails with their maid Laura, I think—but I haven't heard back."

"Cora," I said, taking my seat across the table from her.

She arched her brow. "I'm sorry?"

"Cora. Their housekeeper's name is Cora. You called her Laura."

"Oh." She pursed her lips. "Well, you know more than I do about the family, it seems. Tell me then, how's Gray holding up?"

"I brought you here to speak about the evening of Christmas Eve and the early hours of Christmas morning," I said, thumbing through the papers I'd laid out on the table. "Something you certainly know more about than I, since you were there. With Paul and Gray and a few others, if I'm not mistaken?"

"I was," she answered. Her face turned quizzical. "Do you think something bad happened to Paul? Like foul play?"

I found the blank legal pad I'd been searching for and uncapped my pen. "Ms. Miles . . . Frances, I'd like you to tell me what happened that evening. Start to finish."

She hesitated, clearly not used to having her questions go unanswered. Certainly, not by me. "Well, let's see," she started. "I ran into them at church—"

"Blessed Lamb Baptist, correct?"

"Correct," she replied. "I wasn't expecting to see them. Neither of those girls comes home very often. It was quite a surprise."

I'd begun to make notes. "A good surprise?"

The question seemed to offend her. "Of course. We were all very close friends growing up."

"But you'd drifted apart?"

"I suppose you could say so. But I think it's more like Gray and her sister drifted away from Elizabeth—me and the rest of the town. Even Joanna King talked in church about how she'd raised daughters only to have them run off someplace else. At

117

least Charlotte stayed in a Carolina, even if it was the wrong one. Gray went all the way to Washington."

I tried my best to retain a smile. "So, it was a reunion at church?"

"Oh yes. I promptly invited them out to Ruby's. You know how Ruby's is the nights before Thanksgiving and Christmas. Everyone's there. You can see all your old friends at once without much planning ahead." She'd uncrossed her legs and retrieved her handbag from the floor.

I followed her hands with my eyes. "I'm aware. What happened next?"

"Let's see, I skipped out of the service during the closing hymn to beat traffic to the bar. I mingled for twenty minutes or so before I spotted Gray and Charlotte and Paul walk in through the front door." She rifled through the contents of her purse. Hunting for makeup, I supposed.

"Had you been drinking by then?"

"Of course." She laughed, her eyes meeting mine. "That's the whole point, isn't it?"

"And what about the others?"

She returned to rummaging. "Not yet. In fact, I bought the first round."

"What did everyone order?"

Just as my questions appeared to exhaust her, she finally located the compact she'd been searching for. Retouching her cheeks seemed to renew her interest. "Paul asked for a water. Charlotte and Gray both ordered gin and tonics." She paused. "Come to think of it, Gray asked me to make hers a double. She whispered it to me like she didn't want Paul to hear. Which makes sense."

Her last words struck me. "Why does that make sense?"

The compact snapped closed in her hands like a pricey plastic clam. "I've heard rumors," she answered, lowering her voice. "Rumors Gray might have a drinking problem."

My last few encounters with Gray replayed in my mind. The trembling. The wet brow and flushed cheeks. But her husband was missing. That could more than account for anything unsettling about her demeanor. However, I also recalled Charlotte's hesitation on the topic of Gray's drinking. Charlotte's body language had suggested something beneath the surface.

"How did you hear these rumors?"

Frances offered a wry grin. "In Elizabeth, gossip always trickles back in from the outside world. I'm not exactly sure how I heard—maybe a mutual friend had gone to visit Gray or bumped into her at a restaurant in D.C. or something—but it fits with Gray's personality."

"Her personality?"

Frances spoke matter-of-factly. "Everybody goes through that phase. When all the sudden you don't need your parents out of town to party. We all liked our liquor back then, but Gray liked hers a lot more. When the rest of us began to calm down around senior year, she showed no sign of slowing. I caught her drinking alone more than once myself."

Gray Godfrey struggling with substance abuse? That was something new to me. My next question would be a loaded one. I knew why people drank. They drank to get drunk. To think they needed a reason beyond that was a useless exercise. But Frances might not agree, and whatever she filled in the blanks with could be insightful.

"Assuming it's true, any idea why she might drink?" I asked.

The rain that had become so commonplace the past week resumed, spraying large drops on the window behind Frances.

"I suppose there's the poor-little-rich-girl cliché, but I don't think that holds much water. Her mother might've been a bit cold and her father often gone, but she always had Charlotte." She hesitated, and I could see the spot of joy her next sentence brought no matter how hard she tried to squash it. "And she had your aunt, of course. Matilda?"

"Tilda. We call her Tilda." I let the slight roll off my back. Frances would get no satisfaction from seeing me react. "Why do *you* think she drinks, then?"

The smile fell from her face. "I think Paul drives her to drink. I don't know him well, but he seems awfully controlling. Jealous, too. He proved it that night."

"Yes, I was going to get to that. What happened next?"

Frances answered, "Gray left to use the bathroom. Innocent enough, except she didn't come back. Everyone else was distracted with Paul's conversation. Something political and dull. But I saw where she really went. She went for another drink and took a couple shots while she waited."

I flipped a page in my notepad and continued writing. "With a man named Jonas Hatfield?"

"I have no idea who he was. Run-of-the-mill white trash, it looked like," she replied. "In any case, Jacob excused himself to go to the bathroom, but he didn't go either. He went sniffing for Gray. Paul was oblivious. At first."

"I know Gray and Mr. Wilcox share a history together. What's your understanding of it?"

Frances chuckled, "'History' is an understatement. She lost her virginity to him at thirteen."

"That's awfully young," I remarked. Thirteen years old was more than awfully young; it was statutory. And unfortunate. Despite my efforts to suppress it, a drop of sadness sent tiny ripples through me. Beneath the line where I'd scrawled the words *Possible alcoholism*, I wrote: *sexually active at young age.*

"Like I said, Gray's personality." Frances leaned back in her chair.

"I understand they had an encounter that night?"

Frances' smile and the way she swiveled her high-heel under her ankle made it seem like she was enjoying this. Like she got off on knocking Gray down a peg with lurid details. "On the dance floor. Gray was drunk by then, and if history's any guide, so was Jacob. They made out like a couple barn cats in heat."

"Mr. Wilcox also has a drinking problem?"

"Jacob has an *everything* problem. Gray's not the only girl in town Jacob's fucked," she answered through curved lips. "He may have his issues, but he's the best cut of meat in Elizabeth. Personal opinion, of course."

"Of course." I grinned. "What sort of problems does he have?"

She rattled off her answers, rolling her eyes like she'd personally heard excuses for each one. I didn't doubt she had. "You name it, he's got it. Money problems. Beer problems. Pot problems when the beer's run out. Lives in a carriage house apartment behind his grandmother's place. On unemployment more often than not. And then there's the jealousy."

That word again. "Jealousy?"

She leaned forward on the table. "I guess it'd make Paul's seem tiny by comparison. Once you're his, you're *his*. It might fall apart, and he might move on, but if he comes calling, you better answer."

"You were his?" I leaned forward, too. There was barely more than a foot between our noses now.

"Yes," she answered flatly.

"And if he came calling, would you answer?"

She sat up in her seat, breaking our stare. "Like I said, best cut of meat in Elizabeth. But Gray was the original. And she'll always be the one that got away. Not that he ever had much to offer her."

"And when Paul realized both Gray and Mr. Wilcox were missing together?"

"You mean when I turned Paul's head to the two of them?" Each word she spoke was dotted with ire. "There was a ruckus on the dance floor the next room over. I couldn't see much, but Gray was so hammered that Paul had to practically drag her out when it was over."

I asked my next question more forcefully. "Was there a confrontation between the two men? A physical altercation?"

"I told you I couldn't see much, but I imagine there would've been," she replied, picking at the hem of her sundress. "Someone important like Paul and someone stubborn like Jacob? Talk about an unstoppable force meeting an immovable object."

I sat my pen on the table and closed my notepad. Sammie waited for me on the far side of the conference room door. "Imaginative metaphor. Except, now someone's missing."

Frances smirked. "Then maybe there's no such thing as unstoppable or immovable."

16

Gray

"Like riding a bike," I whispered as I made my way to Charlotte's car. Hattie the Cattie sprawled her aging body on the gravel by the passenger-side door. She purred as I reached down to run my fingers through her tangled black and white fur.

"Hey, girlie," I cooed. "You've got to move, so I can leave." She meowed as I picked her up and sat her in the crabgrass a few yards from the car. I'd decided to bring her home with me when all this was over. Let her live out the few days she had left in the comfort of our townhouse. I didn't give a damn what Paul would have to say about it.

I pulled the driver's door closed. Charlotte's Benz might as well have been a rocket ship, the way the dashboard lit up. Had it really been so long since I'd driven? Folks knew better than to ask me for a lift anywhere. Even if Paul was certain I was sober, he didn't trust me stay that way.

I slung my bag, weighed down with my laptop—just in case—on the passenger seat. I checked the side-view mirror once more for Hattie. She sat perched and alert in the yard, a safe distance away.

Exhaling, I pulled the gearshift into drive. As Piper Point's oppressive pillars retreated in the rearview mirror, an emptiness grew inside me. The joy from leaving Piper Point was nowhere to be found, because I wasn't leaving for good. In a few hours, the house would grow large again. Swallowing me up on all sides.

I turned left onto Atalaya Drive. A high-pitched pinging rang out. *My seatbelt. Of course.* I pulled it across my chest and clicked it into place.

I was doing it. I was on my way to meet Paul's Annie. Not *Paul's* Annie, rather, but the Annie who wanted to help Paul. The woman who wanted to help bring Paul home and ensure he'd be in good shape for the race, too.

I had so few allies in life that the idea of finding one so unexpectedly renewed my resolve in more ways than one. Four days without a drink. The third night was behind me now. No reason I couldn't keep this up. No reason I couldn't keep away from drinking, and then maybe . . . maybe Paul would come home.

We'd be on our way. Away from Piper Point. Out of Elizabeth. Old Hattie nestled warmly in a comfy carrier. I'd never look back—perhaps for good this time. The thought made me smile. Nothing forced or strained about it.

As pines and tall grass whirled by on both sides of the highway, a road sign told me I'd almost reached town. The rain had slowed to a constant drizzle. Not even a drizzle, really. More of a misting. I turned the windshield wipers down.

Cirilo's sat on the corner of Oleander and Percy. A yellow brick building that looked plain enough, but the barrel-tiled roof made it the most exotic in Elizabeth. As far as food went, it was probably the fanciest, but that bar wasn't high in this town. Most folks cooked at home. Nice meals were usually worth the drive into Charleston proper.

None of that mattered. I wasn't here to eat. I was here for answers.

My wrist watch was a rose gold and leather piece I rarely wore, but it was important to be on time today. One fifteen PM. Fifteen minutes to go. I planned to take no chances with Annie. Not when I was finally set to meet her.

People ate lunch early in the Low Country, so I pulled into the near vacant lot framed by crooked palm trees. Their green fronds snapped in intermittent gusts, warning of worse weather to come. A couple pickup trucks by the dumpster likely belonged to the wait staff. The gleaming Cadillac, Luca Cirilo's. Annie had probably come from out of town, so I looked for signs of a rental. I found none in the puddled lot.

A blonde hostess no older than fifteen parted the door as I half ran up the steps and inside. Following her to a back table, I shook my umbrella dry and removed my trench coat.

"Will this be okay?" she asked as she placed a single menu on top of the white linen tablecloth.

"Two," I told her. She paused. "Two menus, please. I'm meeting someone here. A friend."

"Sure thing, ma'am," she replied, setting down a second menu.

I took my seat in the chair she'd pulled out for me. As soon as she'd sauntered off, I concluded this seat wouldn't do at all. For starters, it faced the bar, flanked by row after row of wine bottles. Worse even, I couldn't see the front door.

As soon as I'd switched to the other side of the small table, a college-aged guy in a white button-down and black vest approached me, notepad in hand.

"Welcome to Cirilo's," he said. His dark hair was parted clean down the center. "Have you ever been . . ."

I stared blankly at the young man's face in the sudden silence. *Awkward.*

"I'm so sorry, ma'am," he resumed. "You're Gray King, aren't you?"

"Godfrey," I corrected him, "but yes." I shifted uneasily in the lacquered chair.

"Mr. Cirilo will be pleased to know we've got a King in the house for lunch," he said, a wide grin etched across his face.

"That won't be necessary. To tell him, I mean. I appreciate it, but I'm meeting a friend, and it's quite a private luncheon."

He stiffened his back. "Oh, we'll make no fuss about it. Can I get you something nice to drink?" he asked, handing me a piece of cream-colored paper. A wine list.

I glanced it over from top to bottom out of habit, but I barely stopped to read a word. The young man continued, "We have a nineteen-ninety Riesling import on special today. A great price. Goes well with any of the shellfish pastas."

"No," I answered tersely. It seemed to startle him, so I softened my voice. "No, thank you. I'll have a water, please. With lemon."

"You got it, Mrs. King . . . Godfrey, I mean," he said, scratching my order down. "Sparkling or still?"

"Still," I answered. The waiter snapped his notepad shut with an eager nod and darted off to the kitchen.

*   *   *

By one thirty-five PM, I still hadn't touched my water, and I'd told the waiter I wouldn't be ordering until my friend arrived. He'd brought a basket of buttered bread, but I wasn't hungry. Anticipation squashed my appetite.

Come to think of it, I hadn't eaten much of anything in a couple days now. No wonder my pants hung so loose around my hips. Anxiety was likely masking any light-headedness I might've otherwise felt.

I wiped my damp palms on the table linen for the second time. She'd be here any moment. My eyes stayed glued to the front door. The hostess stood at a podium off to the side. Each time the phone in front of her rang, my pulse spiked. Was it Annie calling? Perhaps to let me know she'd be late?

No, that was nonsense. She had my number. I checked my phone. No missed calls. *Do not let Annie leave here today without getting her number*, I repeated to myself.

"Mrs. Godfrey?" a voice spoke from behind me.

I jumped and turned. The waiter.

"Ma'am, Mr. Cirilo asked me to inform you that, regretfully, he had to leave for a family matter. He won't be able to greet you." He held a tray with both hands.

"I said that wouldn't be necessary—"

"I didn't tell him, ma'am." He frowned. "He recognized you from the galley."

"Oh. Sorry."

The young man's eyes twinkled. "But he's asked me to serve you this." He took a stemmed glass from the tray and sat it before me. His motions sent the wine it carried swirling in circles. "The Riesling. On the house," he announced proudly.

"Thank you," I murmured, stomach twisting at its pale golden color. It's smell, pungent to my heightened sense. *I'm the Spider-Woman of booze.*

As soon as he was out of sight, I pushed the glass to the empty place setting in front of me. It wasn't worth it. I breathed a deep sigh and eyed the door to the ladies room. I could pour it down the sink. I started to slide my chair back but stopped short of standing.

Or I could leave it on the table. I'd let Annie have it. Perhaps she'd think it was a show of goodwill on my part. Maybe it would relax her. From how she sounded in her messages, she could certainly use some relaxing.

One forty-five now. I turned in my seat and spied a side door. If she parked in the opposite lot, she'd probably come in through that one. As I turned back around, the television behind the bar caught my attention. The picture displayed on it did, anyways. It was Paul. The same photograph from before. The one from the Jefferson Hotel gala.

In the bistro's stark emptiness, the voice-over spoke clear as day: "*Still no sign of missing Washingtonian, Paul Godfrey,*" a man's voice announced. "*Calls to the King family have gone unanswered, but a source within the police department has confirmed that a crime scene unit arrived from Charleston. They're sweeping the area where Mr. Godfrey's rental car was found abandoned early Christmas morning.*"

A crime scene unit? My heart seized. Nina never said anything about a crime scene unit. My right hand began to tremble. I grabbed hold of my thigh to still it and released a staggered breath. Protocols, I reminded myself. Nina said the report would initiate protocols. A crime scene investigation would be one of them, no doubt.

On the television, Paul's image had vanished. The voice-over continued: "Our D.C. affiliate obtained the following video statement moments ago from Cooper and Waters, Mr. Godfrey's lobbying firm."

A balding Laurence Cooper appeared, lined face appropriately sullen. He wore a small microphone attached to his pressed lapel, adjacent to an American flag pin. Judging by the granite steps behind him, he stood in front of the firm's building.

"All of us at Cooper and Waters extend our thoughts and prayers to the Godfrey and King families during this time of uncertainty. Most importantly, we expect Paul's whereabouts to be uncovered soon and a speedy return to his wife and family to occur. To my knowledge, there is no reason this cannot happen quickly."

The gaggle of off-screen reporters began to shout questions. I couldn't make out any of them specifically, but I did catch a reference to Mark Sandford, the disappeared politician Nina had mentioned when Mamma and I filed the report. Another asked something about when Paul planned to announce his bid.

Laurence pressed on, "I won't comment on or speculate regarding the circumstances of Mr. Godfrey's absence. I will say, however, that Cooper and Waters is doing absolutely everything in our power to facilitate his return. To that end, I'm happy to announce that we have offered our own investigatory services, and the King family has accepted. Our security contractor is traveling to Elizabeth as we speak."

My head spun as blood drained from it. I grabbed the glass of water and swallowed several gulps, the icy cool down the back of my throat offering little relief. Crime scene investigators. Security contractors. Hell, Annie. It was all too much.

"Excuse me," I called to the bartender who'd appeared beneath the television as Laurence spoke. My voice choked as I did.

The woman creased her brow. I must've looked as anxious as I felt. "Yes, ma'am? Is everything alright?"

"Yes," I answered, words shaky. "Just the television. Could you—do you mind shutting it off?"

She glanced at the screen above her head and back at me, pausing as her mind connected the two. "Oh yes. Of course, ma'am. I'm so sorry."

I struggled to smile. "Thank you," I said, casting my eyes down to my lap. It was nearly two o'clock. Annie was late. Very late.

My eyes darted from one side of the restaurant to the other and back again. Where the hell was she? Calm down, I told myself. She's likely not from Elizabeth. She probably got turned around trying to find the place. It's a small town, but it's old. The streets hardly make any sense.

My heart beat in erratic fits and starts. The discomfort in my chest grew and spread to my limbs as an itchy tingling. I looked down at my watch again. A glaring red caught my attention. My thumb was bleeding. I'd torn the scab from it without realizing.

Christ, my nerves were fraying. Fast.

I wrapped my finger in a napkin and looked around for Annie again. When she did arrive, this was no state for her to find me. Trembling and bleeding. It might scare her off.

The waiter had lit a tealight candle in the center of the table as he'd announced the day's specials. The tiny flame's reflection on the wineglass, the warm undulations across the curved surface, stole my gaze.

It was only Riesling. Practically a dessert wine with hardly any alcohol in it. Pushing all other thoughts aside, I reached for the wine and took a healthy swallow.

17

Nina

I drummed my fingers against the pharmacy counter as the technician turned from the rack behind her. She had a freckled face. A redhead in clean white coat.

"Matilda Palmer. I've got it right here," she announced, scanning the barcode taped to the crinkled baggie. "I'll just need your license and your signature." She slid a clipboard towards me.

"What?" I asked. My thoughts had been wandering from Gray to Auntie and back again while waiting for the refill.

"I need your signature and license, ma'am," she answered. "It's the law. Opiates are controlled substances."

"Right," I replied, collecting my thoughts. "Of course."

Moments later, I was out the door and on Main Street, Auntie's drugs in the book bag slung over my shoulder. I began the brisk walk to my car through a curtain of icy rain. The station was well within walking distance, but I'd driven anyways. I seemed able to control so little of life these days, but wet socks were entirely preventable. As I approached the corner where I'd parked, a man called my name from the sidewalk behind me.

"Nina Palmer?" His tone was as deep as it was snappy. "Detective Nina Palmer?"

I turned to see a well-built man in a knee-length rain coat, coal-colored like his slicked hair.

"Can I help you?" I asked. Something about this guy rubbed me wrong. Maybe it was the interruption. Spending my lunch collecting Auntie's meds meant I'd be eating at my desk. If I ate at all. His dress heels clicked against the pavement as he approached. They must've been expensive. He extended his hand.

"Andrew Huang," he introduced himself. His handshake was firm. I had trouble returning the forcefulness he put into it.

"And am I supposed to recognize your name?" I tried to restrain my annoyance.

Crow's feet formed in the corners of his eyes as he smiled too wide. "Of course, not. I'm an investigator with Security Solutions. We're on contract with Cooper and Waters."

"Paul Godfrey's firm," I added.

"Yes, Detective Palmer, that's correct."

"Nina. You can call me Nina." I gave up on reaching my car quickly and pulled out an umbrella.

"Thank you, Nina. We've been retained to provide . . ." he hesitated a moment as I finished opening my umbrella, "support for your investigation into Mr. Godfrey's whereabouts. The King family has endorsed the effort."

I recalled Laurence Cooper's press conference from earlier today. Private investigators owed loyalty to their clients. Sometimes they were helpful, but things could quickly get out of control, critical information leaked. I thought of Annie. We'd kept that detail out of the press, and I didn't need anyone else deciding otherwise. "I can't comment on ongoing investigations."

I needed to lose this guy and get back to work. "Have a nice day, Mr. Huang."

"You can call me Andrew," he replied, repeating my words back to me. It was clear he had no intention of ending our encounter so soon. "I'm a private contractor now, but I have eight years of federal work under my belt."

"FBI?"

"That's correct." He took a step closer. Personal space was important during polite conversation, and he closed in far too fast.

I threw an edge into my voice. "I'm sure the Kings appreciate your coming down, but it's always been a belief of mine that too many cooks in the kitchen spoil the chicken bog."

He chuckled. At least he tried to. I could see the reference to South Carolina's signature dish was lost on him. "That's cute. Elizabeth is every bit as charming as I imagined it would be. I'm a Pittsburgh guy myself, so this is all quite a treat."

"Goodbye, Mr. Huang." I started to turn around.

His shoes clacked on the sidewalk again. "Hold on, Nina. *Support* is the word I believe I used. I'm only here to support your investigation."

It wasn't that this guy couldn't take a hint. He simply didn't care. "We've got all the support we need. If we didn't, there are channels to acquire more. Official, non-private sector channels."

"Nina—"

"You say you're a former Bureau boy? You should know all about chain of command and how obstructive outside interference can be."

"Cooper and Waters is a powerful firm. Mr. Godfrey's bosses are powerful people. If I was you, I'd welcome the extra hands.

Might make your, what did you call it, chicken bog, taste better after all. Might get it done *sooner*."

"I appreciate the offer. And the power card. But this conversation is over. Nice to meet you."

His lips curved into another grin. He reached into his coat pocket and produced a golden money clip. He slid a white business card from it and offered it to me between his index and middle fingers like a cigarette. "Feel free to get in touch at any time."

I snatched it and stuffed it in my own pocket.

"Have a nice afternoon, Nina," he said as I backed away. He infused his next words with a phony drawl. "I'm going to see if there isn't a spot around here that serves chicken bog. I don't know what the hell it is, but nothing beats Southern cooking."

"Good day, Mr. Huang," I shouted and walked straight to my car without looking back.

* * *

At the office, every phone in every cubicle seemed to ring at once. Since we'd broken the news, the tips had been rolling in steadily and mostly useless, but this was something else.

I sat my book bag on the floor beneath my desk. Sammie must've spotted me walk in and sprinted to catch up because by the time he appeared, he seemed out of breath.

"Everything okay?" I asked as I logged onto my computer.

"Crime scene guys," he replied in staggered breaths. "They've asked for a dog unit."

"What? Why the hell wasn't I informed immediately? Has Burton been told?" A request for dogs meant there was something to be found. Something or someone. The run-in with Andrew

Huang had startled me, but a major development? This knocked me right off-balance.

"Request only just came in. A minute or so before you walked through the door," he answered. "Haven't had a chance to tell Sheriff Burton, yet."

"What was the reason for the request?"

"They found upturned foliage leading from the car through the woods. Said it looked like somebody walked down to the marsh."

I released my held breath. It wasn't as bad as it could've been, then. "They could see that even with all the downpours we've had?"

He shrugged. "They must be pretty good, I guess. Anyways, it's a hunch on their part. That's why they asked for the dogs."

"Alright. Then let's see what happens from here." I looked back at my computer, but Sammie still lingered in the corner of my eye. I swiveled my chair back to him.

"There's something else I've been thinking about, Nina," he said, worry in his eyes. "If this turns out . . . if this turns ugly, I'm concerned about the timeline between finding Mr. Godfrey's vehicle and calling it a crime scene."

"I don't follow you, Sam," I replied. It was a lie. I knew exactly where he headed.

"We sat on the vehicle for nearly a whole day before contacting the Kings. Time is the most critical variable when a person's missing. You know that."

"Thirteen hours. Not a whole day," I corrected him, not that it made any difference. "And we had no reason to believe a crime had occurred. Sheriff Burton agreed. Nobody from the family had reported anything, and there's a record of me checking."

"Still," his voice remained wary. "With the history between your aunt and the King family, folks might question the way we handled this."

"What about you, Sammie?" My heart beat faster. "Do *you* question the way we handled this?"

"No, I mean to say, I'm worried others will. Burton already has at least once. And if those dogs find a damn thing you know he'll be up both our asses," he answered.

Guilt crept up on me. Sammie was right to voice his thoughts, and snapping at him would solve nothing. Certainly, wouldn't satisfy Sheriff Burton's questions, either. Questions we both knew he'd have.

"Look, I understand where you're coming from. As of right now, we don't know which way this is going to go. I think it's clear Paul Godfrey has no intention of returning to his family himself. The best we can hope for is that he turns up in some resort town with this woman. Annie whoever."

"And the worst?"

I puffed my cheeks. "I'm not going to go there yet. That's the crime unit's job. And the K9 guys. We'll wait to hear what evidence they find, and then we'll draw conclusions. We'll move forward from there."

"Sounds good to me, Nina." Sammie softened his voice. "And I apologize. I meant no offense."

"No worries." I smiled. "Do me a couple favors though, will you?"

He straightened his back, hands in his pockets. "Anything."

"Get a hold of Jacob Wilcox. Let him know we can't wait till tomorrow to speak with him. He needs to come in today."

"Sure thing," he said, nodding. "What else?"

I pulled the folded business card—Security Solutions—out of my pocket. Sammie glanced at it as I tossed it on my desk.

"Let the Charleston lab folks know we'll have priority samples coming down the pipe for analysis. We need to get DNA from every person at Piper Point. Cash in on the budget-leeway Sheriff Burton gave us and expedite sequencing to same-day status. I want to get ahead of this. If Jim asks—when Jim asks—I want us to have answers. If the crime unit finds anything with those dogs, we need to be ready to move faster than we did before—than I did before."

18

Gray

"Would you like to use our phone, ma'am?" the waiter asked. "See where your friend is?"

"No, thank you," I whispered.

"I'm sorry, Mrs. Godfrey, what was that?"

I cleared my throat. "No thank you. I have a phone. I'm sure she's just caught up in something. Lost in the rain, maybe."

He tapped his notepad against the side of slacks. "Okay, ma'am. Can I get you another then?"

"What?" My thoughts had been pinned under the unbearable weight of Annie's absence. The woman who'd given me hope. Her message implied Paul was okay. And if he was okay, then the chance to fix things remained. We could return to D.C., and figure it all out far way from Elizabeth. Together.

But if Annie didn't show, I was back to where I'd started—waking up drunk on Christmas morning with no answers. No hope.

"The Riesling. You've finished it," he replied. "Can I get you another?"

The empty wineglass. My next words came without thinking, as involuntary as breathing. "Chardonnay. I'll have the house chardonnay, please."

Moments later, he returned with my drink. I took a large swallow and embraced the familiar fuzziness. The warm blanket. I could thank my nerves for the speedy blood flow.

Hardly five minutes had passed, and I'd polished it off. I knew exactly how long it'd been because I'd become preoccupied with the time. Annie was over an hour late. If she was lost, if she was somehow struggling to make it to our meeting, she would've called.

What information did she have? Was she that frightened?

The more the wine worked, the more open I became to the notion that she truly had gotten lost. If she had, I could start making excuses for her. It was in my nature to make excuses. For Paul. For myself. For this random, faceless woman I'd driven to meet.

I'd driven. *Shit.*

"Would you like another?" The young man had returned to replace my cold bread with a warm basket.

"Yes. Thank you," I answered. I always ordered my drinks in an overtly polite fashion. As if being mannered about it compensated for how many I asked for.

His footsteps stopped, and he turned back to the table. "It's cheaper to buy the bottle, ma'am."

"Excuse me?"

He leaned closer. "Well, by the glass, that wine's nine dollars a pop. Bottle's twenty-eight bucks. There's about five-glasses-worth in a bottle. You do the math."

"I see," I replied as though this information was all brand new.

"Only a two dollar cork fee, too. You can take home anything you don't drink. I'll seal it back up for you," he added.

Moments like this made me question my own disbelief in

God. Or the Devil, rather. I forced a tiny grin. "Yes, that sounds nice. I'll have a bottle then."

"Just looking out for your wallet, ma'am," he laughed. "Not that you need it."

He was only trying to pad the size of my bill, to increase his tip on a thus far entrée-less patron. If only he knew the true face of what he was complicit in. The true, rotten face of it.

A minute later, a pewter bucket of ice stood before me. A minute after that, a newly opened bottle of Napa Valley chardonnay sat nestled inside it. He polished a fresh glass with a linen napkin and placed it on the tabletop.

"Enjoy." He smiled.

19

Nina

I turned the steering wheel, pointing my car down Atalaya Drive, the long, joyless road I'd spent my life avoiding like it held a hoodoo curse or something. It was my second trip in less than a week. I wondered what Auntie had thought each time she traveled down it nearly every morning for decades.

Atop the marshy bluff, Piper Point's white façade stood in stark contrast to all the nature that swaddled it. A beacon calling to something, but what? Something ill. That much was for certain. In the rearview mirror, the evidence van followed close behind.

Sammie came over the radio. "Mr. Wilcox says he can't come in today," he announced. "Can't get Dale to let him off work."

I grabbed the receiver. "Does he know he doesn't have a choice?"

"Apparently not."

I thought for a moment. "I've been meaning to get to Dale's Hardware all week. Auntie's place needs a few things. I'll head there after I wrap this up."

"One thing to know before you speak with him," Sammie said to the sound of shuffling papers on his end, "I finished with

Jonas Hatfield half an hour ago. He knows Jacob. Says he saw him having a physical altercation with Paul on the dance floor. There's more, too. He saw Jacob's truck take off south soon after Paul and Gray left."

I creased my brow. "What?"

"South toward Paul Revere Highway and Piper Point. Jacob's place is northeast of town."

Jacob followed the Godfrey's home? That *was* something to know. "You think he trailed them from Ruby's?"

"It's possible," he replied. "Where are you now?"

"Pulling up to the King house."

"Okay. Good luck, Nina," he chuckled. I clicked off.

My tires ground against gravel as I pulled up. Shutting my car door, I drank in the home. I'd never been so close to it in the daytime. Something seemed off about it, like it was out of place in the present, more fit for the pages of a history book. Yet, here the home stood, defiant as the woman who kept it. Millions of dollars worth of broken-down bleakness.

"We'll be ready when you call for us, Nina," the van driver shouted from his lowered window. He'd pulled up and parked beside me. I'd instructed him earlier to hang back until I had a chance to chat with Gray. I didn't want to overwhelm her or give her mother any excuse to hold things up.

The steps groaned and whined under my boots as I made for the immense front door. A black and white spotted cat, very old by the looks of her, laid sprawled on the porch. Rocking chairs, worn from weather and neglect, stood motionless, frozen in time like everything else about the place.

An ivory doorbell sat inside a brass molding. No noise rang when I pressed it, so I let the heavy bronze knocker fall twice.

The cat skittered off with surprising agility. A wrought iron lamp hung above me—two of its four glass sides gone. A wind-worn copper placard with a stylized "K" was nailed into the door below the knocker. Identical to the label on Auntie's Christmas card.

Severance. Steps echoed from inside as someone made their way to the door. It clicked and swung open.

"Good afternoon, Ms. Palmer." Cora greeted me with a warm smile. She seemed to be the only genuine thing about Piper Point. "How can I help you today?"

"Afternoon, Cora. I'm here with some folks from the sheriff's office. Can I speak with Mrs. Godfrey, please?"

"Oh? I'd better fetch Mrs. King. Do you mind telling me what this is about? She doesn't like surprises. You understand, I'm sure," she replied as she waved me into the foyer.

I swallowed a lump in my throat. "Certainly. I've brought some evidence folks. Regarding the investigation. We're here for voluntary DNA samples from each of member of the family. You too, if you'd be so kind."

Cora appeared understandably taken aback. "One moment. You can have a seat in the salon, if you'd like."

I should've figured Joanna would be gatekeeper to an audience with Gray. I waited in silence, save for the ticking of the sculpted grandfather clock I passed on the way in. A stagnation hung in the air. A musty, almost moist stench. Old homes, I told myself. Low voices from behind the dining room's far wall broke the quiet.

A moment later, Joanna walked into the salon from the other side of the foyer, dressed impeccably in a navy skirt and cream sweater. I wondered if she always wore heels at home or if she stalked around the house in hose just in case.

"Ms. Palmer, what can I do for you?" Her velvet voice matched the floral perfume she wore. Daffodils and obstruction.

"Did Cora not say?" I asked.

She tilted her nose up slightly. "She mentioned something about DNA samples, however, Paul's not related to anyone here, as you're aware. He's only a member of the family by marriage, so I'm afraid none of us would be very helpful."

A woman obsessed with privacy. Nothing about Joanna King was ever easy.

"Forgive me, Joanna, but that's not entirely true. It would be exceedingly helpful to have records from everyone to compare against any material we might find—"

"Material?"

"Correct," I replied, struggling to put my next words delicately. "You're aware of the forensics team sweeping Paul Revere. Were we to find any biological substances we can quickly determine if they belong to Paul or someone he was in close contact with."

She crossed her arms. I'd done nothing but generate more concern—tinged with a hint of morbid curiosity, no doubt. "We can get Paul's DNA from any of his personal items. A toothbrush or a comb, for instance. A shaving razor."

She narrowed her pale eyes. "I suppose, but Cora said you've got a van out front. Don't you just need a couple swabs and Ziplocs for DNA? Seems like overkill."

"That brings me to my second request. I'd very much appreciate it if you'd allow the guys to go through Paul's things and collect them." I clenched my jaw, bracing for a response.

Joanna didn't waste a second. "You've already attracted enough attention bringing some nefarious-looking van to the house. What if a reporter sees them hauling out garbage bags of belongings? What'll they think?"

There were no reporters out front. She knew this.

I did my best to speak in a calm tone. "I assure you, they won't think anything except that we're doing our best to locate Mr. Godfrey," I paused before adding sharply, "and that his family is fully cooperating with our effort."

She hesitated, lips pursed, likely weighing her options.

As we stood face to face in relative quiet, the checks to Auntie Tilda surfaced in my mind. Here she stood, Auntie's benefactor, right in front of me. Those checks were about more than Seamus King. I knew that much. They had to be. I could ask her now, and then I'd have an answer of some sort. True or not, I could work with it.

But I'd be jeopardizing what little goodwill I had with the family and the investigation along with it. It was painful, but I allowed the moment to pass.

"Alright," Joanna relented. "You tell them to take their shoes off on the porch. The way it's been raining, they'll be tracking mud all over the rugs."

"Thank you, Mrs. King," I replied, relaxing my jaw. "May I speak with Mrs. Godfrey now, please?"

She stared blankly at me for a moment before turning to shout up the enormous staircase over her shoulder. "Gray, come down here. Detective Palmer needs to speak with you."

Abrupt footsteps were followed by Gray's younger sister appearing in the salon.

"Gray's preoccupied at the moment," Charlotte announced. "Is there something I can help out with?"

"This is about *Paul's* case, Charlotte. Ms. Palmer needs to speak with *Paul's* wife. And fetch the twins, will you?" She glared at me with disdain. "We'll all be giving DNA samples."

Charlotte turned white. At first, I assumed it was from the DNA request. Anyone would be jarred by that.

Charlotte's hands fidgeted at her sides. "I'll bring the boys down right away, but Gray's not here."

Joanna seemed very startled. "Where the hell is she, then?"

20

Gray

The first of the early bird dinner crowd trickled in as I drained the last few drops of my wine. Between a racing pulse and a hollow stomach, my head swirled as if I'd had two bottles.

Two bottles. There's an idea. What did he say the cork fee was? A couple dollars?

"I'll have my check, please," I called to the waiter from across the room, hand in the air. He looked to be taking another table's order, but I couldn't be certain. Had he even told me his name? Funny I'd sat here for so long and didn't know it.

"Here you are, ma'am," he announced, handing me a black leather billfold.

"That wine, the chardonnay, it was wonderful," I told him. I spoke slow, struggling to enunciate each word correctly.

"I'm glad you thought so," he answered. "Apologies about missing your friend."

Annie. Paul's Annie who'd stood me up. "You know, why don't you add a second bottle to this bill?"

He bit his lip. "I don't think that'd be a good—"

"Keep it corked." I smiled. "I'd like to have it again sometime soon."

"Certainly," he replied hesitantly. "I don't mean to be impolite, but can I call someone to pick you up, ma'am? Maybe a cab or something?" So much for speaking slowly. *He pushed a whole bottle on me and now he's suddenly concerned?*

"Actually, I'm walking," I lied. Mamma was right, lying did come easily for me. Quick.

My lie satisfied him. He retrieved a second bottle and an adjusted bill. I wasted no time paying. Gathering my umbrella, coat, and bag, I made for the front door. I started off walking too fast though and caught a chairback to my hip on the way. The dull pain vanished as quickly as it came.

As I crossed the parking lot, the rain barely registered. Fumbling for Charlotte's keys in my bag, I paused. I shouldn't be driving. But if I took a cab—if I came home without Charlotte's car—they'd all know what I'd done. If I could make it home and get right to bed, they wouldn't. I'd finish the bottle I'd bought locked upstairs and wake up sober. I'd deal with the hangover then. Fuck Annie, I thought as I decided to chance the road.

The Mercedes' headlights flashed as the doors unlocked. A pinging reminded me to buckle up. I exhaled. *I can do this.* In college, I drove drunk often enough to call it a hobby.

Pennies. Frances told me once that if you stuck pennies in your mouth, you could beat a Breathalyzer. Something about the copper, maybe? Not giving it a second thought, I reached into Charlotte's armrest and grabbed a handful. My mouth filled with metallic bitterness followed by an unsettling sweet. I swished the coins from cheek to cheek before spitting them out and cranking the engine. White-knuckling the wheel, I pulled out of Cirilo's parking lot and onto Oleander Avenue.

Not so bad. I shut my left eye so the double lines painted on the road melded into the usual single one. My thoughts went to the bottle in my purse on the seat next to me. Once I started drinking it was impossible to quit. The only thing I could compare it to was forcing yourself to stop urinating before you'd finished. Painful. Unnatural, even.

I pulled the wine out with my right hand. Damnit, I needed a bottle opener.

To my right, I spotted a gas station and turned into it.

I blinked.

Suddenly, I was driving again, wine bottle open. The cork sat impaled by a cheap corkscrew in the passenger seat. The gas station must've sold me one. Where was Main Street? If I could find Main Street, I'd be able to get back to the highway.

Maybe Annie *had* gotten lost. This town was so damn confusing. I took a swig of wine. It held hardly any taste now. Might as well have been water. I cut a left.

When I reached for another gulp, I found the bottle empty. When had I finished it? Maybe I'd had some in the parking lot of the gas station?

My eyelids grew heavy. I began seeing things. Dreaming, maybe.

I was young. Much younger than I was now. *Arms.* A young man's arms wrapped tight around me, belting my trembling body close to his.

"You've seen the Devil, haven't you, Gray?" the man asked. It was Matthew, his voice bubbled as though we were underwater. I couldn't see him, but I knew the crocodile grin he spoke through. The toothy smile that crossed his face. Razor sharp.

"You're a bad girl, Gray King," Matthew whispered into my ear. His breath smelled rancid. Damp onion mixed with metal. "You've seen the Devil, and you're a bad girl now."

I stared deep into the looming mirror in the cellar. The one

Mamma had returned to Piper Point's stair landing. I *was* much younger and with fire-red curls. Matthew had darkened to a black shadow behind me. He kept whispering, but his words dissolved into distant mumbling. His mouth, as if filled with marbles. I only smelled his foul breath.

My eyes met themselves on the mirror's surface. A cracking, splintering pop. The glass fractured in two diagonally across my face.

"I'm a bad girl," I repeated to my broken reflection.

I jolted awake to find myself on Main Street. At least I think it was Main Street. The car hurdled towards a fork in the road. I jerked the wheel to the left but the SUV seemed to slide out from under me as it spun a half circle.

My body lurched in the other direction. A smashing sound tore through my ears. The airbag exploded, striking my face like a mallet. Then silence. Everything stopped. Frozen.

21

Nina

I tripped a bell wire as I entered Dale's Hardware. The scent of pine shavings and cigarettes greeted me as I made for the lone cash register to my left.

"How ya doin', ma'am?" a round man—Dale—nodded as I approached. He roused from a creaking stool and spit a slick wad of dip into a fast-food cup. "Can I help ya?"

I nodded a hello. "Mailboxes. The one I've got is rusted-out from all the rain. You have any?"

He crossed his arms, sucked air through his teeth. "We've got a couple different sorts. Might try a plastic one. Won't ever rust. Head to the back wall and take a right. You'll see them in the corner past the hacksaws."

"Thanks." I smiled, paused. "And someone to help carry it out to my car?"

"Let me radio Jacob," he replied. "I'll have him bring the dolly up."

In the store's back corner, a fluorescent bulb neared the end of its life. It flashed and strobed as I surveyed the collection of mailboxes Dale kept in stock. Footsteps and the mousey squeak of metal wheels turned my head.

"Mr. Wilcox." I extended my hand.

Jacob removed one of his frayed earbuds and gave me a firm handshake. "Nina."

"I'll be buying one of these mailboxes," I announced. "After we talk."

The loose earbud leached music, abrasive heavy metal screaming into the empty space between us. Turning the music off, he respooled the wire and stuck it in his jeans pocket. "I can take fifteen."

"Someplace private?"

He flicked his chin to an exit door behind me. "Out back. Let me grab my cigarettes."

Behind the store, the loading dock sat a few feet above the concrete drive. Bits of paper trash and soggy mulch collected around a grate in the center of the lot, pushed there from all the rain.

"Cowboy killers," Jacob mused, referring to the fresh box of Marlboro Reds he packed against his palm. "You want one?"

"I don't smoke," I answered, before giving him time to put a cigarette between his lips.

"What can I do for you, Nina? Or should I call you *detective*?" A hint of laughter dotted his last question.

"Nina's fine. Do you mind?" I asked, looking down at the tape recorder I'd pulled from my coat pocket.

He shook his head. "By all means."

I pressed record. "I want to talk about Christmas Eve."

A pink plastic lighter sparked alive. The soft color reminded me of Frances' comments. Which lucky lady's bedside had he lifted it from? He tucked the lighter in the same pocket as his earbuds. "And Gray's husband?"

"Yes. I want to know what happened between you and Paul Godfrey that night. I'm already aware of a confrontation."

Cigarette lit, he took a glowing drag. "Not much of one, to be honest about it. The guy flew off the handle at me and Gray. We were dancing, but there wasn't any harm in it."

"You kissed his wife."

The cloud of tobacco he expelled blossomed in my face, and I held my breath. *Cowboy killers.*

"His wife kissed me," he retorted. Emphatic. A point of pride for him, perhaps. Pride made folks behave in all sorts of ill ways.

"Can you explain what you meant by 'Paul flew off the handle'?"

"Shouting mostly." Jacob's face held more than a whisper of apathy.

"Anything physical?"

Another drag on his cigarette. "He stuck his fingers hard into my shoulder. So, I stuck mine right back. Knocked him backwards a step or two."

"And then what happened?"

The ambivalence in his eyes was replaced by smugness. "He sized me up for a fight, best I could tell. Then decided it was a bad idea and yanked Gray out of there."

Interesting word choice. "Yanked?"

"Hard," he answered.

"You could tell that even though you'd been drinking?"

He shrugged. "That's how rough he was with her, I guess. Plain enough to see. Beer or no beer."

That reconciled with the concern Charlotte had expressed, but I'd heard Jacob called entitled, possessive, jealous, all in the past couple days. Time to see if he was a liar, too. "And they left at that point? You had no more contact with either of them the rest of the evening?"

"Yes ma'am, that's correct." Another smoldering drag.

"Do you know a man by the name of Jonas?" I countered, omitting the last name intentionally. When it came to names, people often filled in blanks before deciding if it was in their interest to do so.

"Jonas Hatfield?" he asked, barely hesitating.

"That's correct."

He leaned on the guard rail behind us, one steel-toed boot lifted to a low rung. Flecks of paint and hardened soil spattered them. I pictured those boots trudging through the forest's damp floor of pine and rotting fronds off Paul Revere Highway. Then stomping through saw grass and sinking deep into salty marsh mud. "Yeah. Holds a card night every other Thursday at his place. Texas Hold'em, mostly. I've been a few times. Why?"

"Because he was at the bar, too. I've spoken to him already."

He shifted his weight, suddenly uneasy. "Why's that important?"

I'd maintained eye contact through the conversation, but now I stared. "He saw you, Jacob. He saw you leave the bar right after the confrontation with Mr. Godfrey. He puts you jumping into your truck and speeding off."

"So?" His eyes wandered over my shoulder. His jawline tensed.

I continued, "Your place is north of Ruby's Pub. You took off south. Right behind the Godfreys' rental car."

He moved from the guard rail and straightened his back. "I got turned around. I told you, I'd been drinking a little."

"Did you tail Paul Godfrey?"

"Why the hell would I do something like that? Follow some dick from D.C. just 'cause he shoved my shoulder? I shoved him back. That was enough for me."

"You followed him because of Gray, Jacob. I know about you and Gray. You have a history together. A long history."

"Doesn't mean a thing to me now," he replied, breaking eye contact again.

But I didn't permit him to glance away. "That's not what I hear. I hear you have a tough time letting things go. Letting women go, to be blunt about it. You don't seem to differentiate much between women and things, do you?"

His voice grew petulant. "Who the hell told you something like that? Frances? That bitch is mad I'm not fucking her all the time like I used to. There's no truth to it. Bitch calls me every time she's drunk begging for it. She's crazy. You can't trust her. Once she said she was pregnant and—"

"That's not all I heard, Jacob. I heard you took Gray's virginity. There any truth to that?"

Silence crowded the air between us. It finally broke with Jacob swallowing a stiff lump in his throat.

"Yeah, that's true," he answered, voice lowered.

"You were both about thirteen?"

"I dunno, maybe. It was a long time ago."

I took a step closer. "You want to know something else?"

He said nothing, taking another long pull from what little remained of his cigarette.

I went on, emphasizing each word as I did. "That's statutory rape."

"Like hell it is. I was the same age."

Of course, there'd be no way to stick him with statutory at this point but letting him hear the words might knock him off-balance. I'd seen good liars before, methodical liars whose cold eyes put worms under my skin. Jacob didn't come close. "In the eyes of the law, it doesn't matter."

"Are you threatening me, Nina?"

"Just stating facts."

He tossed his spent smoke onto the concrete, grinding it beneath his boot. "There's limitations or whatever you call it for charges like that. You can't do a damn thing."

I smiled. "That's where your wrong, Jacob. South Carolina's one of a handful of states with no statute of limitations on crimes of a sexual nature."

"A sex crime? Fuck, Nina. We were kids. Both of us."

I struck back with the question I wanted answered. "Did you follow Mr. Godfrey's rental car after he took off from Ruby's?"

He hunched his shoulders and thrust his hands in his pockets. "Yeah. I followed him. Gray wanted me bad, and that fucker couldn't stand it. He thought he could pick a fight with me. I showed Mr. Washington how country boys handle things."

"And is that what you did, Jacob? Did you handle things?"

He went on, eyes gone from spooked to aflame. "I flashed my high beams. I got him to pull off the road, and I whooped his ass, if that's what you wanna know. Gray won't tell you that's what happened. She was too drunk to know one way or the other. Do I need a lawyer?"

"Did you assault Paul Godfrey on the night of Christmas Eve or early Christmas morning?" I touched the button on my tape recorder, ensuring it was still depressed for *on*.

"Call it what you want. I showed him he don't run things down here, and we don't care how important he is. And I'm done talking to you. You got any more questions, I want a lawyer by my side." He began to turn.

"Suit yourself." I reached for the cuffs nestled in the pocket of my jacket. "Jacob Wilcox, you have the right to remain silent.

Anything you do or say can and will be used against you by the state of South Carolina."

"What the hell for?" His muscles tensed like they wanted to fight back, but he held his fists. Turns out Jacob could suss out the difference between a bad idea and good one. If only occasionally.

"Assault and battery," I answered. "For now."

22

Gray

The blackness that had swallowed me up began to recede. It unfolded slowly at first, one frame at a time. Then it crossed some invisible threshold and the dam in my mind broke, everything rushing through.

I stared up at a metal pole. Plastic baggies of liquid and clear tubing strung from it.

I'd gone to meet Annie, but she'd never shown. I'd gotten drunk instead. I drove.

My body jolted, seized. *I drove . . . and I . . .*

To my left and right, there were plastic guardrails. I was in . . . a bed. As I moved my arm, something pinched the back of my left hand. An IV line was attached to me, held by strips of translucent medical tape. I made a fist, and the outline of the needle buried deep in my vein appeared.

Someone spoke to me. A man's voice. "Just Lactated Ringer's," he announced, motioning to the plastic drip bag suspended above my arm. "Fluids. You're very dehydrated."

My vision blurred, but he wore beige scrubs. A nurse. I was in a hospital.

I wrecked.

He went on, "You're woozy from analgesics. I'm not a fan of narcotics," he paused, "especially in these sorts of situations, but doctor's orders. You have a fractured clavicle. And you're going to be sore from the airbag. And the gastric lavage."

A throbbing shot out from my left shoulder as though he'd summoned the pain. Spreading out from my chest, a heavy pressure followed.

"Can I get you anything?"

The man had taken on sharper features now. He was older, but his veined arms looked fit. I closed my eyes and shook my head to indicate *no*.

"Alright, I'll get your family. They've been outside for hours."

My eyes shot open as a wave of nausea rippled outwards from my gut. My family. Charlotte and Mamma and Paul. A painful lump rose in my throat. I swallowed it. *Not Paul. Paul's gone.*

A door clicked open. Heels on linoleum announced Mamma's entrance.

"Hummingbird," she whispered, taking my bruised hand. "My baby girl." By the closeness between our faces, she must've kneeled by the bed. The nurse had vacated the room. Only me and her. The anguish in her words must be real, then.

"Charlotte went for some coffee across the street before they said you'd woken up," Mamma continued. "I sent an orderly for her. She'll be here soon as she can." She gave my hand a second squeeze.

Questions. I wanted to ask questions. Did I hurt anyone? Was the car bad off? Would Charlotte forgive me? Between the aching and a sinking feeling of guilt, I'd lost the ability to speak. Was I in shock? Had they heard any news of Paul?

"I've spoken to . . ." she hesitated, pain still behind her words, "someone. Someone who knows the county prosecutor. He'll take care of everything. There'll be no charges, Hummingbird. No charges, and we're going to get you better. Your body *and* your mind."

The fogginess that shrouded my thoughts prevented me from processing what she'd said. Then a second click from an opening door broke my attempt at concentration altogether.

"Gray," another voice called. *Charlotte.* Mamma stood as my sister rushed to my side. Her warm lips found my forehead.

I forced words out. "I'm sorry. Your car—"

"Quiet," she said, index finger to my mouth. "Things are things. They're unimportant. You're going to be okay, and that's all that matters."

She offered me a tiny smile. I wanted to return it, but I couldn't. I had nothing to smile about. Truthfully, I wasn't happy to have woken up at all.

23

Nina

"**S**hit, is she okay?" I asked.

"Beat up a bit," Cora answered, discomforted. Likely unsettled to be the one communicating on behalf of the family. "She'll make a full recovery, I'm told."

I'd phoned Piper Point to inform Gray of Jacob's arrest. I had more questions, too, hoping the details of a fight between the two men on the highway might jog her memory. Instead, Cora told me she'd struck a streetlamp in town.

What Frances disclosed replayed in my head. "Was alcohol involved?"

Cora ignored the question. "As I said, she's expected to make a full recovery, Ms. Palmer."

I sighed. "Thank you, Cora."

"You're welcome," she replied before she hung up.

My next call would be to the station. If alcohol was a factor in the accident, they'd be sure to let me know.

My gaze wandered to Auntie Tilda, asleep in her hospice bed. It'd been half an hour since I'd administered her meds, and I needed to get back to work. If I had to guess, Gray looked the exact same right now.

As I walked back into the kitchen to retrieve my book bag, my phone vibrated in my pocket. Virginia area code. Andrew Huang. He'd called twice already. He must be scanning the sheriff's office website. Jacob's mug shot would've been posted by now.

Jacob had lawyered up courtesy of his grandmother, so I didn't have anything new yet. Even if I did, I didn't owe Andrew information. I played his voicemail anyway.

"Nina, it's Andrew. Give me a call at this number when you can. I've got some things I'd like to discuss with you."

Of course, he did.

"Maybe we could meet for a drink this evening? Let me know."

As I started to tuck my phone back into my pocket, it vibrated once more.

Damn, this guy was persistent. But instead of Andrew, it was Sammie. "Nina, you need to come back in now."

"I'm about to be on my way," I replied, book bag slung across my shoulder.

Sammie didn't miss a beat. "The dogs found blood down by the marsh." My heart stopped. "Running it against the samples from Piper Point now, but my guess is DNA's gonna match Paul Godfrey."

* * *

The baying of German Shepherds met me as I stepped out of my car on the shoulder of Paul Revere Highway. Their handler guided them back into the truck bed kennels beneath the strobes of silent flashers. Taut yellow police tape wound from tree trunk to tree trunk to tree trunk.

I swallowed hard and approached the man waiting to speak with me, a Charleston Crime Scene Unit insignia emblazoned on his windbreaker. The constant hum of cicadas soon overwhelmed even the dogs' barking. Loud and hostile.

"Detective Palmer," he said. "This way, please."

I remained silent as I followed him off the road and into the woods. Piles of decaying broad leaf and pine needles cushioned my steps. The smell of damp rot mixing with the saline marsh air lent a sinister air to an otherwise peaceful scene.

"Upturned foliage suggests the movement of two individuals coming this way from the road."

"Can you tell where they originated?" I asked, thinking of Jacob's truck. "If they came from the same car or different ones, for instance?"

"Not for certain. Asphalt's not really great for footprints, detective. Not unless there's a bit of gravel on the surface. And with the rain . . ." He paused to find his footing in the swampy soil.

A few more yards, and he spoke again. "But they terminate down here," he said, side-stepping down the slope to the tall grass and the foamy water's edge beyond it. I followed his lead.

Ahead, the burst of a flashbulb accompanied the man photographing a patch of salt meadow and saw grass—all of it staked and cordoned off with more ribbon. A woman knelt by his side, picking through leafy matter with a pair of forceps, a bundle of Ziploc baggies by her side.

"Hopefully those'll fit you." My companion motioned to an empty pair of rubber boots a couple feet from where I stood. I took the hint and slipped them on, leaving my own hiking boots behind.

"Down here's where the dogs led us," he announced, waving to the staked-out patch. My feet sank deep into the festering marsh mud as I traced the man's steps. "Sure enough, we found quite a bit that tested positive with Luminol."

"Oxidized in the presence of blood," I stated.

He nodded. "Mr. Godfrey's iron-rich hemoglobin to be exact. Two sets of tracks, but his is the only sample we've found."

"Results back already?"

"Confirmation came in just before you got here."

So, at the very least, Paul was presumably injured. If there'd been a fight, blood from Jacob might have been found, too. He hadn't displayed any obvious signs, bruises or otherwise, but then he'd been wearing jeans, long sleeves. Sammie had told me he was processing the warrant for Jacob's DNA right now. As soon as he got the lab techs a sample to compare with, some of Jacob's blood could turn up.

"How much is 'quite a bit'?" I asked. "I used to slice my legs up all the time on saw grass as a kid. The stuff's practically serrated."

"Not a whole lot," he answered. "And you're right. Mr. Godfrey could've cut himself on the grass, but I'm not inclined to believe it."

I wiped sweat from my brow. The closer to the water I drew, the more the air turned jungle humid. "Why's that?"

He glanced towards the ash-colored sky, swollen with rain. "The way it's been pouring the past week, to find anything suggests there was a lot of material present at first. Most of it would've been washed out. Diluted."

"We're looking at a transition, then?" I folded my arms across my chest. "Missing person to homicide?"

He shrugged. "Hard to conclude homicide without a body, but given the circumstances and the fact Mr. Godfrey hasn't turned up anywhere, that's my hypothesis."

My thoughts went to each of the people I'd spoken with so far. People like Jacob Wilcox and Charlotte. Gray and Joanna. The woman, Annie, who I couldn't find.

"Nice to have a body for a homicide," I agreed. "We need divers."

"Already sent for," he replied. "I've got an oceanographer coming up from Beaufort, too. Tides and currents have been a mess with all the bad weather, but they'll know where to look."

My question from earlier—*who stood to benefit from Paul's absence?*—took on a newer, darker meaning. *Who stood to gain from his murder?*

24

Annie

I consume news of Gray's accident with the same gleefulness that I had when Paul's missing persons report came down the wire. I set events into motion, and there's no stopping them now. They'll evolve and escalate and assume a chaotic life all their own.

They already are.

I spin a lock of my hair into a ringlet around my index finger.

I should tell her. I should tell Gray. There's no reason Gray can't know the truth. At least some of it. Or maybe she *can* know the whole truth. The nasty, awful, rotting truth.

Releasing my ringlet, it bounces once like a spring before straightening itself out.

No, that's not fair. It isn't right to do that to her. At least not all at once. But I could give it to her in tiny doses. Little bits and pieces of truth. Spoonfuls at a time. Like medicine. Or poison. She won't realize the effect they have because they're too subtle. They might even feel good at first. And by the time she realizes the answers are killing her, it'll be too late.

Too fucking late.

25

Gray

There were no windows in my hospital suite. A digital clock above the doorway said it was half past six in the evening. The only light came from soft bulbs beneath a row of cabinets on one side. Everything reeked of sterility.

On the tray extending over my legs sat a collection of Styrofoam containers. Peas and chopped carrots. Greek yogurt. A cup of melting shaved ice.

The nurse—the man with the self-righteous attitude towards painkillers—insisted on leaving the food. "It'll do you good to eat something," he'd said as he made notes on my chart. "Your blood sugar's too low, and you're underweight as is. You're also Vitamin B deficient. Common for folks who drink . . . a lot."

He was right about needing calories, but the idea of eating repulsed me. Charlotte and Mamma had gone for dinner themselves, and I'd been alone for the past half hour.

To be fair, I'd tried for the yogurt, but the throbbing in my collarbone prevented me from reaching it. The movement my arm sling permitted was deceptive as far as pain went, but there was no point in ringing *that* nurse for more than the ordered Percocet. A single tablet every four hours. Not a minute earlier.

Murmuring voices outside the door interrupted my thoughts. As the handle turned, I closed my eyes. Feigning sleep, my only way to hide.

Clicking dress shoes told me whoever entered wasn't a scrubbed-up nurse or doctor. Mamma and Charlotte hadn't been gone long enough. And Mamma wouldn't eat fast food. She'd have found a booth for the two of them to sit down and eat casually.

Besides, I heard only one set of shoes on the tiled floor. Maybe it was someone with a clerical job to do. Coming for insurance information, perhaps. As the person drew closer, keeping my eyes shut became harder. The tighter I held them, the more they twitched.

I detected a man's cologne, expensive like Paul's but not the same brand. Behind it, the scent of musk. The way a man's suit smelled after a long day at a desk. Perspiration mixed with Old Spice and office.

As soon as I opened my eyes, my heart stopped. Standing before the hospital bed was my cousin.

Matthew.

My face flushed hot as my heart crawled up my throat.

He wore a tailored suit subtly patterned in a dark plaid. His loosely curled locks shined from hair product. His Roman nose, distinctive.

"Hello, Gray," he said, setting a glass vase of yellow tulips on the table beside my food tray. "I'm so sorry," he added as he stood a card next to the etched crystal.

I couldn't speak. My blood froze solid in my veins, and now my bottom lip trembled. Just like my hands beneath the scratchy quilt.

I'd awoken to a nightmare. This wasn't supposed to happen.

You wake to escape, to leave terrors behind in a place where they can't find you or hurt you.

"After everything that's happened—Paul and the rest. This?" His eyes appeared sullen and anguished. Despite the shock, I retained the wherewithal to doubt the sadness in them was for me. Not *only* for me.

He continued in a softened voice, slow and deliberate and stomach-turning. "Aunt Joanna phoned me to let me know what happened. She described the circumstances of the accident. Police were first on the scene so a report had already been filed by the time she called. You were very intoxicated."

The person she spoke to—the one who would take care of everything. It was Matthew. *How could she? How could she have done this to me?* She knew everything. I'd told her everything that'd happened. *For Christ's sake, I'm her child!*

"I know we haven't spoken in a long time, but Aunt Joanna was frightened you'd be arrested," he said, taking a seat at the foot of my bed. As he sunk into the padding, the whole room pulled in closer. "And she was right. The county prosecutor was prepared to move forward with charges."

A fire grew inside my chest. My organs burned within my ribs. I willed my mouth to speak, but nothing came out. I couldn't move my lips.

"You've nothing to worry over," he said with a smile. "I made a few calls and the county prosecutor agreed to drop it. I changed his appraisal of the situation. With all the stress of Paul's case, there was no point in piling it on when no else was injured. Of course, you'll still need to show you're making an effort to get help, but nothing more."

I began to flinch with every movement he made. Brushing his slacks, adjusting his collar. I jerked each time, and he appeared to take note. He avoided my eyes as though they might melt him.

He finally stood from the bed, and his look suggested he realized it'd been a mistake to visit me. "In any case, I stopped by to say hello and wish you well. I wanted to let you know myself that everything was squared away."

He lingered at the bedside for a moment more. My nails dug into my palms like knives.

"Goodbye, Gray," he said, turning to leave. As he opened the door, he paused and added, "I'm sorry again."

The door clicked shut, and he was gone.

The flames inside my chest raged like a frantic fire searching for more oxygen. More fuel to burn.

I reached for the crystal vase he'd brought and a searing flash of pain crackled from my fractured bone and down my arm. But the bolt of adrenaline carried me as I hurled the vase at the wall, screaming. It struck plaster in a shattering crash. Glass shards rained to the floor as water and yellow petals splashed in every direction.

The moment I stopped screaming, the pain became unbearable. I buried my face into my pillow and wailed.

"What happened?" The nurse shouted as he bolted through the door and raced to my side. "Mrs. Godfrey! Are you okay?"

I let the pillow fall to my lap but couldn't speak through my sobbing.

"What happened here?" He asked again, eyeing the glass, broken and strewn.

I trembled from head to toe. The pain from my broken shoulder turned from white-hot to dull and deep.

"Mrs. Godfrey, are you okay? Talk to me, please!"

Looking into his eyes, I spoke in a raspy whisper, "How could she have called him?"

The nurse knotted his brow, struggling to understand. "How could she have called *who*, Mrs. Godfrey?"

*   *   *

Two doors led to Piper Point's cellar. A wooden aperture, gnarled and splintering, from the backyard, and the clean white paneled one in the kitchen.

On *that* day, my hands trembled by my sides. Damp like Matthew's had been when he led me to the kitchen, away from Charlotte watching cartoons upstairs. I'd second-guessed myself as I followed him, fought to squash my fear with every step. If Matthew could face the Devil, so could I. And if he was tricking me, then I'd show him how tough I was. It wasn't so easy for him to fool me anymore.

"Why would the Devil live down there?" I asked, turning from the cellar door towards my cousin.

"Might have something to do with what happened down there," he started.

"What happened?"

"It's past. It's history, Gray."

I opened my mouth to speak, but Matthew pressed on, taking my hand again. The sweat collecting on our palms mixed. "After the Civil War, Sherman was burning everything from Atlanta eastward. So, the women of Elizabeth hid down there." He stroked my palm with his knuckle as he spoke. "Children, too. Babies."

He reached over my shoulder and turned the whining brass handle. A gentle push and the door creaked open. The first few steps, crooked and rotting, vanished into the blackness below. A rush of ice-cold air washed over me.

"Go on, Gray," he spoke into my ear, warm breath whistling inside my head. Matthew nudged me onto the first step. Knees locked, I almost toppled. Matthew's hand found my shoulder and steadied me.

"But the Union soldiers were on the hunt for folks hiding. And in Elizabeth in those days, there weren't too many places to hide. They stomped through Piper Point, tracking mud all over with their big leather boots. And they found them—the women and the children. Found them hiding down here. And they didn't like the fact that traitors—in their opinion—thought they might escape what was coming to them."

The second step.

"What happened next? Did they hurt them?" My voice caught in my throat. The chill spread to my teeth and my bones, and they chattered and trembled.

"They told them, angry as sin, 'You wanna hide in the dark?'" Matthew's voice grew demanding and deep. "'Then you can stay in the dark!'"

I jolted on the third step. The wooden plank lurched, groaned. Wisps of damp mildew bloomed into a wet stench

Matthew's voice grew matter-of-fact. "So, the soldiers stuck hot sewing needles into their eyes. The women. The children. The babies, crying and hollering. Red hot needles into the soft whites of their eyes."

"They did not!" A burst of courage as sweat beaded on my brow.

"They did." Matthew shrugged.

A fourth step, and my stomach flipped. My own eyes burned. He *was* tricking me. His story wasn't true. Daddy would've told me if all this happened. Still, if I played along—even if the fear was real—the game would go on. Maybe after, when I'd proven to Matthew he could let me in on it, we could even spook Charlotte, too.

"Chopped their fingers and toes to bits, too. Tore out the tongues of the ones that wouldn't shut up. Tortured them. Showed the mother's what their babies' insides looked like, and then laughed at the wailing women 'cause they couldn't see.

"They locked all the blind women down here. Yep, the Union soldiers made quite a home for the Devil in this cellar. Nothing the Devil likes more than bits and pieces of babies strewn about.

"But it was cold being locked down here back then, just like it is now. And the women needed to stay warm. With no kindling, they had to burn what remained of their children in the furnace or they'd freeze to death."

On the fifth plank, nearly to the bottom of the rotting cellar stairs, I froze. The brave face I'd worked up dissolved, and I became a petrified piece of timber—an extension of the wooden step. As darkness swallowed us both, I started to blame myself. I'd begged to hear a scary story, and I'd taken it too far. Believed too much of it. But it was too late. The damage was done, and the ghosts Matthew spoke of, real or not, had been conjured. They swirled and breathed around me as shadows dancing across the cellar's stone walls.

Matthew goaded, "Go on, Gray." Another gentle push and both of my feet found the cement floor, cracked and uneven like the moist ground beneath it.

"I don't want—"

"So that's where the Devil lives now. Among all those burnt babies. Go on and have a look in the furnace. You can see him for yourself."

My heart thumped wildly beneath my tiny ribs. I took a deep breath. My eyes were teary, but I was almost there. Matthew would be so proud if I took a look. If I showed him I wasn't scared. I couldn't let him see that I was afraid.

Stepping across the floor, I imagined my feet sinking into the wet gore of baby pieces. Blood like inky black paint. My legs slowed, wanting to turn back. To run up the steps, to the rest of the house swaddled in sunlight. Back upstairs to Charlotte.

But behind me, Matthew formed an impenetrable wall. His chest, swelling and shrinking in anticipation, forced me onward. Around the corner. Towards the furnace. Where the Devil lived.

Something moved to my right. My reflection, barely visible in the dark. The landing mirror—the one Daddy had taken down—stood propped against the river stone foundation. I paused, squinting at its cracked surface just to make sure the girl looking back really was me.

"Almost there," Matthew said, pushing me forward and away from the enormous mirror.

I'd seen the furnace before, but this time was different. This time, it materialized from shadow like an evil thing. A creature sprung up from the uneven ground. Black cast-iron like soot or tar. When it was turned off, it melded with the shadows, but even in the darkness it gleamed, swollen like the belly of a pregnant woman. A grate crossed its potbelly, splitting it open at the seams like the people from Matthew's story. The grate curved upwards at the edges, like a smile. Wicked. Carnivorous.

"Just me and you, Gray. We're the only ones who know. A secret for the two of us. Have a look. I dare you."

My shoulders jumped. In the span of a few seconds I'd

forgotten Matthew stood behind me. The furnace had drawn all my thoughts.

The air changed. My ears felt plugged or muffled, but as I crept closer, a sound grew. A sharp, constant sound. Hissing. A hissing like a—

"Do you hear him?" Matthew asked. "If he looks you in the eye . . ."

I nodded, swallowed the stiff lump building in the back of my throat.

"Well, we'll deal with *that* if it happens."

I was nearly to the furnace now. The constant hiss of gas feeding its unending hunger grew louder and louder. Like a snake.

"Look inside."

If the grate was a mouth, then the caged bars within were sharp teeth, dripping with long strings of black saliva. It seemed to open, to call me. To swallow me whole.

"Don't look him in the eye."

The tip of my nose nearly touched the iron. The hissing came from a metal rod buried deep within the creature's belly. It hypnotized me.

The hissing became a sudden tick-ticking. A spark. A swooshing roar. Flames erupted within as a searing blossom. I screamed and stumbled backwards.

A blast of fiery heat and light drew the rest of the room pitch black. Streaks from the sudden brightness formed and floated across the inside of my eyelids.

I saw him. A glimpse. A mere fraction of a second, but it was him. Crocodile grin. The Devil. And he looked like Matthew.

Matthew, who'd caught me with both arms. They latched

around me then like a too-tight belt, his fingers interlocking just below my belly button.

"You've seen the Devil, haven't you Gray?" he whispered. His breath, hot like the fire. "You're a bad girl now."

I'd broken out in a sudden fever. My cheeks were flushed, hot to the touch. A tear rolled down my cheek, and Matthew caught it with his index finger.

"Hush now, Gray," he cooed. "Hush now." I thought he might've sucked his finger—the one with my tear on its tip—but I couldn't be certain. I breathed in staggered heaves.

He knelt, pulling me down halfway in his lap. I lost my balance and turned, catching myself with my right palm pressed against the ice-cold floor. When I looked up, I saw my reflection in the cracked mirror again. "I saw him. I saw the Devil."

"Shhh . . . quiet down now."

"I saw the Devil, and now I'm bad. I am a bad girl."

"You are," Matthew said, his cheek pressed to mine. "I can't tell you otherwise. I'd like to, but I can't. I can't change that you've seen him."

I coughed and a dollop of spit ran down my chin.

Matthew went on, "I gotta ask you a question now, and I need you to tell me the truth. It's very important you be honest with me, you hear?"

A broken nod.

"I know you saw him, but did you look the Devil in the eyes?"

The fire was so hot, I'd clenched my eyes shut. But then I'd opened them. The blinding streaks that floated before me had formed an image—a face. And the face had eyes.

"I . . . I think so."

Matthew breathed heavily. "This is serious."

His words spiked my pulse. I'd never heard him so worried before. I couldn't collect my thoughts. I couldn't tear the image made in the furnace's flash from my mind's eye. Matthew's face. My cousin, who I sat clinging to like a life raft.

"We've gotta get him out of you, Gray, do you hear? We've got to get the Devil out."

I didn't know what he was saying. His words became distant and garbled. I watched Matthew speak, as if from afar. Another nod. Empty. Blank.

My throat had tightened. Breathing became almost impossible. Matthew paused as though searching for a solution, a cure. Should I tell him the Devil looked just like him? I opened my mouth to speak, but he turned my head back towards the glass.

As my eyes readjusted, my cheeks now appeared splotched and wet in the mirror. I clenched my hands.

"Look at yourself, Gray," Matthew whispered. For a flash, his wet breath seemed . . . wetter. Queasiness rippled through me. Did he touch my neck with his tongue?

"Look at yourself," he said again. My eyes met themselves in the glass. Damp, wide with terror. "Look at yourself, and tell me what you are."

I'd never stared at anything so hard before.

"Tell me what you are," Matthew repeated. "Tell me you're a bad girl, and we can get the Devil out. We can leave him in the mirror. Trapped."

My voice caught in my throat. I couldn't form words. Nothing Matthew said made any sense.

"Tell me what you are. Tell me you're a bad girl."

"I . . . ," my voice cracked, "I—I'm a bad . . . girl."

"Say it again."

"I'm a bad girl."

"That's right. You've seen the Devil. You're a wicked little girl now." Matthew's breath grew hotter on my neck. Then his lips pressed against my skin.

My eyes remained locked on my reflection, my mouth repeating the phrase over and over and over again. Matthew's icy fingers ran beneath the elastic waistline of my skirt. The girl in the mirror became magnetic. We shared an unbroken stare.

"I'm a bad girl."

26

Nina

In the hospital corridor, Matthew King stumbled towards me. Even from yards away, he appeared distraught. An unusual look for someone like him. He must've just left Gray's bedside. He held his head down, and I doubted he even saw me.

"Matthew..." I said. He ignored my greeting and pressed onward to the elevators, brushing my shoulder as he passed by. Why was he so obviously upset? From what I'd heard, his request for the county prosecutor to decline charges against Gray had been successful.

As soon as I'd finished with the crime scene team, I'd learned the exact circumstances of the accident. Her blood alcohol content—taken in the emergency department—measured point three. She'd been behind the wheel of a large SUV possibly going in and out of consciousness. It was a goddamn miracle that a streetlamp had stopped her—and not a pedestrian.

I turned the corner, noting the room numbers painted above each doorway. Through the open door of what I guessed was Gray's suite, a custodian swept broken glass from the floor. Another wiped down the wall with a wet rag. A nurse appeared, drying his hands off with a paper towel.

"This isn't a good time to visit, ma'am." His face was worrying.

"Detective Palmer." I flashed my badge. "What happened in here?"

He sighed. "There was an incident. Mrs. Godfrey had an outburst and broke a vase against the wall."

Did she and Matthew have an argument? That would have fit with his demeanor in the hallway.

"I still need to speak with her," I said, looking over his shoulder.

Gray's chest rose in regular intervals. She was awake but appeared dazed. Her eyes were purpled with bruises—likely caused by the airbag—and a sling held her left arm up by her side. Her cheeks glistened from sweat, and the tips of her ears reddened like they were on fire.

"I have to tell you she's been given an antianxiety medication and additional painkillers, so nothing she says can be," he hesitated, "you know, *used* or whatever by you folks."

"Not a worry of mine," I replied, waving him off.

I stood to the side, allowing the custodial staff to leave with a garbage bag of clattering glass. When the last person exited the room, I gently closed the door. Gray and I made eye contact.

"How are you doing, Gray?" I asked, stepping closer to the bed.

Her dry lips twitched as though she intended to speak, but she stopped short of words.

"I'm here to tell you we made an arrest. Jacob confessed to assaulting your husband early Christmas morning."

Still only silence from Gray. My words seemed to have no affect on her. I decided not to disclose the blood we'd found in the marsh. Now wasn't the time for that.

I continued, "I thought maybe if I told you Jacob had admitted to being on the highway that night, you might remember more. A new detail?"

Her eyes remained trained on my own in an unsettling way. Every time we'd spoken over the past week, she'd avoided my eyes. I'd chalked it up to anxiety, or perhaps the drinking. But now those dark eyes seemed to want to say something to me. Something she couldn't bring herself to speak aloud.

I smiled as best I could and took a seat in the chair by her bed. With my elbows on my knees, I leaned closer. "Do you recall seeing Jacob on the highway that night or what he did to Paul?"

When I reached to take her hand, she finally spoke. "Why did he do it?" Her palm was frigid and clammy, and I gave her a reassuring squeeze.

"Why did who do what?" I asked, eyes narrowed. "Why did Jacob attack Paul?"

She glanced towards the freshly cleaned wall. "Why did Matthew do it?"

What had the two of them fought over? What could have prompted her to break a vase despite her own injuries? Unease washed over me.

"Do you want to tell me something, Gray? Is there something you're struggling with?"

She fell silent again.

"Look, I know about the drinking. I know it's a significant problem. Do you want to tell me what's been happening? Did Paul hurt you? Did you argue with your cousin over it?"

Her hand clenched at my last question. "Gray, you can talk to me. We've known each other a long time, and I'm here to help you. Tell me how I can help you. Did *Matthew* hurt you in some way?"

Her breathing became erratic at the second mention of his name. She needed rest, desperately, and my presence wasn't helping. The nurse had tried to caution me about the drugs and their effects, but I hadn't listened.

She wasn't going anywhere and neither was Jacob Wilcox. There'd be chances to talk tomorrow. A pang of guilt struck me for visiting her now. My burning questions no longer justified being here, torturing her. I stood to leave.

"Nina, wait," Gray called out. I stopped, and she added in a shaky voice, "I want to talk to you. I want to tell *you* what happened."

* * *

I sped down the highway on my way back to Auntie Tilda's, the revving engine barely keeping pace with my thoughts. Pine trees flickered by my window as Elizabeth's steepled silhouette grew smaller in the rearview mirror.

Gray's allegations reverberated in my mind. Matthew King, respected defense attorney and her first cousin, sexually assaulted her in her own home when she was nine years old, and he was a senior in high school.

Did I believe her? What reasons would she have to lie to me? Of course, if she did have anything to do with Paul's disappearance, a story like this would be both distracting and paint her a victim. Or had her medication simply led her to allege something so unexpected? But then remembering the look on Matthew's face as I passed him in the hallway . . . One word came to mind to describe it: shame.

Her nurse said she'd been medicated heavily after the incident during Matthew's visit. *After the incident.* That meant something had *incited* the hostility, independent of any drug. I considered the possibly that the medication might've coaxed her to tell me. The visit from Matthew combined with lowered inhibitions could've spurred the disclosure.

And if it was true, then had her parents known? Or suspected, maybe? A tingle swept over my shoulders. Auntie was more a caretaker to Gray than Joanna or Seamus, would she have something to add to any of this?

But as disturbing as Gray's allegations were, they got me no closer to determining what had happened to Paul.

Then there was still the matter of Annie. Gray's accident only occurred because she'd gone to meet the woman. A shaken Gray had told me so afterwards, played the second voicemail she'd received from her. Annie didn't seem to fit anywhere.

My own phone rang from inside my bag. I started to reach for it, but thoughts of Gray's car wreck had me pulling over before answering. Andrew Huang. Again.

"This is Nina," I said, making no effort to hide my exasperation.

"Hello, Nina," Andrew said. "You're a very difficult woman to get a hold of."

"Do you need something?"

"It would benefit you to meet with me," he answered. "I have information that'll help you." His voice had an earnestness I hadn't detected when we first met in the street.

"Then tell me right now. We don't need to meet," I said. What had his message said he wanted? A drink?

"It'd be far easier in person," he replied. "A lot of nuance to discuss."

"I bet. You've got me on the phone. Give me something. Make me want to meet you."

"You're finally speaking my language," he chuckled. "For starters, Jacob Wilcox isn't your guy."

"You've been keeping informed, then."

"Doing my job, same as you," he answered.

"He confessed to assaulting Paul Godfrey on the highway where we found his rental. A physical confrontation moments before a person vanishes is a tough thing to look past, Andrew." I glanced at my watch. I needed to be back at Auntie Tilda's in less than half an hour.

"He's not your guy, and I can prove it," he replied, his tone certain. "And I've got more for you. We're on the same team, Nina. We want the same thing more or less. Will you meet me tonight?"

I challenged him to make me want to meet him, and he'd done just that. No matter what my opinion of the guy was, I'd give him a chance to talk. More than likely, this was an opportunity to ply me for information, not the other way around. But after today? Between blood by the marshes and Gray's allegations, I'd give Andrew a shot. Nothing he said could make this day any more surprising.

"When and where?" I asked.

"I'm staying at a hotel right off the interstate. The James Plantation Inn."

"I know the place."

"There's a bar downstairs, the Magnolia Lounge. Seems to be about as classy as it gets in Elizabeth. Can you be there in an hour?"

"No. I've got something. How about ten o'clock?"

"See you then, detective." He hung up.

*   *   *

The hotel was two stories of white siding and black shutters. Four pillars stood in front of the main façade, evoking the look of a neoclassical plantation.

Each Sunday, the hotel's restaurant, a country buffet, became a popular lunch spot for the church crowd. I'd been once, but watching the all-black waitstaff scurry to fill sweet teas for dressy whites kept me from ever going back.

The deviled crab wasn't so bad, I thought, walking up to the entrance.

Sammie wouldn't like the idea of me meeting Andrew. I didn't tell him about our first encounter outside the pharmacy, but he'd seen Andrew's business card. *We're partners, Nina,* I imagined him saying. *When it comes to a case, we tell each other everything. It's the only way we'll get it done right.*

He might make a connection where there wasn't one between our—or rather, my—hesitation to contact the Kings about their missing rental and this city-slicking former agent from D.C. And would he be right? Was I overcompensating for bungling the start of the investigation by giving in too much now?

The darkened restaurant's French doors had been closed and locked, but the bar next door was alive with piano music and soft, yellow lighting.

The Magnolia Lounge was more bustling than I'd expected. Clinking crystal met with laughter, as a sonata played from a baby grand. Ornate potted palms sat on the burgundy carpet, and the tabletops were all oak.

My watch read nine forty PM. I came early on purpose to pick our table. I wanted to make sure I had a line of sight to the bathrooms and the exits. If Andrew excused himself at any point during our chat, I wanted to see everywhere he went. I didn't care where Andrew was from or what he'd done before coming here. He was in Elizabeth now. My town, my turf. I'd worked too hard to get where I was to cede ground to anyone.

An enormous portrait stared out from behind the piano. Scarlett O'Hara, in a pink ruffled hoop skirt, stood beneath an arching oak. Only instead of Tara, the house in the background mimicked the front of this hotel. I returned a pastel Vivien Leigh's smirk with one of my own.

"Can I get you something to drink, ma'am?" A waiter asked as I took my seat at a corner table.

"What blushes do you have?"

"We've got a zinfandel '05, and a '99 white merlot," he replied, uncapping his pen to take my order.

"The zinfandel would be great."

"And will you be having something to eat, as well?"

"No." I smiled. "And do me a favor. I'm meeting someone. Don't offer him a menu when you take his drink order, we won't be staying long."

Moments later, my drink sat before me. As I sipped it, my head tingled. I didn't often drink, but a day like today didn't come often, either.

As I swirled the pink wine by the stem, my thoughts went to Gray. What was only a simple drink to me, to so many people, was everything to her. Did I believe her allegations? Were they relevant to Paul's case? If anything, her near-constant inebriation seemed to be her alibi.

But at the same time, I got it. I understood what drove her to drink. Life was overwhelming at the best of times. And at the worst? I took another swallow, allowing myself to enjoy the euphoric warmth.

"Hello, Nina." Andrew cracked a wide grin as he took a seat across the table. His hair perfectly shellacked into place. The cologne he wore, too strong.

"Good evening, Andrew." I failed to blunt the sardonic edge in my voice. The waiter had followed him to the table.

"Balvenie scotch, neat," he ordered. "No more than a finger or two, please."

"A conscientious drinker?" I laughed.

He smiled sideways. "All things in moderation, detective."

I got right to the point. "Why is Jacob not my guy?"

Andrew straightened the silverware in front of him as he answered. "His truck. He bought it used in Beaufort. One of those guaranteed credit lots. They finance high-risk customers, but the catch is a starter cut-off device."

"If someone skips a payment, they shut the car off remotely," I concluded. With the sorts of problems Jacob had, why hadn't I thought to look into this?

Andrew went on. "And nearly always, these devices include GPS tracking for the repo folks."

"Which you checked . . ."

"Which I checked. I'm not quite as *regulated* as an officer of the law like yourself." Was he offering me an excuse for my oversight? Reaching into his pocket, he produced a piece of paper. Printed coordinates covered both sides.

A sinking feeling gripped me. "Jacob's truck didn't make it to Paul Revere Highway, did it?"

"No. Maybe his intention had been to follow the Godfreys, but he didn't make it that far." Andrew pointed to a single line he'd highlighted. "All the way to a second bar a few blocks south, in fact."

"Shit." The sinking feeling began to turn my stomach. He'd let his temper get the best of him. It wasn't the first time he'd been hauled in, so the idea probably didn't frighten him like it might someone else. Not while his head was hot, anyways. He was likely revising his story to reflect to truth as I sat here. The chance to laugh at me may've even been worth it to him. *Sheriff Burton's going to have a coronary.*

Andrew shrugged. "Probably couldn't stand the idea of someone like Paul taking what he believed was his."

"It fits with everything else I know about him." My cheeks grew hot. Partly from Jacob's dishonesty. Partly from embarrassment that this man had been the one to figure it out. "Shit."

"Sorry, detective."

Eager to move on from my mistake, I spoke forcefully. "You said on the phone you've got something else?"

He grinned again. "I do. But I need information from you first."

Here we go, I thought to myself. His opening salvo had knocked me completely off-balance. Now came the part where he started to dig. The look on his face suggested he sensed my hesitation.

"Don't dismiss me so fast." He tapped his finger on the paper sitting between us. "I think I've proven I don't mind playing ball."

I sipped my wine. "What do you want?"

He followed my lead with his scotch. "The crime scene unit. What've they found?"

"Blood," I answered tersely.

He arched his brow. "Paul's?"

"Yes."

The tone of his next question surprised me. "Has Paul's case transitioned to homicide?"

"Not officially, but you can do the math." We locked eyes.

"Why do you care what label the case has stuck to it?" Joking, I added, "He's no good to Cooper and Waters dead?"

Andrew's face became stolid. "In so many words, no."

"I see." Beltway business was cut-throat and cold. No reason to be surprised, I guessed.

He continued, polishing off his drink in the process. "When Paul's undamaged return is no longer a possibility, they'll recall me. Dead men can't run for congress. Dead men can't vote in the firm's interests on Capitol Hill."

"No concern for his family? Beyond the portrayal of worry in public, of course." I sighed. "But there's still a possibility of his return. The blood we found was trace at best."

Andrew corrected me. "His return? Perhaps, though unlikely. Undamaged? Not a chance."

I leaned forward on the table. "What do you know? If Jacob's bad credit alibis him, then the last person seen with Paul the night he disappeared was his wife." I paused for a moment. "But Paul was stone-cold sober, and Gray was blackout drunk. The picture witnesses paint had her nearly immobile. Being dragged off a dance floor."

"That's true." Andrew ran a manicured finger around the rim of his tumbler. "But Gray wasn't the only woman with Paul at Ruby's that night."

My heart fluttered. "I'll ask again. What do you know?"

He lowered his voice to just above a whisper. "Like I said, I'm not as regulated as law enforcement. We've done forensics on Paul's work computers. Maybe even some devices in their Georgetown place."

"You broke in?"

"The firm has a copy of the keys in case of emergencies. Courtesy of Mr. Godfrey. All above board." His tone grew playful. "Unfortunately, no one could recall if the Godfreys kept any pets that might need care during their unexpectedly prolonged absence."

Access to Paul's work computer? Devices from the home? The warrants for all these things were working their way through the system, but with the amount of coordination between jurisdictions . . .

"You've seen the debts. That's what you meant by *damaged*." I found myself whispering, too.

Andrew nodded. "Alive or not, Paul Godfrey is no longer a viable candidate as far as the firm is concerned."

His previous words replayed in my mind. *Not the only woman.* "What else did you find?"

He lowered his head. "We uncovered a large trove of personal correspondence between Mr. Godfrey and an IP address in Raleigh, North Carolina. He'd gone through proxy servers to cover his trail, but our IT department followed the breadcrumbs."

My heart beat in my throat, and I spoke slowly to make up for it. "Charlotte."

"Correct."

Gray's sister. Gray's diligently supportive sister. My mind went straight to Annie. Annie, a name no one in the Godfrey or King families recognized. Someone who had intimate knowledge of Gray's self-destructive habits.

I decided to keep the details of Annie to myself. Instead, I spoke of Charlotte. "She's recently divorced. A case of infidelity on the husband's part with a woman named Florence or Florencia or something."

"Not quite." Andrew shook his head as he spoke. "We've interviewed the husband. Will Barfield. There was an affair, but not on his end. The knowledge of it was enough to unravel their marriage, but with whom, he couldn't be sure. I don't think he suspected Paul."

If what Andrew had said was true, then Charlotte lied about her husband being the one who cheated. On its own, it was a common thing to do. No reason to take responsibility for sinking your marriage if it's not germane to the discussion. But in this instance, it was definitely germane.

"Someone who used proxy servers to mask IP addresses would be careful. Does the correspondence confirm an affair? Between Paul and Gray's sister?"

"Most definitely." Andrew puffed out his cheeks. "Those emails? Lewd is an understatement."

27

Annie

I slip the USB—the one with my private collection of photographs—out of a tiny drawstring sack I keep hidden at the bottom of my bag. Black satin and utterly fitting.

I should tell Gray about Paul. Tell her all about Paul. The things about Paul she *thinks* only she knows.

Like his dick. Limp like cooked spaghetti when he drinks too much. Gray's not the only Godfrey who likes their liquor, though Paul likes to lie that he's a teetotaler. Then there are his *hobbies*. The way he likes to be tied up. Tight enough for him to struggle, to really struggle. He likes it to hurt when I hit him. No playing around.

"Leave a mark," he'd tell me right before I'd stuff his own silk tie into his mouth. While flames from dozens of candles painted the room in flickering shadows. Once the candles had burned down far enough, once enough hot wax had collected at the wicks, I'd mark him from head to toe.

I should tell Gray. Privileged, entitled Gray. Gray who's been afforded the entire world only to squander it with booze and a passivity entirely out of place in modern society. Did she even know women could vote now? Hold property? I'm not certain she knows she solely owns their townhome.

As I open the USB's contents on my laptop, graphic images fill my screen. I scroll through them, unable to stop smiling. My pulse races as I recall the circumstances of each one. Paul was a dolt, but he made me wet. Even now. *Especially* now.

I continue to scroll. Not once do I appear in a single photo. He, on the other hand, is front and center. Bound every which way, from hogtied to spread-eagle. I stop at one particularly satisfying row of images: the one with the toys.

Men are fools when pussy's a possibility. A lobbyist running for congress putting himself in front of a camera? In these ways?

I shake my head.

Clicking the browser, I open ShadowMail, an anonymous email account. Ostensibly for folks who don't want their personal addresses linked to passwords for online services. A "spam-avoidance platform" is how ShadowMail sells itself, but everyone knows its real use.

I begin highlighting files to attach to the email I'd composed, but pause for a moment. Grinning, I click *select all*.

Then I press *send*.

28

Gray

It was a sunless early morning. A single night in the hospital, and I'd been discharged. Whatever they'd given me got me to sleep, but all my dreams were nightmares. Home invasions, liars. People cutting me open for organs only to discover them shriveled from booze.

Charlotte placed her hand atop mine in the backseat of Mamma's Jag. She'd convinced Mamma to ride in front with Cora who drove in polite silence as Mamma smoked a cigarette. She cracked the window, but it hardly helped.

The cigarette's not what burned me up.

What the hell was Mamma thinking? I sat motionless, but my mind raved. Worms wiggled and crawled under my skin. Matthew's face at the foot of my bed had summoned them, and they moved relentlessly.

I didn't even choose to pour everything out to Nina. It happened as naturally as breathing, and as I spoke, relief washed over me like a cleansing river. A baptism of truth. But moments later, the worms had resurfaced.

No one had mentioned Paul since I'd been picked up.

"I've got your phone and computer with the rest of your

clothes from the accident," Charlotte said. "You can get them back at home after we've gotten you settled in." She hesitated. "No missed calls."

No missed calls. No progress. And now I was back to *settling in* at Piper Point.

"Do you think you'll be able to eat something when we get there?" Charlotte asked, rubbing her forehead. Her eyes appeared weary, too.

I tried my best to give her a nod, but I wasn't sure if she noticed my reply.

I knew she'd been torn up by all this. Fresh off her divorce from Will, raising two boys as a newly single mom, and now this? My shit show? Worried sick over Paul on my behalf, she'd given into my pleas to borrow her car, despite her best judgement, and I'd totaled it. The slight smile her lips always held must have been so hard to maintain. But somehow, she did it.

My head buzzed, see-sawing down and then wildly up again.

Maybe I didn't hate Matthew most of all. No, I hated myself more. *I'm a drunk. A manipulative, conniving drunk.* The way I fell over Jacob at the bar made me unfaithful, untrustworthy. The liar Mamma and Paul always knew I was. Wedding vows as meaningless as the promises I made to Charlotte when she handed me her keys. I hated myself, and Charlotte deserved none of this.

The sedatives I'd been administered were draining away like an outgoing tide, and the sharp bite of non-existent alcohol tickled my nose. Mamma kept hand sanitizers in the back-seat pockets. I reached into one and retrieved the clear, plastic bottle. What the hell was I thinking? I couldn't *drink* this. Instead, I squeezed a dollop onto my hand and rubbed my palms together, inhaling the scent deeply.

Mamma ground her cigarette out in the front ashtray and turned her head to the backseat. "Soon as we're home, you need to eat, Gray. The doctors were almost as concerned with your eating as your drinking. I know you've been stressed, but—"

"What are *you* concerned with, Mamma?" I demanded. She sat silent in the face of my outburst, shock creasing her brow.

Charlotte's hand reached around my wrist as if to hold me back, but I pressed, "You called Matthew. You sent him to my room!" My lips quivered. I imagined what the hand sanitizer would taste like. Soapy, but the burn down my throat would feel good. My whole body began to shake.

"I did no such thing," Mamma retorted, pale eyes locked onto mine. "I did not send him to your hospital room."

"You called him, Mamma."

She shouted back, "You were going to be arrested, Gray. Arrested! You think you'd be able to do a damn thing from behind bars? Get better? Find Paul? Anything?"

Charlotte slid over in her seat so our shoulders met.

"You were stark-raving drunk," Mamma continued, turning to face the front again. "You could've killed somebody. Multiple people. You think a judge would go easy on you because of who you are? I got news for you, Hummingbird, this family isn't what it used to be. I had one card to play, Gray. One card to save you. And I damn sure played it."

As Mamma spoke, the blood drained from my head. Spots danced before my eyes as my chest squeezed. Her voice became distant and vague, and Charlotte's soon joined in.

"Gray? You alright?" My sister asked.

I couldn't speak. I'd lost control again. The harder I fought for breath, the more I hyperventilated. Was I dying? *This is a panic attack*, I told myself. *This is what panic feels like. This is what it's always felt like.*

Muffled to my ears, Mamma said, "Go faster, Cora. We need to get Gray home. I'll call *our* doctor to meet us there."

* * *

Mamma turned down her own bed for me when we returned to Piper Point.

"Nonsense," she said when I told her my old bed was fine. "Mine's more comfortable. Bigger, too." As she pulled the down-filled duvet up to my shoulders, she wiped her left eye. She squinted and turned away quick, but I saw a tear cut a trail down her cheek. I'd never seen Mamma cry before. Not when Daddy passed away. Not with Paul's disappearance. Never.

It dawned on me then that not having seen someone cry was unusual. Particularly if that someone happened to be your own mother. Just as bizarre, it'd only been seeing her cry now that caused me to note a lifetime's worth of absent tears. Absent or perhaps, unseen.

Sniffling, she straightened her back and said, "Press the pager on the phone hook there if you need anything." She closed the door behind her.

She had the look of a deeply wounded woman. A corner of me felt sorry for her. Had it pained her at all to call Matthew? Was it a desperate attempt to keep me from jail like she'd said?

Then I remembered the first time she'd brought up reaching out to Matthew for help, and any pity that had collected for Mamma vanished. There was no threat of jail-time lurking in that scenario. Just the possibility of injured pride as public news of Paul's disappearance broke.

What had happened that night on the highway? I racked my

brain, struggling to carve out some kind of memory. Something beneath the surface of my subconscious. Nina told me Jacob had confessed to being with us on the shoulder of Paul Revere early that morning, but nothing about that detail seemed right. No, I was sure Jacob hadn't been there. My top teeth clanged against my bottom ones as my mind turned to the one outcome I'd been running from since Christmas morning: Was Paul dead?

* * *

Voices from downstairs woke me. The clock on Mamma's wall said it was morning, which meant I'd slept for almost twenty-four hours. But I hardly felt rested. It was more like my body had simply given out. A bowl of stone-cold grits sat on the nightstand. The pain in my shoulder had dulled, but I still winced as I lifted myself up.

Shadows from the tightly-closed shutters obscured the room's garden mural in darkness, the painting of a placid outdoor space skewing into a haunted one. Weeping trees, twisting and thorny. Sliding off the large bed, my feet stung when they touched the icy pinewood floor.

I took a gulp of water from the faucet in the bathroom, catching the medicine cabinet's reflection in the sink mirror. No point going through there again. Mamma had removed the good stuff already, and there wasn't a chance she'd put it back with me still at home. At least I'd been discharged with a handful of Percocet. Even if Mamma or Charlotte rigidly dispensed them, they'd only help stave off the cravings. *Cravings.* The thought pushed an invisible needle into the back of my neck. I was stuck in a bone-dry desert with only tiny white pills. Would they *actually* take the edge off? Mornings weren't so bad. I'd have to wait for the afternoon to find out.

The doorbell rang, and the voices downstairs paused as

someone went to answer it. The needle stuck me again, and my whole head ticked.

Who had Mamma called over? In the midst of my panic attack during the ride home, she'd said something about calling the family doctor—Mary-Ann Conner. The aging woman whose name was all over the rattling pill bottles in Mamma's cabinet. But I heard more than a single visitor. A range of voices spoke in muted chatter.

My thoughts went to those television shows about interventions. Would Mamma do something like that? Certainly, not right after I was released from the hospital. Who would they even call? Frances? Interventions were all about disclosures and feelings. Telling anyone anything about our family didn't fit with Mamma's personality. Not if she could help it.

Curiosity gripped me as I crept down the hall towards the staircase. From the landing, I could remain hidden from whoever sat in the salon but still hear most of the discussion. I squatted, avoiding my reflection in the cracked mirror. My body ached like it'd been beaten with a baseball bat.

"Thank you for calling," an older woman said. "Sorry I couldn't get over here sooner."

"I'm at the end of my rope, Mary-Ann," Mamma replied. So it was Dr. Conner.

A man spoke up, "No coffee for me, Cora." I recognized his voice from church the night my life unraveled. And from school many years earlier. A bellicose drawl unchanged over time. Pastor Charles Calcutt.

"Thank you all for coming. Gray's in serious trouble, and as hard as it is to admit, I'm in need of advice," Mamma said.

So, this is *an intervention.* I nearly laughed aloud. Only, it apparently wasn't to include me. An intervention organized by Mamma sure looked an awful lot like a scheming cabal: plotting what to do with me while I slept, voiceless, in the master bedroom upstairs.

"She needs *real* help," another voice announced—Charlotte's. I breathed a relieved sigh. At least I'd have a semblance of advocacy down there.

"God's help is the best sort of help there is," Pastor Calcutt rebutted. "We run a program, you know. Reformed Disciples. All folks who've struggled with addiction and turned to Christ to do something about it."

"I didn't know that," Mamma exclaimed.

"Indeed, Mrs. King. The way the Great Recession tore through Elizabeth, nobody's immune to the relief drugs and drink promise. I can't tell you who attends regularly. That's confidential, of course." I imagined Pastor Calcutt nodding with self-satisfaction as he spoke that last sentence.

"Of course," Mamma concurred.

"Joanna," Dr. Conner spoke again, "I agree with Charlotte. No disrespect, Pastor, but Gray needs serious help. Medical help."

Mamma answered, "If I'm not mistaken, the agreement with the county prosecutor requires her to attend Alcoholics Anonymous meetings in South Carolina. She'll have to sign in and everything. Maybe a church-based organization would be helpful, too—"

"AA is a wonderful program, but that's not the sort of medical help I'm talking about." Dr. Conner sighed. "She needs to see someone who can work with her regularly. Someone who can dive deep, emotionally, and prescribe medication."

"A psychiatrist," Charlotte said.

"Yes. Gray needs to see a psychiatrist," Dr. Conner replied. A brief silence passed through the room before the doctor continued, "None of this comes as a surprise to me, Joanna. The substance abuse. The risk-taking behavior."

Still crouching on the stair landing, my heart fluttered. How the hell would Dr. Conner be surprised by *none of this*? I hadn't seen her in years. How could she have any idea what I was going through?

"Mary-Ann, I understand your concern, believe me, but . . ." Mamma paused. "Would you all excuse us for a moment?"

"Of course," Pastor Calcutt answered. The floorboards creaked as Mamma and Dr. Conner exited into the foyer. I shrank further back on the landing and froze as the creaky parlor doors slid closed. A cabal within a cabal. Typical Mamma.

Dr. Conner picked up where the conversation had been left, straining to whisper. "I haven't slept, Joanna. Not from the moment I heard what happened to Mr. Godfrey. And now the car accident?"

"How do you think I feel, Mary-Ann? She's my child."

"I regret everything I did," Dr. Conner said. "Everything I didn't do."

My heart beat in erratic fits and starts. Eavesdropping on this conversation would pair nicely with wine. Glasses and glasses of wine.

"What's done is done," Mamma said, seeming to reassure herself as much as the doctor. "Believe me, regrets are about all I have left."

"Then fix it, Joanna," Dr. Conner implored. "Make it right. Get Gray to a doctor. One who specializes in these sorts of things. The lying. It was out of control back then, and I'm afraid to ask if she's kept it up. From the news report, I'm worried—"

"Don't you dare go down that path. Gray has had problems, but they have nothing to do with this. Besides, what good will it do now? So many years later? It'll dredge up pain and heart-break, and it won't get anybody any closer to finding Paul. Wherever the hell he's gone off to. I swear, I'm starting to hate that man. I don't use that word often, but I truly hate him. Putting Gray through all this. Pushing her to a breaking point. He'd be better off dead."

Paul dead? As Mamma spoke, I ground my back teeth and picked at my scabbed nailbed. My husband is fucking missing, and she's telling people she wished he was dead?

Dr. Conner hesitated, then said, "Regardless of the circumstances now, Gray needs a specialist. I almost . . ."

"You almost what?"

"I could go to her myself, Joanna. Confront her again about the lies."

"You wouldn't." More shuffling. Mamma must be stepping closer to Dr. Conner. "It could destroy her at a time like this."

"It could jar her into getting help. Maybe even *save* her. I don't know why I let you talk me into sitting on this all this years ago."

I struggled to remain still. My legs turned numb and my heart pounded strong enough to shatter my ribcage.

Mamma grew indignant. "Do you hear yourself, Mary-Ann? Years ago. Decades, in fact. The situation was delicate back then. Seamus was running for president and discretion was the only way."

Dr. Conner scoffed, "A lot of good discretion did for Seamus."

"Regardless, it's too late now. You've been compensated for your troubles." Mamma's voice quaked. "We've all got regrets. We've all made difficult decisions, but circumstances called for them. What's important now is getting Gray better. And I don't believe for a second that digging up skeletons is gonna help my daughter one bit."

Dr. Conner exhaled loudly. "Maybe you're correct, but now you've got a chance to make things better moving forward. None of this Reformed Disciples bullshit. Get her into a psychiatrist's office. Under whatever pretenses you have to."

Mamma's silence suggested careful thinking. "Okay, Mary-Ann. You're right. I'll need a day or two to come up with a reason. You think she'll be okay till then?"

"You know I can't answer that question, Joanna. I'm an internist. I don't have the training."

My trembling ceased. If they were speaking about a psychiatrist specializing in addiction, I'd given them more than enough reason to see one. Was something else being considered here? The heels of both women clacked against the pine as they made for the kitchen. And what had Mamma meant by saying Dr. Conner had been compensated?

Here I was, hiding on the stairs like a child listening to other people bicker over me as though I was a child, too. Sure, I had problems, deep problems, but I could take control. In the hospital, they'd recommended a psychiatrist, but Mamma hadn't made an appointment for me. Still, I didn't need Mamma's permission to see one, and after the accident, I had nothing left to hide. Drinking was no longer a poorly kept secret, but an open wound. The discretion that'd kept me from help in the past had vanished. All I needed was a referral from a willing primary-care doctor. One like Mary-Ann Conner.

Breathing deep, I opened the door to the Yellow Room, scanning it for my phone. I spotted it on the dresser, likely placed there by Charlotte when we returned to the house. She'd been holding onto it for me. I pressed the home button, and the screen lit up. There was a notification. An email, to be exact.

From Annie@ShadowMail.com.

29

Nina

I rang Andrew up the morning after we'd had drinks, asking to meet again. He flew out today, and I still had questions. He suggested the highway Waffle House across from his hotel. A Waffle House. His last day in Elizabeth, and he wanted to wring every last drop of Dixie from this experience on his way out. Like the night before, I made sure to beat him there. By the time he arrived, I was pushing what was left of my hash browns around my plate with a fork. Smeared ketchup like blood spatter.

"Good morning," Andrew said as he made his way to my corner booth. He tapped a server on the shoulder on his way, ordered a coffee. His smile still came off too wide.

"Hello." I checked my phone once more before returning it to my pocket. A text from the hospice nurse I'd requested for Auntie confirming she was fine—at least as fine as circumstances allowed. And a couple from Sammie indicating the divers had arrived on the crime scene.

I'd have to lie to Sammie when he asked how I learned about Paul and Charlotte's affair. I didn't believe that Andrew had the information "above board," but there was no reason to pull Sammie into a gray area.

"Heading back already, then?" I asked Andrew as he sat down.

"Cup of joe at your request, then it's off to the airport."

"Right." I smirked. "Paul's damaged goods. Your job is done."

"Correct."

"Tell me something." A thought had gnawed at me since my last encounter with Andrew, and if I wanted an answer, it was now or never. "Why tell me what you found? You already knew Paul's shot at congress was done after what your team found on his computer, and you obviously had a flight home booked before last night."

He paused for a moment, sipping coffee from the chipped brown mug that was placed before him. "Honestly?"

"Honestly."

We made eye contact. "Because I respect you, Nina."

"Bullshit."

"It's true. Completely true." The look on his face said he meant it. He held out his right hand and began to count fingers. "Look, in any small town, there are three centers of power. Local money, local politics, and local police. Money? That's the Kings. Politics? Well, that's the Kings again. But the police? You're young, you're black, you're a woman, and *you're* the police."

"Four," I corrected. "Four centers of power. You forgot local religion." Blessed Lamb Baptist conjured itself inside my head.

"Fine. But in a town like this?" He cocked his head. "You're some kind of woman. And if that's not worth a great deal of respect, I don't know what is."

He stood, draining his coffee in three large gulps, and placing his mug on the tabletop.

"Then humor me one last time."

"How so?" he asked, his forehead creasing.

I edged forward in my seat. "Aside from a few details, you know mostly what I know about Paul's case."

"That might be true."

From his incredulous expression, I wondered if he knew more—if he knew about Annie. Pushing the thought aside, I went on. "As a former agent, what would your next move be? You'd go after the sister, but how?"

He glanced towards the window for a moment. To the silvered sky, swollen with rain. When he looked back, he spoke matter-of-factly. "I'd lie."

I grinned sideways. "Go on."

He brushed his lapel with his palm, leaned in over the table, and lowered his voice to a near whisper. "You need to get all the phones in that house wiretapped. Track emails, cell phones, the works. There's a great deal of pressure on every member of that family; conversations are bound to happen."

I scoffed. "Joanna would never allow it. The lies about the affair might justify a warrant, but that family would circle the wagons like you've never seen."

He matched my smirk. "That's why you lie. You tell them the investigation is now focused on kidnapping. Tracing the ransom call is still the easiest way to catch a kidnapper."

"They *might* consent to the phone wiretapping, then," I agreed. "Might."

"Come up with a cover story so they'll buy the delay," he mused. "Then you—"

"Play them off each other. See what the wiretaps catch."

He hesitated, then said, "Except you're in a time crunch."

"The blood found on the scene. It's a race against the body divers. If Paul's recovered, the kidnapping rouse is shot."

Andrew stood once more, and tossed a crisp twenty onto the

table. "I'd wish you good luck, Nina, but I don't think you need any." Before turning around, he added, "Have a nice day, detective." With that, Andrew was gone. For a moment, I thought a tiny part of me might miss that smile. Then the moment passed.

I laid my head back against the torn leather cushion. Staring at the mildewed ceiling, I recounted the revelations over the past twenty-four hours.

Paul's rain-diluted blood in the marsh meant he might be dead. Politician Paul, who'd been engaged in an affair with his wife's sister. His wife who nearly drank herself to death, possibly as a result of being sexually assaulted by her cousin. Oh, who also happened to be a venerable defense attorney.

Then there was Annie. Annie whose real name may be Charlotte.

My initial instincts might've been right all along. Annie was Paul's mistress, and the calls were meant to torture Gray. Annie had always struck me as a pseudonym, and, according to Andrew's findings, Charlotte had a knack for making up names. *Florencia.*

But what would Charlotte's motive be?

There were two possibilities. The first had to do with Paul's congressional run. Someone as unstable as Gray would be an immense political liability. More so than debts, perhaps. Could he and Charlotte have concocted this scheme in an elaborate attempt to push Gray off the edge? It sounded crazy, but if so, they'd nearly succeeded yesterday.

If Gray had died in the wreck, what might've happened? Paul could've suddenly surfaced, rich from his wife's inheritance. He might even have public sympathy on his side. Certainly, he'd have publicity, and that'd be more valuable than support from Cooper and Waters at the ballot box. In fact, were

Gray to die, nearly all Paul's problems would vanish. Charlotte's hands would be clean, too. After all, a woman named Annie had tormented Gray, not her.

But the second possibility cast an even darker shadow over Gray's sister. A jealous fight by the highway turned ugly. Perhaps Charlotte murdered Paul—we had her DNA in the lab if we found anything at the scene—but why antagonize Gray? I recalled our coffee shop conversation. She'd looked me in my eyes and lied to me about her divorce. About Paul. Was she also lying about how much she cared for Gray? And she was more than a good liar. She was almost flawless.

Was she good enough to play the part of Annie?

Drowning in motives and opportunities, I reminded myself the simplest answer was usually the right one. But there was nothing simple about any of this. Did Auntie Tilda know something that could help me? Was there a connection to Joanna's checks? As I thought of Auntie's relationship to the King girls, my head swirled.

Tapping all the communications coming in and out of Piper Point would be like kicking over a rotten log. There was no telling what unsavory things might slither out. And that was *if* the family even bought the kidnapping angle and allowed me to do it.

* * *

Back at the station, Burton summoned me to his corner office before I could flag Sammie down. The eight mounted deer heads turned the paneled space into a redneck natural history museum. Counting Burton's glower, nine pairs of eyes bore down on me.

"Jacob Wilcox," Burton started, pausing dramatically between the first and last name.

"Admitted to assaulting our missing person—"

"Wasn't on the goddamn highway."

I shifted in my seat. Regardless of his point, the dressing down felt obstructive.

"Sheriff—"

"You are walking the line, Nina," he said, placing both elbows on his heavy desk and clasping his hands together. "Walking a fine line."

I sat back. *Let him talk, let him get it all out.*

"One more." He pointed his index finger to the ceiling. "One more fuck up and you're off this."

I hesitated, met his eyes, said, "Yes sir."

"This is Paul Godfrey we're talking about, *detective*. Not some Dixie Outfitters trash picking fights down at Ruby's. A fucking politician. The King Family."

"I understand—"

"You aren't right for this case. Not with that aunt of yours."

My cheeks flushed. "That's not a fair statement."

"I want to be wrong, but you're making my position easier every damn second. I've got the paperwork filled out to bench you. All I have to do is pull the trigger."

I opened my mouth to reply, but he excused me with a patronizing flick of his wrist. As his office door closed behind me, I puffed my cheeks. The *lub-dub* of my heartbeat made thinking hard, but I pushed the confrontation aside. No time to dwell on what he'd say about my next plan.

Ten minutes later, Sammie sat across from me in the conference room, stretching a rubber band with both thumbs. Shirt wrinkled. Almost as dubious as Burton had been, only for different reasons.

"How'd you know, Nina?"

"A hunch," I replied, avoiding his eyes.

"You had *a hunch* that Paul Godfrey and Charlotte Barfield were engaged in an affair? Bullshit." He leaned forward, fingers steepled on the tabletop. "You expect me to believe that *a hunch* had me cross-referencing business trips on Paul's calendar with purchases on his Navy Union card—the one Gray knows nothing about, mind you—to determine which trips he'd lied about?"

I looked up from the table. "Yeah—"

"You know, I might've believed you if *your hunch* hadn't been so damn spot on."

I sprang up from my chair. "There's something there, then? Something that links the two of them?" My pulse raced. He slid a manila folder across the table, and I slapped it open.

He flicked his chin. "I found thirty-eight instances of travel in Paul's schedule this past year. During most of those trips, absolutely zero purchases were made with the Navy Union card, which makes sense. Paul had a Cooper and Waters expense account for every sanctioned trip."

I arched my brow. "Except . . ."

Sammie held up his fingers. "Except five. Five trips were recorded as business travel on his calendar even though his Navy Union card was used. Interestingly, the destinations are all Canadian cities. Vancouver, Calgary, Montreal, you get the idea."

I cracked a grin. "Paul had a system to keep things straight for himself."

"Sure looks like it. Because each time Paul's calendar indicated he took a 'trip' to a city in Canada, his Navy Union card was used for purchases in the Raleigh-Durham area."

I thumbed through Sammie's notes in the manila folder. "When was the most recent trip?"

"A couple months back. Listed as Toronto. The purchases

don't appear to have been suspicious themselves so we haven't flagged them for further investigation. Groceries, restaurants, gasoline. That sort of thing."

"But we've got a link. We can put him in Raleigh."

Sammie tried to temper my excitement. "You think Charlotte's good for this, then? Paul's disappearance, Annie, everything?"

"Best break we've had yet."

"Besides the blood." Sammie shrugged.

I stood up from my seat, uncapping a dry-erase marker. I paced to one of the glass walls and began to write. "Correct. Which brings me to my next point."

As I wrote, Sammie's eyes burned into the back of my neck, but even he couldn't argue with results. Not results like these. The marker squeaked across glass, and I took a step back.

"Our next move," I announced. Behind me, in large red letters: Kidnapping Hypothesis.

Sammie narrowed his eyes. "A kidnapping with no ransom demand this late in the game? Not impossible, but sure as hell unlikely."

"That's right." I grinned. "Which means we have our work cut out for us if we're going to make the Kings believe it."

Sammie shook his head. "You think lying to the family is the best course of action at this point?"

I clasped my hands together in a fist and exhaled. "I've made a mistake. I moved too slowly on this from the start. I take responsibility for that."

Another headshake from Sammie. "Making another mistake won't fix that."

"We need to make up for lost time. Wiretaps are the quickest way to do that. Joanna King deals in half-truths and lies. And now we've learned Charlotte does, too. Go with me on this one, Sammie. If it doesn't work out, then it's on me. Not you. I give you my word on that."

Sammie grew quiet as he considered my argument, then spoke, "Your word. Given the course of this investigation, the delays, your family history—" He hesitated once more. "I hope your word is as good as it used to be."

The sentiment hurt coming from Sammie. It hurt because it was true.

* * *

Enormous raindrops struck my windshield, and my thoughts went to the body divers that were no doubt scouring the marsh beds as I drove home to Auntie Tilda's. The weather and water chop might prove an obstacle, but nothing was insurmountable. If there was a body to find, they'd find it. And I needed them to find Paul—a homicide case built without a body was hollow— but not too quickly. It was an ironic position to be in as an investigator.

Doubts aside, Sammie gave my plan the buy-in I needed. After we'd sketched out a false timeline to follow, we'd settled on how we would switch the focus to kidnapping and determined precisely what information we wanted access to. We would hold off on confronting Charlotte until after the monitors were secured in the home. Importantly, our rationale needed to be airtight, both for the Kings and Sheriff Burton. Even if we got Joanna's signed consent to listen in, I wanted deniability regarding wiretapping under false pretenses. That's where Annie and her calls fit perfectly.

So much work to be done, but at least we were finally getting somewhere.

My turn signal clicked as I hung a left into Auntie's driveway. James from next door waved at me with a garden-gloved hand as he weeded his flowerbeds beneath an umbrella. What an odd man. Exiting my car, I nodded hello and ran to avoid getting wet. My keys stuck more than once in the front door.

Inside, a sermon played on the TV, which meant Auntie was having a good day. Good enough to get up from bed on her own. The refrigerator door rattled from inside the kitchen. Was she feeling well enough to eat something, too?

Auntie greeted me as I sat my bag and keys on the kitchen table. She offered a small grin and turned back to the open refrigerator. I snatched a dishtowel off the wall rack and wiped the rain from my face.

"Can I get you something, Auntie? Fix you something to eat?"

"Oh no," she protested. "I can do it myself. I woke up this morning thinking of fried eggs. I might not be able to eat a whole one, but I couldn't get the thought out of my head."

As she fumbled with the egg basket, I reached into the cupboard for the skillet. She shouldn't be doing anything herself, but I had no intention of taking this away from her. The next time she crawled into that hospice bed might be her last.

Gnarled hands trembling, she cracked an egg into a bowl and shuffled to the stove. I'd already melted a slice of butter in the pan.

"I'll take care of it," she told me. "Go on and take a seat. You want one, too?"

I couldn't help smiling. "No, Auntie. I'm not hungry."

As the egg sizzled, a thought I'd been carrying around for two days grew louder. I had to question Auntie Tilda about Gray's allegations. I needed the corroboration, of course, but the decades of severance checks got me thinking: Were they connected in some way?

For all the reasons Auntie might take severance money from Joanna, only one possibility came up over and over again. Did Auntie know about the abuse? Were the checks really hush money? My stomach tightened. Was Auntie the kind of person who'd actually take it?

She slid the fried egg onto a plate and hobbled to the table. Today was a good day for her. The best she's had in quite some time. There may not be another chance to ask her. But as she took a seat across the table, I decided to let her finish her food first. She'd woken up thinking of fried eggs, after all.

Golden yolk oozed out as her fork sank into the egg. She'd fried it to perfection in spite of the cancer choking her organs. After a few bites, Auntie rested her fork next to the half-eaten egg on her plate. "Do you mind helping me up?" she asked. Before she finished her question, I'd already slid out of my chair to give her a hand.

One foot in front of the other, we made our way to the bedroom together. It occurred to me that this might be the last moment I had with a faultless Auntie Tilda. Tilda who'd never take money for a cover-up. For everything she was, everything she'd done, I'd put her atop a pedestal. If she came off it, I'd grieve the loss.

Pulling her knitted quilt over her chest, I swallowed a hard lump in my throat and took a seat on the bed beside her. "Auntie, I need to ask you something. Something very important."

"What is it?" she asked, closing her eyes. The simple act of making an egg had drained her.

"I need you to tell the truth. I need you tell me the God's honest truth."

I gave her a moment to respond, but she stayed silent. Something told me she knew what I was going to ask. My involvement with the Kings had been all over local news and radio. Maybe the brief pause permitted her to gather herself. As the moment stretched, my heart fluttered. Fearless Auntie Tilda may not be as fearless as I'd believed.

I took another deep breath. "Does Joanna King write you checks for your silence?"

Still no words from Auntie. She rustled uncomfortably beneath the sheets. Maybe if the question was more specific, she'd answer. Hearing the allegation might startle her into telling me. I didn't want the checks to have anything to with this, but I needed to rule it out with facts.

Pulse racing, I asked again, "Did Gray's cousin once touch her inappropriately? Did Joanna want you to keep quiet about it? On account of Seamus' run for office, maybe?"

Auntie breathed a staggered sigh and opened her eyes. They glistened wetly. "No, Nina."

I dug my nails into my palms. Why did I have to do this? Why did I have to push her? I spoke forcefully, "I need you to be honest with me."

I held my breath as Auntie looked into my eyes. Regret welling in hers.

"That boy didn't touch her just once." She choked up as she spoke, trembling. "It happened so many times."

Something uncomfortable stirred inside me. Questions searching for answers bubbled to the surface like bits of leafy matter in marsh water. "How do you know?"

She drew a long, pained breath. "I had my suspicions. The way that boy's eyes lingered on her. The way her drawers weren't flush in her dresser after he'd been over—their contents not the way I'd folded and tucked them. But I had no proof. I followed him around that house as best I could, but I couldn't be everywhere."

I winced, biting my lip as she continued speaking.

"More than once," Auntie paused, as if to gather strength for her next words, "I walked in on them alone in a room, and I knew. I just *knew*. I tried to tell Seamus and Joanna. They wouldn't hear any of it."

A prickly knot grew in the back of my throat. "What sort of parents cover up abuse of their own child?"

"It was all about that damned election. I've never seen such willfully ignorant people. Matthew's daddy was the campaign lawyer, if I recall right. Between that and being family, they wouldn't hear it."

"What changed?"

"When Gray spoke up herself. She told her mamma what happened, and even a woman as cold as that one is couldn't deny it any longer. Mrs. King was keen to have Gray seen by the family doctor. Wanted to make sure that boy hadn't given her little *Hummingbird* any venereal diseases. I was glad to learn Joanna had a soul, because you best believe I seriously doubted it."

"And Seamus?"

"Mr. King was mad as hell—he even threatened Matthew's life if he ever showed his face again at Piper Point—but what was done was done. He didn't think it made sense to drag the whole family down."

Taking a deep staccato breath, she continued, "The checks are to keep my mouth shut, but not for the abuse itself. I agreed to sign my own name to the paperwork so there'd be no record of having a child tested. It was the only way to get that girl some care. Doctor took samples right there in Joanna's bathroom.

HIV, syphilis, all of it. Tubes of drawn blood, urine, all bearing my name."

That's when it dawned on me. "You stuck a tape recorder in her pocket all those years ago. That's why you knocked over a drunk Seamus King's dinner tray."

"I had to get the truth out in some way," she said. "If not the actual truth, then I could at least let the world know what sort of folks the Kings were. I waited till the South Carolina primaries to do it, Nina. I waited till it would do the most damage."

It didn't make up for what she'd done, but I understood why she'd been complicit. She did care for Gray. She'd wanted her tested, and she'd wanted the Kings to suffer for how they handled it.

"Who was the family doctor? Who forged the STI tests for Joanna?"

"Dr. Conner," Auntie replied. "Mary-Ann Conner. A selfish woman whose medical oaths aren't worth the paper they're written on."

"Can I get you to make a statement? Declaring what you've just told me?"

"You write up what I told you, and I'll put my name to it," she answered. Her eyelids sagged. I had to move quickly. "I don't have a thing to lose by telling the truth now."

As I made for Auntie's desk for a pen, Auntie cleared her throat again. "The doctor wasn't the only call Joanna made that night. Not even the first one."

I paused. "Who else did she call?"

"The police."

"So Joanna called the police on Matthew?"

A cough from Auntie. "She tried. Sheriff came to the house, but Seamus convinced him to put it away. Told him it was handled and things were best left alone."

I braced, asked, "Which sheriff?"

"*Deputy* sheriff," Auntie replied. "Funny what details you cling to after all the years. I'll never forget how the man looked me up and down as he introduced himself."

"What was his name?" I whispered.

"Your boss, Nina. Deputy Sheriff Jim Burton."

30

Gray

I'm terribly sorry to hear about your mishap, Humming-bird. Please know you're in my prayers. So is Paul. When we lose loved ones—and it does seem likely that Paul's been lost—it's often helpful to gather all the photographs we have. To misplace any memories would only add unnecessarily to grief. As such, I've included some pictures of Paul that were in my possession from the happy times we spent together.

Warmest regards,
Annie

* * *

She'd slept with Paul. Annie was Paul's sociopathic lover.

The first picture put me on my knees in front of the toilet, my broken shoulder throbbing as I steadied myself against the porcelain rim. Later, I lay on my back atop a made-up bed in the Yellow Room, frozen from head to toe. I couldn't unsee them, the glimpses of Paul's affair attached to Annie's email. Thoughts of separation and divorce surfaced before vanishing again beneath the filthy images—so many of them—things even the darkest corners of my mind could never create. And calling me Hummingbird? That meant that beyond the affair, the bizarre fetishes, they'd spoken about me intimately. Mocked me.

Invisible spiders danced up and down my limbs. Needle legs prickling my skin. Tickling in between my toes, behind my ears. I imagined turning up a bottle of dry red. The slippery glass mouth on my own. The glugging sound. Swallowing gulp after gulp till the green bottom appeared, and these fucking spiders fell off me.

I was wrong about Annie. So wrong. She never wanted to help me or Paul. She didn't get lost on the way to Cirilo's. She intended to stand me up. Taunted me *because* of my husband. Sour acid climbed up from my stomach. I didn't want to vomit again.

My heart stopped as I considered a new possibility. The facts flashed across my mind in rapid succession as I dug my nails into my arms.

And it does seem likely that Paul's been lost.

She was right. The goddamn bitch was right.

Annie hadn't reached out to me until *after* Paul vanished. She knew about the accident, too. Even if she stood me up, that still meant she was in Elizabeth. She'd at least been down Oleander Avenue.

Paul could very well be dead. Murdered in cold blood that night off the highway while I'd been slouched over in the passenger seat, passed out from drinking. Annie might've killed him. But if that was true, why hadn't she killed me at the same time? *Unless this is what she wants, to torture me.* Killing me would've been too easy. It would've spared me from all of *this*.

I shut my eyes tight, placing myself back in the bar. Back in Ruby's Pub on Christmas Eve. I'd just finished my first drink, my mind focused on getting another with laser-like intensity. I searched my memory of the crowd for a woman's face. One that stood out from everyone else's. Even if I didn't recognize Annie, there must've been something off about her. Someone who'd do something malicious to Paul and *still* come after me? She must hate me. Could she have concealed her loathing if I'd walked by? But I'd avoided looking at other patrons as I made my way to the counter. I hadn't wanted to catch a glance from a familiar person and delay my next drink. *Damnit, Gray!*

Frantic and quaking, I leapt up and reached for my phone. A confluence of anger and fear had my hands trembling and sweating. Wet fingers smeared and smudged the screen of my cell. Scrolling through my contacts, I finally landed on Nina Palmer's mobile.

She needed to know about this. All of this. The email, the pictures, everything. No more keeping secrets from her. I learned that lesson, and my arm rested in a sling to prove it. There must be some way to trace the email or the photos. Something the police could do. Someway Nina could help me.

The sooner we found Annie, the sooner we'd find Paul. Or at least find out what had happened to him. The not knowing was eating away at me. The not knowing might kill me.

31

Nina

Any doubt that Charlotte was Annie disappeared as soon as I opened the images Gray forwarded from her phone.

"Let me weigh our options, and I'll call you back this afternoon," I'd told Gray as I hung up. She'd been desperate for answers. I didn't blame her. Annie possessed intimate knowledge of Gray and had obviously been sleeping with Paul. Only one woman checked both boxes.

"Goddamn." Sammie cringed as he flipped through the photos at my desk. "That's some shit if I've ever seen it. And I've seen a lot."

"Ain't it though?"

"The hate isn't what unnerves me most. It's the charade. The way Charlotte acts as though she's Gray's only true ally in all this," he replied, handing my phone back.

"No kidding," I said, plugging it into my desk charger. I hesitated, then added, "I feel for Gray. It's a wonder she's held it together this long. Matthew, Paul, and now Annie tormenting her? Possibly her own sister."

He nodded. "If anyone deserved a drink, it'd be her. I still can't wrap my head around Matthew. No statute of limitations, but it'd be a hell of case to build from here."

I bit my bottom lip. "Short of a confession, no. It's all hearsay. He said, she said . . ."

"Your aunt said, too."

"Her statements are a starting place, but we need more than that. We need witnesses, corroboration on the STI test samples, additional victims if they exist."

"Speaking of," he replied, "you gonna clue Gray in on her sister?"

"When I figure out how to broach it. She's pretty broken up at this point."

"Are you worried about how she might take it? How Charlotte might respond to her if confronted?"

Shaking my head, I changed the topic. "To tell you the truth, talking with Auntie Tilda's been the only thing on my mind. Tough to game through anything else. It was a whopper of a revelation." *And not the only one.* Joanna had brought the police to Piper Point, before Seamus intervened. Whether money exchanged hands à la Auntie or it was a wink and a smile on Burton's part, the fact remained: Burton had heard these allegations before. And done nothing.

Now he was turning the screws on my handling of Paul's case.

Sammie shoved his hands in his pockets. "If Matthew was a pedophile back then, he likely hasn't changed. We might have a predator loose in Elizabeth."

"Not just a predator," I corrected him. "A defense attorney. A privileged predator."

"Should we pursue it?" Sammie asked.

"I think so. These aren't two entirely separate investigations. Charlotte was left unsupervised with Matthew the same as her sister, and that warrants an inquiry."

My desk phone rang. I knew why before I answered. Joanna King had arrived at my invitation. I puffed my cheeks and stood. Time to convince a woman with a pathologic aversion to disclosure to let me tap her phone lines.

* * *

For the second time in a week, Joanna sat at the conference room table. The look on her face—a barely concealed scowl—said she was none too pleased about it.

"Good afternoon, Joanna." Her floral perfume enveloped me. This time, peony and entitlement.

"Detective," she answered tersely. "You got any air in this building? I'm about to burn up alive in here." She removed her blazer and rolled up the sleeves of her silk blouse.

"I'll see what I can do about the temperature in a moment."

Crossing her legs beneath the table, she muttered, "My tax dollars hard at work."

Disregarding the slight, I continued, "I've asked you to come in today because we've had a break in the case." A lie—sort of.

The scowl dissolved into a look of surprise. "Really? What sort of break? Shouldn't Gray be here to hear this, too?"

"This is a sensitive matter, and until we can be certain, the information is only to be distributed on a need-to-know basis."

"What could be so sensitive?" she asked, arching her brow. I'd piqued her interest—a good start since appealing to the woman's sense of intrigue might be my only chance.

"Annie," I said.

"What about her?"

I folded my hands together atop the table. "We have reason to believe Paul's being held against his will, and she's an accomplice."

Mamma shifted in her seat. "Held against his will? Like kidnapping? That's preposterous! If Paul had been kidnapped, wouldn't there have been a ransom call or something? We've heard nothing from anyone."

"That's incorrect, Joanna. We have heard from someone. We've heard from Annie."

Joanna rolled her eyes. "Barely. The woman leaves nonsensical voicemails and doesn't show up to meetings *she's* arranged. That hardly qualifies as a ransom demand."

Did she know about the photographs on Gray's phone? Perhaps Gray had hidden them from her out of shame.

I kept my voice steady. "To the contrary, we believe those instances were botched attempts at delivering a ransom demand. As I said, we only believe Annie to be an accomplice, not the actual kidnapper."

She cocked her head to one side, eyes narrowed. "Then who the hell's the kidnapper? And how have you learned all this?"

"We've been coordinating with Security Solutions, the private security firm," I answered. "They've been working the case in Washington. The abduction occurred in Elizabeth, but we believe it was planned in D.C."

This appeared to take Joanna by surprise. "I know who Security Solutions is, but why haven't I heard any of this? Don't they work for me?"

"Technically, they don't work for you," I said. "They work for Paul's firm, Cooper and Waters."

"Well, what have they learned?" Joanna sounded desperate now. Starving for information. So hungry for it, she'd agree to wiretapping for no other reason than to satisfy her own morbid curiosity.

"Paul's fallen into debt with some very bad people." I tossed carefully selected bank statements from the Navy Union account across the table. I wanted Joanna to see a lot of red numbers. "We believe the kidnapping is an attempt to extort funds from the family. To get their money back. I know it's a simple answer, but simple is usually correct."

She thumbed through the statements, clearly fighting to maintain her composure.

My heart beat faster. "As such, we need to monitor all communications at the house. When Annie calls again, we need to be ready to trace the call."

Joanna knotted her brow. "Monitor all communications? Like our telephones?"

"Telephones, internet, all of it."

For a brief moment, the woman sat speechless, fidgeting with the knot of pearls suspended from her neck. "This still doesn't make any sense. Paul's been gone for days now without any word. Where would they be keeping him? Do you think he's been harmed?"

I shook my head. "I can't say for certain, but I do know the longer these things go on, the slimmer the chances become of recovering the victim. That's why it's critical to get the monitors in place now."

She reached into her purse and retrieved a pack of cigarettes. She made eye contact in lieu of asking permission to smoke inside a police station. She'd never ask me for permission to do anything. I nodded, and her silver lighter sparked a tiny flame at its tip.

Finishing a long drag, she spoke up. "I don't know how Gray is gonna react to all this. She's very fragile right now."

"She can't know," I replied before emphasizing, "and neither can Charlotte."

"Why on Earth not?" She ashed into a cup of coffee she'd brought with her. A wispy blossom of cigarette smoke lingered between us.

The true answer to Joanna's question was two-fold. Most importantly, Charlotte needed to remain in the dark or the recordings would be useless. She'd already proven to possess impressive acting skills. But also, leaving Joanna with a sense of control—by being the only one at Piper Point with knowledge of the tapped lines—was the key to getting her consent.

"We need Gray and her sister to act naturally if and when the ransom demand comes through. The kidnappers must not suspect they're being recorded or that we can trace their location."

Joanna's cigarette hissed as she dropped it into her coffee cup. "Isn't it illegal to record people without their knowledge?"

"We only need one party's consent," I answered, "and the phones, the internet service—it's all in your name, anyways. Your house. Your name."

Recrossing her legs, she appeared to think for a moment. "If Paul's been kidnapped, it stands to reason Annie will make contact again. She's obviously not a professional. Perhaps monitoring communications will be the best way to catch her and whoever she works for." She slipped a second cigarette out from her pack. "Paul has plenty of political enemies, and then of course, there's the family money. Like you said."

I breathed a heavy sigh and produced the consent forms from my folder. "I've marked each place needing a signature."

"Seems like an awful lot," she complained as she flipped

through the papers. She hesitated and glanced up. Her next question caught me completely off-guard, a jarring reminder that when it came to Joanna King, I'd never be the only one playing games.

"These monitors, will I be able to use them? Even after the investigation?"

32

Annie

The marshes smell like soggy, salty mud. Like shit. I can't see them on account of it being nearly midnight, but the lapping water sloshes like the words of a drunk. Like Gray when she speaks.

I make my way across the crabgrass, passing through swirling clouds of buzzing gnats. Dew gathers on the ground, and tiny droplets tickle the in-betweens of my toes. A singing cricket grows quieter and quieter as I creep closer to its hidden nook. Then silence.

I turn back towards the house—a sprawling, darkened shadow but for the light in Gray's room. I was raised not to play with my food, not to toy with it, but I can't help myself. Besides, I'm not playing. Not at all.

An expected rustling in the courtyard. Training my eyes on the hedges, blackened by the night, I find the movement's source. A black and white cat deftly moving my way.

I stand perfectly still, let her steal her way close to me. Feline caution gives her pause, but I came prepared. Reaching into my pocket, I grab a handful of dried kibble and scatter it onto the cold bricks before my naked feet.

The aging cat hesitates—a scrupulous old girl—then sniffs and starts to nibble. I stretch my fingers and stroke her back. People aren't so different from animals. They can be distracted. They can be manipulated.

"That's a good girl," I whisper. I run my hand up Hattie's spine to the nape of her fragile neck.

I reach into my other pocket. The pocket holding my paring knife.

"You wouldn't let me get so close to you back then, would you, old girl? You could sense something was wrong. Not so smart anymore, are you, Hattie the Cattie?"

I tighten my grip and brace for the struggle.

33

Gray

I sat at the kitchen table with Charlotte and Mamma. Three cups of morning coffee and three unfinished pieces of toast between us. I guess they'd lost their appetites, too.

"AA's going to be a new start for you," Charlotte said. "When's your first meeting?"

"Noon tomorrow," I answered, tightening the strap on my shoulder sling. A dull pain radiated down my arm.

As great as it sounded, a new start seemed impossible. AA might show me the right direction, but did I have the strength? Just don't drink, I'd repeated to myself. Drinking is an active behavior: I've got to find one and pour one and bring it to my lips. *Just don't do any of those things.* But in the wake of Paul's affair, what the hell else was I supposed to do? In his selfishness, he'd disappeared before I found out so there'd be no way to parse the differences between cheating and vanishing and Annie. All while I was supposed to remain fucking sober? *He's gaslighting me from god-knows-where.*

Charlotte scattered my thoughts. "Do you think you'll stay here for a while longer, then? Maybe I could help you find groups in D.C.—"

"I can't go home anytime soon." I shook my head. If I was left alone at our house, I'd drink myself dead. Horrible as it seemed, staying at Piper Point was safer for me. "Besides, Nina wouldn't let me even if I wanted. Not with everything happening."

"Speaking of, the police are coming over for a bit today," Mamma announced, bringing her porcelain mug to her lips. "Detective Palmer, too."

"Why are they coming?" Charlotte asked, wide-eyed.

Mamma returned her cup to the table. "They've got more questions for the family."

Charlotte pressed, "What sort of questions? Have they learned anything new?"

"To be perfectly honest, I'm not sure," Mamma answered. "I only know they have questions. It's normal." Her eyes met mine. "All things considered."

Charlotte might be surprised by the visit, and Mamma disinterested, but I knew exactly what questions Nina wanted answered. "The pictures from my phone," I said aloud.

"What pictures?" Now Mamma seemed surprised by me.

"Gray, don't." Charlotte grabbed my hand on the table.

I'd shown them to Nina and Charlotte, but not Mamma. They were too mortifying. When Paul returned—if Paul returned—I'd wanted to maintain his dignity. Especially in Mamma's eyes. But there was no sense keeping them secret now. She'd learn about them as soon as the police arrived, anyways. Besides, what did I care about Paul's dignity? He hadn't given two shits about mine when he let Annie do . . . those things to him. While he'd mocked me and made fun of me and told Annie all about how Mamma called me Hummingbird.

Picture after picture reappeared in my mind. Here I sat, struggling with a decision that only had one answer: If Paul ever turned up, I'd divorce him. I was done making excuses for him.

Mamma creased her brow, eyes dancing between the two of us. "What pictures? Do you know what she's on about, Charlotte?"

I spoke matter-of-factly. "Annie sent me pictures. Graphic pictures of Paul. They'd been sleeping together like we suspected, and she wanted me to see them."

Mamma's eyes grew wide as her mouth dropped open. Cora slid by the table, garbage bag in tow, and out back through the conservatory.

Mamma lowered her voice. "Like nude photographs or something?"

Before I could answer Mamma, a sharp scream shot through the house like a pistol. It came from outside.

34

Nina

By the time I parked in front of Piper Point, two other squad cars had already arrived, lights strobing blue and red across the home's white pillared front. A mansion that looked to be moving in slow motion. The effect was unsettling.

My plan had been to visit the King home today anyways. I'd intended to gather Charlotte and Gray in the salon for questioning while Sammie accompanied our technician—with Joanna's guidance—as he installed the appropriate hardware. But this new development would create even more of a distraction. It also represented a startling escalation in violence, not against Paul, who'd likely been victimized already, but directed at Gray.

As a horrified Cora led me through the foyer, tingling fear inched up my spine. Everyone who lived at Piper Point was in danger. I ground my molars. Everyone who slept under the same roof as Charlotte Barfield.

A uniformed officer greeted me and guided me down the long hall towards the kitchen. "It's right back here. In the courtyard."

Walking by the salon, I spotted Charlotte on one of the couches. A twin boy under each of her arms. Needles pricked the back of my neck at the sight of her young children. Was her hatred contained to Paul and Gray? Or was she capable of harming her boys, too?

I nodded at Gray as I passed her seated in the breakfast nook. She appeared shaken, her face wet from crying. Splotchy and dazed.

"And what exactly happened?" I asked my escort as we stepped into the conservatory. Iron scaffolding—begging for a fresh coat of white paint—framed the glass walls in intricate swirls, evoking a Victorian feel.

"From what I understand, the family kept a yard cat. Name was Hattie, I believe," he replied.

As we stepped between rows of heavy planters, the officer continued, "The housekeeper, Cora, went to take out the trash after breakfast and found it." He waved me onto the courtyard. My ribs contracted, pressing on my lungs. Stealing my air.

The black and white carcass hung suspended by its matted legs from a stone angel. Crimson blood splashed and spattered in all directions, running down cracks and grooves. Flaring across the fountain's stone. Staining the basin water red.

"Throat's been slit," the officer reported. "The cat was hung and exsanguinated. Not unlike a hunter might do."

"Jesus. Hell of a lot of blood," I said, surveying the clotted puddles.

The officer shrugged. He didn't seem the least bit perturbed, or if he was, he concealed it well. Perhaps he hunted himself. "We're checking the property for any possible weapons."

"It's Annie," a tepid voice called from behind. "I know it's her. I know she's in Elizabeth." Gray walked up beside me, her face stark white. The woman looked three-days dead. "I was going to bring Hattie home with us when Paul . . . when we found him—"

I turned to her. "Why don't you go inside for now until we get this bagged up and cleaned?"

"Annie killed my husband. There's no doubt in my mind." Her bottom lip quaked as she spoke.

An interesting leap on Gray's part, though it wasn't uncommon for loved ones to jump to the worst conclusions. Still, at this stage in the investigation, I was inclined to agree with her about Paul's fate. *Whoever* Annie was.

"Come on in the house, Hummingbird," Joanna called from the conservatory. "Let the police do their work." That woman appeared eerily unshaken by the incident.

Gray followed her mother's voice inside. Every one of them was behaving in a manner that left me uneasy. Understandable, I figured, given the circumstances. Still, I found myself wishing to be anywhere else but here. At Piper Point. The conservatory door swung back open.

"Jesus," Sammie exclaimed, taking in the scene. He must've pulled up minutes after me. The disgust in his voice said he wasn't the hunting type.

"You have everything ready?" I asked, refocusing on the task at hand.

He placed his hands on his waist, scowling at the sight. "Technician's out front. Just waiting for the go-ahead. We've got standard taps for the landline, and the internet provider's given us access to the Wi-Fi."

"No problems with the consent forms, then," I said, relieved. "And cell phones?"

"Tech bragged about that all the way here. An IMSI-Catcher. They call it the Stingray. Overnighted from our counterparts in Columbia."

"An IMSI-Catcher?"

236

"Don't know what it stands for, but from what I understand, it imitates a cellular base station. Any cell used within a few hundred feet will communicate with it. Double-checked with County, and we don't even need probable cause on account of it not being a traditional line tap."

I nodded. As morning evaporated, sweat beaded on my brow. "Good. Charlotte might be blocking her number, but I doubt she's driving out of town to make the calls."

Behind Sammie, a police photographer arrived and began to snap pictures of the cat, its fur matted in a sickening, glossy wet. "What's our next move?" Sammie asked, rubbing his stubbled chin.

Another officer joined the photographer, a black lawn bag in his gloved hands. "Auntie gave me the name of the family doctor. The one who saw Gray after her parents uncovered the abuse. If we find evidence, or if this doctor can verify that there were other victims, we might be able to get something hard on Matthew."

Sammie shrugged. "Joanna seems to have been oddly cooperative so far."

"No way she'll even corroborate the doctor's visit," I replied. "She covered up a crime against her own daughter. If she makes a connection, there'll be no more assistance from her. I wouldn't put more obstruction past that woman."

"Agreed," Sammie said.

Standing on the fountain's cement pedestal, an officer unsheathed a long knife.

With a snap, the cat was cut loose. It struck the ground with a muffled thud, and its limp head rolled my way. Hattie's dead eyes met mine.

35

Nina

The tapped lines were in place just a couple days before two divers discovered the body of Paul Godfrey. What remained of Paul Godfrey. They dredged the cadaver from the marsh bed in a tidal basin some fifteen miles south of the blood we'd found. After weeks of bad weather, the Beaufort oceanographer had underestimated how aggressive the currents had grown—a low-pressure system pushing and pulling the roiling seas in all sorts of unnatural directions.

A swollen leather wallet had been found on Paul's person alongside a set of rental car keys. Aside from the fact the body was in no state to be IDed, the lab quickly matched the DNA to the samples I'd collected, so the family wasn't needed for a positive identification. We'd dispatched uniforms to Piper Point to officially notify the Kings. They were no doubt on their way.

Nevertheless, I insisted on seeing the body myself, and the assigned medical examiner obliged. Fluorescent bulbs strobed overhead as I followed him to the autopsy rooms of the Medical University of South Carolina in Charleston. The corridor was illuminated by brutal lighting and surrounded by nothing but cream-colored cinderblocks and stainless steel.

"We'll hang a right at the next hallway," The ME announced as we turned down a second bleak corridor. "Autopsy's not been done, so I can't offer any official answers, but I'm happy to give you a look anyways. Let you draw your own conclusions."

"That obvious, then?" I prepared myself for the worst.

He shook his head. "The sooner you see what happened to Mr. Godfrey, the better. As far as your investigation is concerned."

Swinging open a windowless door designated Examination Room One, we entered an antechamber filled with racks and racks of personal protective equipment.

"P.P.E. requirements are double booties, gown, double gloves, cap, and mask." The ME pointed to each chrome-wire shelf, respectively.

I was already tugging a second pair of disposable booties on over my sneakers. "I've been through this before."

"It's standard operating procedure to say it every time, Nina," he quipped as he snapped his mask in place. Once dressed, I followed him to a second door exactly the same as the first.

In the exam room, formaldehyde mixed with the biting scent of bleach, soaking the air in solvents. Two stainless steel platforms stood—one empty, one supporting a draped, man-sized heap. As pungent as the smells were, I clung to them. They'd be joined by something far worse soon.

He wheeled a stool next to the occupied table and motioned for me to take the second one on its far side.

"You ready, detective?" The surgical mask muffled his words.

Taking a deep breath, hot and damp behind my own mask, I nodded.

Pressing a button, he initiated a hydraulic lift that raised the table and permitted a more comfortable viewing posture. In a single, sweeping motion, he withdrew the drape down to Paul's torso. I winced.

I'd seen a handful of decaying bodies, but nothing like this. Nothing that had festered in salt water for days. I cringed at the putrefaction. The mask, once a frustrating inconvenience, became my only way to blunt the rot.

Before me lay what remained of Paul Godfrey. The bloating had inflated him like a balloon and rendered facial recognition impossible. Covered by a waxy sheen, his bubbled face glossed beneath the lights and his translucent skin splotched blue in places.

I'd never admit it aloud, but the investigation had seemed surreal until that moment. Missing a body, I had been operating without fully grasping the horrible thing that had occurred. The heinous act someone had committed. Confronting the ugly truth would be good for me. It filled me with urgency. Gray's face scrolled through my mind. Then Charlotte's children.

Lives might depend on it.

"He looks," I hesitated, "better than I expected, actually." On the drive into downtown Charleston, I'd recalled scenes from *Jaws*, imagining that feeding sea creatures had carved the body into a cavernous husk before it washed ashore.

"It's a consequence of the time of year," the ME explained. "The water's quite cold. Low temperatures inhibit the bacterial growth required to strip away the epidermal layers. Decomposers like crabs and sea lice can't gain access to underlying tissue as quickly so the body remains intact longer."

"I see," I replied, swallowing the stomach acid inching up my throat.

"Formation of adipocere also helps," he added, pointing to

the glossy slime. "It's a soap-like substance that forms from fat tissue underwater. It acts as a preservative."

I gulped a second time before my mind returned to my task. At first, I'd wondered why he'd only pulled the drape halfway down. Modesty, I figured. Then I realized I only needed to see his upper body. His neck, specifically.

"This the injury that killed him?" I asked.

"A single puncture wound a few centimeters below the right ear."

I leaned closer to the spot beneath Paul's ear. The slivered hole was no wider than an inch.

"Likely," he continued, "the blade was small, shorter than a switchblade—a pocket knife, perhaps—but at this location, it didn't need to be any longer to inflict a mortal wound. He's been dead for a week."

"Christmas Eve or early Christmas morning, then?" I asked.

"A strong possibility. The strongest, in fact. Stabbed this way, his external carotid artery was likely severed. Exsanguination would've been rapid. He'd have been instantly incapacitated."

After days of incessant rainfall, we'd still detected blood in the saw grass. There must have been buckets of it.

"No chance to fight back," I said. My mind ticked through each of the people I'd interviewed. None of them displayed any injuries, which fit with the lack of a struggle.

"It's difficult to say until I perform the autopsy, so don't take my words for gospel," he prefaced, "but there don't appear to be defensive wounds. If the assailant was right handed, as most people are, the location suggests a frontal attack. In this case, the knife may have been thrust with a sideways motion." He mimed the action with his right fist.

"And if he didn't fight back, that means he may not have seen it coming," I offered. This squared with the idea that there'd been a shared intimacy between Paul and his killer. Charlotte's face came to mind.

Through the cap, he rubbed the top of his head. "That's right. And as I said, a wound like this wouldn't have permitted him to do much of anything after. I'm guessing his attacker knew this. No repeat stabbing. A one and done."

I finished his thought. "Then the killer waited for him to die and dragged his body to the marsh. They expected the rain and the seawater to do the rest."

I imagined Paul, eyes wide and swirling with terror, as he fell to his knees in salty marsh water, putting together the impossible events that had transpired seconds before when a knife had plunged into his neck from out of nowhere. A faceless person stepping back to watch him bleed out from a distance, drinking in their work the way a painter or sculptor might.

In a morbid sort of way, Paul's murder got me off the hook. Or rather, his quick death. Calling the Kings sooner about their abandoned rental wouldn't have made a lick of difference, and Sheriff Burton would have to agree.

As I exhaled, I looked over Paul's face as it was now. Or where his face had been, anyways. He built his entire life around impressing others, maintaining an image of success until he could secure it for himself. A fake-it-till-you-make-it syndrome of pathologic proportions. But this was the last impression he'd give anyone.

"Thank you for accommodating me, doctor," I said, standing. "I'm anxious to read your report, but I think it's clear this was no accident. Drowning or otherwise."

As he drew the drape back over Paul's body, he sighed. "No accident at all. But certainly not a professional job."

Behind my mask, I bit my bottom lip. "Crimes of passion rarely are."

I opened the door to let myself out of the stinking room. My next task would serve two purposes: consoling a grieving family and sussing out which one's grief might not be so real.

36

Gray

The deal with the county prosecutor required local Alcoholics Anonymous attendance. The chapter I'd chosen met weekly in the theater classroom of Pickens High. Thoughts of Hattie, languidly sunning herself, hung heavy. And the blood. The hate. *I was going to take her home with me.*

Charlotte volunteered to drop me off in her new rental car. My fractured collarbone jolted as the car halted outside the gym, and I winced.

"Mamma will have to bring you to the rest," she said as I stepped out of the passenger seat of the compact SUV. "Winter break's over in a few days. I'll need to be getting back to Raleigh with the boys."

I offered her a nod of understanding and made for the school's gym entrance. White-knuckling my handbag, my heart beat faster as I drew closer. I wanted to bottle up poor Hattie, shove her memory into a weighty trunk and drop it in the marsh. It wasn't fair, but it was how I dealt: replace one pain with another.

Attending AA surpassed jail time, but the prospect of sharing anything panicked me. The value of openness had been neglected in the King household. Unsurprisingly. Breathing unevenly, I reminded myself I didn't have to share if I didn't want to. My attendance had been ordered, not my participation. A phantom scent of chardonnay tickled my nose.

Clutching a blue pen, I wrote my name on the sign-in sheet at the front of the room. Only those needing to prove they'd shown up bothered signing. The rest remained, well, anonymous. I'd scrawled *Gray Godfrey*, but reading it back made me queasy.

I'd grown to hate Paul and the name he gave me more with each passing day. The gaslighting. The affair. *Annie.* I hated him for everything he'd invited into our lives. I had a drinking problem, no denying it, but it paled in comparison to what he'd done.

In a rush of anger, I scratched out my last name. Hastily, I wrote *King* instead.

Regaining my composure, I searched for a seat. Chairs had been arranged in a semi-circle. Coffee and bagels sat on a folding table by the door. People of all sorts trickled in.

By the coffee dispenser, a middle-aged woman with cropped brown hair hummed as she filled her cup. She could've been a grade school teacher. Nothing about her suggested she struggled with anything. Certainly not drinking.

Next to her, an elderly man spread softened cream cheese across a bagel. He wore pressed chinos and a black cap designating him a veteran. He might've come straight from central casting, called for the role of Grandfather with Kind Eyes.

Despite my fears, seeing other people—what they did and did not look like—calmed me. I didn't know I'd carried expectations about this meeting until then. I'd pictured myself as a weak creature, a sheep maybe, wandering into a den of hungry wolves. People hardened by years of drinking, probably to mask the pain of the horrible things they'd done. Crimes of all kinds. Maybe even murder.

I had expected bandannaed biker-gang types. Hell's Angels or something. Maybe tattooed women with voices broken by cigarettes. Gaunt skin and skull-like faces. Everyone sunken and husky and dank. But these folks weren't anything like that. In fact, the only person here who'd committed any sort of crime that I could personally attest to was . . . me.

The woman who could have been a teacher offered me a warm grin as she took a seat next to me. She introduced herself as Barbara.

"Gray," I replied, taking her hand. She noticed mine was trembling, and I snatched it back.

"First time at a meeting? You don't have a thing in the world to worry about. Don't you dare say a word, either. Not if you don't want to."

"Thank you," I whispered, unclenching my jaw.

It occurred to me that she must have known exactly how I felt, but that shouldn't have been surprising. She was like me, after all. An alcoholic. All these perfectly normal people chatting with each other and finding their favorite chairs were like me. For the first time in a very, very long time, I relaxed. My chest loosened at the thought that maybe, just maybe, I was right where I should be.

"I see you didn't get anything to eat or drink," Barbara said, pointing to my empty lap. "First meeting's always tough. You feel like every pair of eyeballs is looking right at you. Will you let me fetch you something?"

Now that she mentioned it, I did feel a slight pang of hunger.

"A bagel," I answered. "If you don't mind, I could go for half a bagel with a bit of cream cheese."

"You got it, darling," she replied, leaving her seat for the front.

The woman made no mention of who I was, though it was

unlikely that she'd failed to recognize me, either from my family or the past week's news. My name and my photograph had been splashed across the *Elizabeth Gazette* as intrigue surrounding Paul's case grew.

Then it dawned on me. This was Alcoholics *Anonymous.* Even if she did know who I was, she'd never say so. I decided Barbara was right. At least right now—in this very moment—I had nothing to worry about.

As the meeting commenced, first with a prayer and a recitation, the floor was opened for sharing. A rustle in the next seat, and Barbara stood.

"My name's Barbara, and I'm an alcoholic," she told the room.

"Hi, Barbara," the room repeated back in unison.

Every face was turned our way. I shifted uneasily being so close to the center of attention. Thankfully, I'd finished my bagel before she raised her hand to share.

Barbara fished a coin from her left pocket. A gold or bronze piece about the size of a half-dollar.

"This," she started, "is my ten-year coin." A round of applause tore through the space. Oddly thunderous given the crowd size. "Most of you know what these coins say on them, but I'm gonna read it aloud for those who don't. It says 'To Thine Own Self Be True.'"

She paused and silence covered the room. It took a moment, but I soon realized why. Barbara's eyes had welled up with tears like gutters in a rainstorm. Taking a worn tissue from her other pocket, she dabbed at them.

"You know, I got this coin six months ago. Six months and fourteen days to be exact." She chuckled then lowered her voice. "About one month ago, however, my first husband passed away.

A twisted bowel. But I'd lost him once already to drinking. It'd been over a decade, but his mother still barred me from his funeral."

She paused for a moment, collecting herself. "It infuriated me at first. Didn't she see I'd gotten better? That what's done is done, and it's today that counts? And tomorrow? In my anger, I experienced cravings. Intense cravings. To fight them, I held onto this coin so tight the letters engraved in my palm."

My stomach knotted. I couldn't imagine how anyone, much less family, could deny Barbara. But she said it had been ten years. The woman standing next to me now wasn't the same one from back then. What had this benign woman been capable of in the past? She must've done terrible things to have been turned away from a funeral.

My thoughts darted to my own behavior. The terrible thing I'd done, drunkenly behind the wheel of an SUV. If I had harmed anyone with Charlotte's car, I'd have killed myself by now.

Barbara pressed on, "I didn't break. And if I didn't break then, it gives me hope that I might not break in the future. But the fact that my addiction crept up on me ten years out reminded me to take nothing for granted. To never fool myself into thinking that time has made me invulnerable." She balled her hand into a fist around the coin. "To thine own self be true."

As she took her seat to a chorus of clapping and whistling, the words replayed in my head. I was true to no one. Most of all, I was untrue to myself. Perhaps honesty made for a good starting place.

And not just any sort of honesty, but honesty with myself. I'd buried and suppressed and denied and pretended daily. The drinking. Paul and his affair. His money problems, too. He thought he'd hidden that, but I knew. *I'm a drunk, not stupid.*

And Matthew. I carried him around like a festering wound. I'd never confronted it, never allowed it to heal. Instead, I scratched and picked at it. Unbandaged, it collected dirt and grew inflamed. A thought crossed my mind: What if my wounds were on the outside? I shuddered to think of what they might look like.

It was time to be honest with myself. To be true. And it started today.

As I leaned back in my seat, a movement in the corner of my eye caught my attention. Someone was frantically waving their hand in front of the door's square window.

Charlotte?

What was she doing here? The clock suspended at the front of the room said it'd only been thirty minutes. I told her the meeting lasted at least an hour.

A creeping unease spread inside me, and I broke out in a cold sweat. The window and the distance blurred her face, but she waved me over. Beckoning me to leave.

My pulse quickened, and I stood shakily. The man who was sharing paused as I gathered my things and slung my purse over my shoulder. I offered him an apologetic nod and did my best not to meet Barbara's eyes as I slid out of our row.

As I neared the door, Charlotte took on sharper features. She looked as though she had no blood in her face, but her eyes burned. I gently turned the handle and stepped outside, careful to shut it quietly behind me.

"What's going on?" I asked, straining to whisper. It was a question I knew I didn't want answered.

"We've got to go. Now." Her voice snapped like a dry twig. Something had happened. Something very serious. "Mamma's waiting for us at the door. Cora's got the car pulled around."

Some dark corner of me—shadowy and wet—knew exactly what this was about. Disregarding the coin's proverb, I sought to squash the dread, struggling in vain to shove it back down into whatever abyss it had crawled out from.

Squeezing my arm with a vise-like grip, Charlotte practically dragged me through a dim hallway flanked with lockers. My broken collar bone throbbed, and I stumbled once, twice.

Charlotte choked. "The police—they came to the house."

The agnostic in me began to pray. *Please, God. Don't let it be this. Please,* please, *God.* Useless.

As we turned the corner, I sensed my nightmare shudder and shake, unleashing itself from the cage deep within my mind one flimsy bolt at a time. Then Charlotte breathed life into it fully.

"They've found Paul."

* * *

It was as if I'd detached. Like I floated above myself, looking down. Only then did events become clearer. Sharper. Strangely, even the pain in my collar bone had dulled.

Ahead, I spotted Mamma standing inside the gym door. Enormous sunglasses, round and black, obscured nearly half her face.

Through the window behind her, I detected movement. Blurry movement and a melding of voices. Shouting as to make none of them discernible. Somehow, Charlotte tightened her grip further. I didn't know she possessed that sort of strength. Nothing about her bony stature suggested she did.

"This way," Mamma barked as Charlotte passed me off to her. "They followed us from the house. Police in this town seem to leak like damn faucets. Cora's got the car already running."

She took a deep breath as though preparing to go to battle and pushed open the door to the outside.

Who's they?

As we crossed the threshold to the parking lot, lights flickered from every direction. Photographers' flashbulbs burst, making me squint even in daylight. The strobing made me feel like I was moving in slow-motion.

"Mrs. Godfrey! Mrs. Godfrey!"

"Do you have a comment—"

"Are you aware of the circumstances—"

Ahead, the family car took shape, but everything else blurred like a dream. Defined details—the school, the parking lot, the gathered crowd of reporters—became abstract and swirled together. The whole world melted.

"Mrs. Godfrey!"

"—Paul's body!"

"Any comment? Any idea what—"

"—Mrs. Godfrey! Gray!"

More flashbulbs. More shouting. More strobing lights and reporters shouldering this way and that. Climbing over one another like panicked lobsters in a tank. Locked in some frantic fight. Clawing at me, desperate to rip me apart limb from bloody limb.

Someone bumped my elbow, and a bolt of pain shot through me. I winced. Pressed on all sides, the sharp burning had nowhere to go. Everything turned claustrophobic.

"Make way," Mamma shouted, indignant. "Move out of our way!" Her knotted pearls swung wildly.

When we reached the car, Charlotte leapt into the front passenger seat. Mamma swung the rear door open, thrusting me inside and stepping in behind me. The door slammed hard, muting the

clamor. Tires squealed. Cora appeared nervous, face dancing from
one direction to another then back again.

"Run them over if you have to," Mamma shouted. Cora fidgeted behind the wheel as though unsure if she should take the
order seriously. I bounced in my seat as the car struck speed-
bumps at high speed.

"Where are we going, ma'am?" Cora asked, her voice catching.
"Home?"

"No," Mamma replied, her tone still fiery. "The police station.
Take us to the police station."

* * *

I sat at the same conference room table. The place I first sat with
Mamma to report Paul missing. A lifetime ago now. How
quickly things had changed in a week. I didn't have the mental
fortitude to keep up with the changes. It was probably for the
best.

A numbness from deep inside my chest extended down my
limbs and swathed by fingers and toes in tingling pricks. AA
had given me a strange high. Like I no longer wanted a drink, and
better yet, that I didn't need one. But as good as the feeling had
been, it'd vanished.

"Here, Hummingbird." Mamma took one of my pain pills
from her purse and placed it in front of me. "Take this."

The sight of it set my shoulder throbbing. What kind of state
was I in? To not even know I hurt? Before me sat a cup of orange
juice, but I imagined the bitterness of that pill slipping down with
a cool grapey white—both making the other more potent. My
quaking hands rippled the juice as I gulped, chasing the Percocet.

A wool blanket, thick but scratchy, covered my shoulders
and upper back. Nina had placed it over me as I exited our car.

She and her partner—Sammie—ran out to meet us in the parking lot. They'd brought a handful of uniformed officers with them to tame the pack of journalists that had gathered and roiled out front.

I sat frozen in my chair. Charlotte and Mamma took seats on either side. Nina watched me from across the table. Her tensed jaw muscle suggested the situation pained her, but she kept her face mostly vacant.

"Do we," Mamma spoke, paused, "do we need to identify him?"

"No, Joanna," Nina answered. "That won't be necessary. We matched the DNA to samples we obtained from Paul's personal belongings."

"I see." A relieved sigh escaped Mamma. "So, there was no kidnapping?"

"It appears not," Nina replied. "Or, if there was, the scheme was abandoned."

"Kidnapping?" Charlotte's voice grew edgy and terse. "What do you mean kidnapping?"

My vision blurred around the edges. Everything moved in slow motion. Words dulled then sharpened then dulled again. People talked over me, across me. No one spoke *to* me.

Joanna shifted in her seat. "Detective Palmer . . ." I watched her eyes meet Nina's. Mamma appeared to retool what she planned to say. "Detective Palmer indulged a theory of mine. I thought Paul might've been kidnapped. She was kind enough to humor me, but it would seem I was mistaken. Gravely so."

Nina gave Mamma a nod and a small, closed-mouth smile.

"Humor you?" Charlotte asked, incredulous.

Mamma stiffened. "She heard me out, my theory that is. Made mention that she'd come up with options to pursue it. But before she could, well, this happened, I suppose."

"That's correct," Nina added.

Charlotte leaned back in her chair. Judging by the way she bit her lip, I doubted her concern was satisfied.

A sudden burst of curiosity sprang from me. "How did it happen?" I asked. My dry eyes burned. I knew they were bloodshot. "How did Paul die?"

Nina glanced down for a moment before speaking. "He was murdered, Gray." She steadied her voice. No doubt her profession required her voice to be steady when delivering bad news. Steady and utterly devoid of feeling.

Ironically, like me. Like the pain in my shoulder, news of Paul's murder hardly registered. My ability to feel anything had shrunk to almost nothing. Of course, I had assumed murder to be the case. Annie had no doubt killed Paul, but all sorts of questions stemmed from that fact. I asked only one. "How did he die?"

Drawing in breath, Nina answered. "Stabbed. He was stabbed once in his neck with a small knife. His passing was . . . very fast."

The last bit was meant to assuage me. Nina intended to ease my grief, but when I became aware that I didn't care—that I felt nothing but apathy towards Paul and his suffering, however little or much there had been—I realized something else.

Paul's disappearance may have shaken me to my core, sending me into fits of panic and depression and self-destruction, but it wasn't my affection for him that spurred this. Not love or admiration or any other feeling of attachment. It was the jarring change to my world that had unmoored me, when denial was snatched away by events beyond my control. Abrupt change, pure and simple.

I'd never handled change well. And for all our problems, for the way Paul made me miserable day in and day out, I had treasured the routine my life had fallen into. The structure Paul provided. He'd given me a refuge from home and the hurt that surrounded it. And his emotional distance gave me the space I'd needed to drink my pain into numbness. Paul enabled my denial, and when he vanished, my vulnerabilities flared up like a recurrent infection.

As it turned out, I didn't really care that Paul was gone. And now I didn't care that he was dead.

As Nina and Mamma discussed the circumstances of Paul's murder—Charlotte chiming in with questions of her own—I couldn't help but think something morbidly ironic. At first, I blamed it on the painkiller—the lack of alcohol and the head-squeezing void it left—but the more I dwelled on it, the more I actually believed it.

Maybe Annie had done me a favor.

37

Nina

Hidden from reporters, the station's back doors closed behind the King family, and thoughts of Matthew persisted again. I couldn't seem to break from them. Not that a pedophile was a thing to be disregarded. To the contrary, I believed him to be a danger to the people of Elizabeth.

"I'm so very sorry for your loss," Burton had offered the Kings as they left. What would he say about Matthew and the danger he posed? Joanna had called the police that night. What did *Deputy Sheriff* Jim Burton know?

If I wanted to take down Matthew—and whoever else was involved—I needed to determine what had happened to Paul. I needed to confront Charlotte with evidence. If I could get a confession out of her—maybe in a moment of heated emotion—then I could close Paul's case with three accounts of Matthew's crime in my back pocket: Gray's allegations and whatever Charlotte might know, plus the statement I'd taken from Auntie Tilda. Those first two—a reckless alcoholic and an alleged murderer—might not scream reliability, but at least one of them was a victim. And victims always deserved to be heard. No exceptions. Besides, a jury would see Auntie's corroboration and know a woman at death's door had nothing to gain by lying.

And if I spoke with the doctor, if I could get tangible proof the STI tests for Auntie had contained Gray's samples—

"Autopsy report's in," Sammie announced.

I rubbed my temples. "That fast, huh?"

He threw a folder down, thick with pages stapled and paper-clipped every which way. "Paul's career, priority number one—all that jazz."

Judging from the size of the report, the ME had been thorough. That was nothing to complain about. The more airtight the case against Charlotte, the greater our chances of getting her to comment on Matthew.

Sammie noticed I'd yet to even touch the folder. "You don't want to have a look?"

"Does it say anything new?" I asked. It needed to be read. But I'd only be wasting my own valuable time if I went through it with my head somewhere else. If I could avoid reading it thoughtlessly, I would.

"Mostly confirms what we already know, but I thought you'd like to get a start on digging in. You enjoy this sort of thing, don't you?" I consumed details, and Sammie knew this better than most anyone. Details were why I became a detective. Details and the fact that folks quietly said I couldn't. Burton most of all.

I sighed, rubbing my head again. "I still can't shake it, Sammie. I can't get Matthew out of my mind. Paul's case unmasked Gray's allegations."

"Don't forget about Charlotte. If our hypothesis is correct, she's Annie. There's a chance she might also have been victimized by Matthew," he added. "At the very least, she was left unsupervised with him as a kid."

"That complicates things quite a bit. Did Charlotte confirm? For our interview later today?" I bit my lip and looked at the folder again.

"She did." Sammie lowered his voice, circled back to Matthew. "You know he's got a little girl himself, don't you?"

My heart sank. "No. I didn't."

"She'd be about Gray's age when . . ."

I shook my head as a new discomfort spread through me. I made fists by my side and tightened my jaw. I had to do something, but what?

A thought—born from the bottled rage building in my chest—struck me. I could put him on notice. I could let him know we were closing in and that it was only a matter of time until . . . There would be consequences for confronting him, no doubt. Despite some of the deepest roots in Elizabeth, it could send him running. He had the cash for it. And I could only imagine what Sheriff Burton would say. But what about the consequences of doing nothing? I had seen those flare up time and time again. In horrifying ways.

If I put him on notice, it might startle him. Prevent him from hurting his little girl or anyone else's for that matter. Paranoia might protect them until a real case could be made.

"Where are you going?" Sammie asked as I stood and began to pack my things.

He took a step backwards, clearing a path from my cubicle. "I'm going to clear my head." I stuffed the folder in my book bag. "So I can give this report the attention it deserves."

* * *

I pulled up to the law offices of King, Floyd, and Powers. The second two names were alphabetized, but every alphabet in Elizabeth started with "King."

As I slammed my car door, I noticed my awful parking job. I'd angled my way into the space, back tires stretched over into the next slot.

Stay cool, Nina, I repeated to myself.

The downtown office occupied a Georgian-style townhome, narrow and leaning to one side atop its centuries-old foundation. A receptionist greeted me as I walked in through the front.

"Good afternoon, ma'am." She smiled through bleached teeth. "Can I help you?"

In other places, it might appear odd for an officer to visit defense counsel, but in Elizabeth, familiarity permeated all facets of life.

"Detective Nina Palmer. I need to see Matthew King." Impatiently, I added, "I don't have a scheduled appointment, but tell him it's important. Urgent."

The woman frowned. "Unfortunately, Mr. King isn't here at the moment. Is there something I can help you with? Perhaps, I could take down a message for you or you could speak with another attorney?"

"I'm afraid I have to speak with Matthew, specifically," I replied. "Can you tell me where he is, please?"

She withdrew, guarded. I easily imagined Matthew chastising the woman for revealing his whereabouts. The man never struck me as the sort to handle interruption well.

"Um," she stuttered and fumbled through a calendar on her desk.

I tapped my badge, scattering any doubt the woman held onto.

"Of course, detective," she said, relenting. "Let me just check his schedule." She turned to a computer, clicked the spacebar a handful of times, then whipped around. She grinned as though she hadn't done anything worth second-guessing.

"It looks like he's taken his family to lunch," she announced. "At the country club."

Ah. There it is. She assumed he'd be protected within the gilded halls of a club house.

"Thanks." I smiled, turning to leave. Unfortunately for her and Matthew, I rarely played by the antiquated rules of a small southern town. Not when they worked against me. And not when I was angry.

* * *

"Ma'am, I'm afraid I can't allow you inside," a balding man in a dark blazer announced as I approached the club house. The gold crest stitched into the front of his jacket must've given him a profound sense of authority.

But I had my own gold crest. "Police," I told him, flashing my badge as I strode by.

"Ma'am," he called from behind. "Ma'am! There's no denim permitted!" I brushed the front of my jeans with my palms and swung the front door open.

Inside, I followed elegant signage to the restaurant, the heels of my boots clacking against the white and black checkered floors. The paneled walls and mahogany pillars smelled like money.

The maître d' guarding the restaurant's entrance called out, "Miss, can I help you? Miss?" His voice dwindled as I made my way from table to table, scanning for Matthew.

I could almost feel his presence. Maybe it was all the expensive cologne and perfume, but my heart thumped inside my ears as I drew nearer.

"Stay calm," I whispered under my breath. "Stay collected."

Maintaining some sort of composure was crucial. After all, no one in their right mind would've advised me to come here.

Burton would bench me if he knew. Someone like Matthew would misconstrue it later. Later when he sat before a jury of his peers.

"This was entirely personal," I imagined him stating from the witness stand, eyes darting from one hapless juror to the next. "All of it. Every bit. My Uncle Seamus made a mistake years ago when he said those things to Matilda Palmer. But the man's dead now. Detective Palmer needs to let it go."

That's when I envisioned him turning to me—seated somewhere in the gallery—and pressing, "But you couldn't let it go, could you, Nina? And when you found Mr. Godfrey's abandoned vehicle, what did you do? You sat on it. While Paul's body decomposed beneath the water, pride prevented you from reaching out to my family. It's almost like you got off on causing us pain. Is that what you're doing to me now? Getting off?"

He'd turn to the judge next. "And you should've seen her, your honor. The way she hunted me down at lunch with my family at the club. Blinded by rage. A reckless bull in a china shop."

A high-pitched giggle sharpened my focus. The squealy laughter of a young girl. Ahead, Matthew sat before a white linen tabletop, arrogant in his seersucker suit.

I slowed my pace, taking note of everything. They'd finished lunch by the looks of it. Dirty silverware was strewn about, but the plates had been cleared. He swirled his martini with a skewered olive—of course, he'd feel entitled enough to drink at lunch.

A woman, I presumed his wife, sipped an after-meal espresso from a tiny bone china cup. Her blonde hair was loosely curled and shoulder-length. Her floral sundress, perfect.

Something sour spread through me. The source of the spritely laughter. Her hair had been wrapped in a French braid. Her small hands held a crayon which she used to color on a notepad. The crayon was red. She wore a school uniform, too. A pressed skirt and polo. The color had changed over the years, but the embroidered insignia was the exact same. Elizabeth Baptist School.

It was a uniform like I'd worn years ago. Like Gray had worn.

"Detective Nina Palmer." Matthew met my eyes as I approached the table. He smiled with cheeks full of color. Hair coifed and kept, he looked nothing like he had when I last saw him, fresh from Gray's bedside. In the corridor of the hospital, he'd appeared wracked with guilt and shame.

I gave a subtle nod.

Polishing off his martini, he placed the olive between his teeth and slid it from its spear. Still chewing, he nodded to the woman next to him. "Have you met my wife, Ellen?"

"No," I whispered.

The blonde turned to me. "Pleasure to meet you. Nina, is it?"

A second nod.

Matthew appeared to note my silence. With a creased brow and eyes lingering on mine, he motioned to the little girl. "And this is my daughter. Susannah," he said warily. "Is there something I can do for you?"

"No," I answered tersely. "There's not anything you can do for me."

He cocked his head, perplexed. "But you made a beeline right for me. I watched you come in."

I held my silence. I could almost see his mind working. Neurons firing to determine my purpose. If my presence alone hadn't knocked him off-balance, my odd behavior likely would.

Everyone knows getting away with something can only be measured by time. A thing is true until it isn't any longer. *You're hidden until you're found.*

Tiny beads of sweat collected on his brow.

"Nina?" He leaned forward. I'd gotten to him already. Seeing Gray the other day must've done a real number on him, instilling paranoia. I planned to stoke it further.

"I know what you've done, Matthew," I finally said. "I know what you did to Gray."

He narrowed his eyes. "I don't understand—"

"At Piper Point. She was nine. You were seventeen."

His wife, Ellen, turned in her seat. "Darling, what's she—"

"The cellar? Going on a hunt for the Devil down there? Is that little detail correct?"

His cheeks reddened. A vein cutting vertically down his forehead swelled. "You're not supposed to be here," he said through a clenched jaw. "I'm having lunch with my family. If you'd like to schedule some time to chat, you can contact—"

"You took it much farther than a silly game though, didn't you?" I wanted to push him, but I wouldn't come out and say it. Not with little Susannah blinking up at me from the table.

He stood, scooting his chair out with force. Other patrons turned towards us, startled by the commotion. "I am asking you kindly to leave me and my family alone, detective. This is entirely inappropriate." He struggled to speak softly.

"Matthew, what's she saying?" Ellen asked, clearly concerned by the unfolding scene. "Why's she asking you about Gray?"

He ignored his wife. "Leave, Nina."

"I'll leave as soon as we talk. Step outside, and then I'm gone."

He glanced at his family and then turned to meet the eyes of everyone staring at him. "Fine," he shot back, throwing down his linen napkin.

"Matthew, what's happening?" Ellen raised her voice, glowering at me.

"I'll be right back," he replied. His brow glistened.

He had no other option but to follow me to the club house's veranda. As soon as the door closed behind us, Matthew exploded.

"What the hell do you think you're doing?" His face shook. His eyes lit up like a pair of matches.

My own fire grew. "Putting you on fucking notice," I answered through gritted teeth.

He threw his arms up. "For what, exactly?"

"For the sexual assault of a minor. Gray Godfrey."

He opened his mouth as though he planned to shout back but stopped. He had to be careful now. He was speaking to an officer of the law about allegations against him. Allegations which were not constrained by any statute of limitations. The attorney in him took over.

Turning a half-circle, he ran both hands through his hair. He'd become disheveled. He exhaled loudly, then spoke. "I'm sorry, Nina. I have nothing to say to you."

"That's okay," I said, unclenching my teeth. "I expected you wouldn't. I came here to let you know what I know. That's all."

He scoffed. "Gray's a drunk. You know that as well as I. What she says can't be trusted."

I stared deep into his baby blue eyes. "Like I said, Matthew. I know."

As I turned to leave, he called from behind. "A drunk, Nina. Probably three sheets to the wind when she said whatever it is she said. She's sober now, though. Guess the accident scared her straight." His voice grew fainter as I reached for the door handle to return inside. "In fact, she called me earlier today. Said she wants to catch up. Doesn't sound like someone who's been assaulted to me."

The door shut behind me. Crossing the dining room to the

exit, I caught a glimpse of Susannah, and my heart clenched. As her mother leaned in next to her—maybe to see what she'd drawn—I wanted nothing more than to leap to her side. To whisk her away from the man pacing back and forth on the veranda.

Could I tell Ellen what sort of man her husband was? She wouldn't believe me if I did. I pushed the thought from my mind. To do so was difficult. Unnatural. It went against every fiber of my being. But I did it.

Making my way back to the parking lot, I understood Auntie's decision a little better. The difference between being principled and being pragmatic could sometimes be measured in miles.

As I sank back into the driver's seat of my car, I released a heavy sigh. Holding out my hands, fingers outstretched, they shook badly.

Okay, Nina. Your mind's clear. Get the autopsy report read. Then get half the rise out of Charlotte that you got out of Matthew, and you might just wind up with a confession.

38

Gray

I tugged the parlor doors closed, sealing myself off in the library. We'd arrived home from the police station hours ago, but the spinning wheels in my brain were just gaining traction.

Did Annie's sudden presence in my life actually *help* me? A slanted thought. Broken. Even if Annie's actions had pushed me closer to getting help—AA for instance—she was still a sociopath.

Annie hadn't really done me any favors. Not on purpose. And mutilating Hattie after killing Paul suggested she wasn't finished. Hattie was the last of the yard cats. The only one to survive that year's tragedies and traumas. Like me. But how would Annie know that?

I thought of Charlotte. The way she hated Hattie. Hated when I brought her inside as children. But that was outrageous; she'd been allergic. She'd never do something so horrible. Would Mamma? Would Tilda Palmer?

In the grand scheme of things, Paul's death had been easy. Nina said so herself. A quick knife to the neck. All his suffering had ended days earlier. Me on the other hand? My pain had only grown since Christmas morning.

I had to do something about her.

Annie wanted me to panic and grieve and writhe. Like a hook-pierced worm. She wanted fear to permeate my flesh every waking moment—right down to the muscle like a confined veal. Everything she'd done had been designed that way.

The phone call, vague and cautious, with no information or callback number. She meant to send me off the path, and she'd succeeded. When I played her message for the police, I took them with me on a wild-goose chase assuming my husband had run off to the Caribbean or the Azores or Italy with his mistress.

Wincing, I let my leather purse fall from my unbroken shoulder. I sat it atop Daddy's claw-foot desk.

Then there was Cirilo's. Annie didn't merely know how to push a person over the edge—she seemed to know exactly how to push *me*. And she pushed and pushed and pushed. The Riesling brought to my table courtesy of the house. Had Annie arranged that, too? No. That had been Luca Cirilo himself. The waiter had verified as much. I couldn't fall into paranoia on top of everything else.

I shuddered as Annie's email came to mind. The wild-goose chase to find Paul had only been half of what we thought. Maybe he hadn't run off with her, but she was his mistress. Or they'd slept together in the past, at least. The fact she'd saved the photos to send me meant she'd been planning this for quite some time. If not plotting to murder Paul outright, then torturing me in some way.

And now she drew closer. So close she'd stood on this very property. She'd likely watched me in my bedroom from the courtyard while Hattie bled out atop the inlaid brick.

I took a seat in the leather high back chair, sinking into its worn cushion.

My arms goose-bumped, and I grew expectedly thirsty. It was the afternoon, and a drink was completely out of reach. The pain pills burned off some of my anxiety, but I craved the *glug glug* of an upside-down bottle. My thoughts darted to hand sanitizer, mouth wash, maybe even rubbing alcohol. If I just smelled it, I might feel better.

I'm coming apart.

I placed my palms to my cheeks and pressed inwards, shaking my head. I also craved information. I wanted to know who this woman was. If I stood any chance against her, I needed to know.

And I planned to put up a fight. It had taken Paul's death and Matthew showing up at my bedside, but now I spoiled for one. For once in my life, I refused to go down easy. I wanted to get better—like Barbara. And I wanted to fight Annie—to the death if I had to.

Daddy's portrait over the mantle caught my eye. Billowy tufts of white gave him a look like Teddy Roosevelt in need of a trim. I hadn't noticed it since being back. The last time I stood in the library—when Charlotte told me Paul hadn't come home—my mind had been twisted with panic and pills. A wet rag wringing fear from itself. No surprise I'd missed Daddy looming over the mantle.

His nose, Roman like all the men in my family, was capped by gin blossoms. What an ordeal that little detail had stirred. He'd demanded the artist touch it up, but Mamma insisted it stay. The woman who polished the family's reputation so fiercely had passed up a chance to spit-shine it further. I'd always wondered what her motives had been. Why she'd wanted to reflect life as it was, rather than as Daddy wanted it to be. Likewise, I questioned why I'd been drawn to this room in the first place.

I'd grabbed my bag containing my laptop from my bedroom, but rather than opening it there, I'd come down here. I'd walked past the landing mirror—this time looking into it—and come to the room where Daddy's portrait hung.

I came down here because I wanted to rip the band-aid off. I needed to confront my enemy—Annie—and I wanted Daddy to see me do it. The man who'd buried everything so selfishly. Who'd encouraged Mamma to do the same. Whether he'd be proud or turn in his grave, I wasn't sure.

I didn't fucking care.

I closed my eyes, recalling what Daddy once said to me in this room. Late at night.

"You have to fight, Gray. Somebody knocks you down, you gotta fight." He'd slurred his words. The smoky tang of bourbon on his breath had stung my young eyes. I hadn't been sure to what or whom he was referring to at the time. It could've been anything. Contention had filled his life. His career path had been littered with fallen foes. "We're Kings, you hear me? We weren't put in this world to live up to its expectations. It's the world that needs to live up to ours."

I'd never made anything easy for anyone. I certainly wasn't going to stop now. Not with Annie. Not when it came to taking me down. As my computer powered up, I considered the possibilities; what were the sorts of questions police asked during homicide investigations? First, they always suspected the victim's significant other. The boyfriend or girlfriend, the wife or husband. But I didn't kill Paul.

Then they inquire about enemies. They ask if the victim had any. Paul undoubtedly had enemies. A liberal lobbyist throwing his hat in the ring for congress? There'd be enemies on every corner.

But Paul wasn't the *only* intended victim here. The question now was, what enemies did *I* have?

With my drinking, I'd managed to anger more than a handful of folks up and down the east coast. But my run-ins were of the casual sort. Nothing resulting in a burning desire for me to suffer endlessly. The D.C. museum director who fired me, for example.

Only one person kept coming to mind. One person I'd angered enough—and enough times—to want me dead. That person was Paul.

And if I'd made him mad enough, then maybe he communicated that to Annie. When he wasn't mockingly calling me Hummingbird during pillow talk, he might've expressed his fatigue with my behavior.

I found myself back at square one. The lover was usually guilty, and this case seemed no different. More than likely, Annie had killed Paul.

But who the hell is Annie?

I stared blankly at my welcome screen. A balmy sixty-eight degrees according to my weather app. Partly cloudy. No new emails. Headlines from around the world, the typical mix of depressing and even more so.

As I bit my thumbnail, a thought occurred: the security firm. The one Laurence Cooper hired to assist with Paul's case. I assumed they'd been called off because Paul was no longer missing. They worked for Laurence, not me, so it didn't seem strange to not have heard from them and besides, my mind had been so frantic, they might've checked in with Mamma, and I missed it.

But none of that mattered. They'd been working alongside the police. How much coordination occurred between their contractors and the Elizabeth County Sheriff's Office? Were they still on the case? Did Nina tell them about Annie? They were an unexplored lead, and if I could get an investigator on the phone, I could ask what they'd learned. Maybe they'd IDed Annie, or at least had a short-list.

I couldn't recall the firm's name, so I typed "Cooper and Waters, security contractor, Paul Godfrey" into my search browser. Surely there'd be an article or something naming them in the context of Paul's case. I'd spoken briefly to a man who said he planned to travel to Elizabeth himself. If I couldn't remember the name of his company, I certainly wouldn't know his. But if I saw a list of employees, perhaps I could pick it out?

Bingo. Security Solutions. I clicked on the link to their website. I scrolled through contact information for Security Solution's investigatory services. I recognized Andrew Huang's name and dialed his number.

An administrative assistant answered on the third ring. "Andrew Huang's office, Robin speaking. How can I help you?"

During my brooding, my throat had grown dry, and my voice caught as I started to speak. I coughed instead.

"Hello?"

"Yes, I'm sorry. Hello." I cleared my throat. "I'd like to speak with Mr. Huang. Please."

"I'm afraid he's on a call at the moment, can I take a message?"

I hesitated, suddenly feeling a bit foolish. "Sure," I answered. "Could you tell him Gray called."

"Gray Godfrey?" The woman—Robin—asked. She sounded taken aback. The clamor behind her abruptly stopped.

"Yes. That's me."

"Hold please." She clicked off, not giving me the chance to respond. A soft concerto played from the other side of the line.

As I waited, Mamma peeked in on her way out the front door. Cora and the twins trailed her. "We're taking the boys for an outing. Ice cream sundaes and a movie. They've been through the wringer themselves this past week," she said. "I've also got some shopping to do. We may be gone for quite a while. You'll be alright alone?"

I nodded.

"Charlotte should be back from the sheriff's office before long. Nina had a few questions for her. Nothing too serious, I'm sure," Mamma added before heading out. Cora locked the door behind them.

"Mrs. Godfrey?" A man asked, cutting off the hold music.

"Yes," I repeated.

"This is Andrew. It's nice to hear from you." He paused for a moment. "My sincerest condolences to you and your family. I've been keeping tabs on the news out of Elizabeth."

"Thank you," I whispered as his comment sank in. "You're no longer investigating? If you're only watching the news, that is?"

"I'm afraid not, Mrs. Godfrey—"

"Call me Gray." The taste Paul's last name left in my mouth had only grown sourer, curdling like month-old milk.

"Of course, Gray. As I said, no, we're no longer providing services. Not since news of Paul's death surfaced."

"I see. That makes sense."

"Is there anything I can help you with?" He sounded genuinely eager.

I stiffened my back in Daddy's chair. "Yes, actually, there is. I was wondering if you might've found anything over the course of your investigation that pointed to Annie's identity?"

Andrew hesitated. "I'm sorry, who?"

"Annie. The woman who's been . . . terrorizing me."

"A woman's been terrorizing you?" His surprise came off as real as his eagerness had.

I dug my nails into the palm of my free hand. "Didn't you know? The phone calls, the car accident? The photographs?"

Another hesitation. "Mrs. Godfrey . . . Gray, could you tell me what happened? Precisely how this woman—Annie—has been tormenting you? If you don't mind."

I started from the beginning. From the innocuous voicemail left on my phone on Christmas Day. As I recounted the events for Andrew, my cheeks grew hot. First from the shock of hearing myself say them aloud, then from shame. As I finished with what happened to Hattie, anger supplanted all other feeling.

A pause lingered on Andrew's end of the line. I assumed he took his time digesting the whole story. If it sounded crazy to me, I could only imagine how it came off to him, hearing it all for the first time.

"And you knew none of this?" I asked. Nina must've withheld news of Annie from him. It had been withheld from the public, too. A police trap, maybe? If it came out someone knew about Annie, then they must be involved in Paul's disappearance.

"No," Andrew finally answered. "No, I didn't."

As silence resumed on his end, I spoke up. "I'm sorry to bother you. I thought you might be able to help me identify the woman—"

"I can."

"I'm sorry?" His response jarred me. Surely, he meant to say . . .

He repeated himself with certainty. "I can help you identify the woman. Annie."

I said nothing, but my blood began to rush, reddening my face further. As my breath quickened, the receiver played my exhalations back like a static-filled echo.

"I don't believe Annie's name is actually Annie," he began as I held my breath. "What do you know about Paul and your sister? How much do you really know about Charlotte?"

39

Nina

As I turned the corner towards reception, I spotted Gray's sister. Charlotte leaned on the front desk with one elbow as she signed her name onto the clipboard sitting there.

"Charlotte," I said tersely. "Follow me, please."

"Hello, Nina." She started to smile but stopped when it became clear I wouldn't be returning the gesture. As we strode through the office, we passed the Fish Bowl to my right. Her head turned as though she expected me to lead her into it.

"Are we not speaking in there?" She asked, her tone wary.

"No," I replied.

She hesitated, my answer clearly unsatisfying. "But didn't you ask me here to talk? That's where we spoke last time. And that's where you've spoken to the rest of the family."

It was unusual for someone to show concern for where I opted to speak with them. But Charlotte wasn't usual. She had something to hide, and someone with something to hide would be shaken by the unexpected. Even something as insignificant as a room change.

It only solidified my read of the woman. At the very least, she had conducted an affair with a married man. Her sister's husband. Her sister's dead husband. And the worst-case scenario?

"We'll be chatting in a formal interview room," I replied, holding open a heavy door to a second hallway. As I beckoned her through, she fidgeted with the strap of her purse. Her eyes darted from one direction to another.

"A formal interview room?" Her voice cracked like a fallen vase.

"Yes," I answered matter-of-factly. "This is a formal interview. Recorded, etcetera."

"Recorded? You never said anything about recording our conversation. You asked me to come in for a chat." She paused, gulping perhaps. "Do I . . . Do I need to have an attorney present?"

I opened the interview room door, revealing a cramped space with a single table against the wall and plastic chairs. "You're welcome to have one present if you'd like. Although, I'm unsure why you would need one. If you did, it might change my approach."

Hovering in the doorway, her mind appeared to race, likely second-guessing every decision she'd made before this moment. Perhaps even the ones that had gotten her here in the first place. Her eyes went to the ceiling. To the camera with the blinking red light perched in the corner.

"Charlotte? Would you like an attorney present?" I asked for the camera's benefit.

White-knuckling the strap of her bag, she said, "No. No, thanks. That won't be necessary. Not for a chat."

She came off as genuinely nervous. But if she was playing a part for me . . . I recalled the ease with which the woman had lied to me in the past. *Florencia.*

"Have a seat, please." I motioned to one chair and took the second one for myself. Her folder sat waiting on the table. I reached for it.

Charlotte blinked at me in silence. She let her purse slide to the linoleum floor.

After half a minute or so passed, I spoke up. "What can you tell me about your relationship with Mr. Godfrey?"

She bit her lip. "He's my brother-in-law. Was my brother-in-law. You know that. I thought you'd want to talk to me about Gray—"

"We'll get to Gray," I interjected. "But right now, I want to know about Paul. I want to know about you and Paul."

"There's not much more than that . . ."

I shifted in my seat. "Let me adjust my question. I want to know about you and Paul from *you*."

Charlotte tensed her jaw. "I don't know what you mean."

"Well, let's see, I've heard about you and Paul from others. And now I want to hear about you and Paul from *you*."

She ground her teeth as she spoke. Confusion, pretend or otherwise, marked her face. "Me and Paul? Others? What others?"

"From the private security firm contracted by Cooper and Waters, for instance." I flipped my folder open on the table. A printed email sat deliberately on top.

"The private security . . ." As her voice trailed off, she grew pale. Even her lips purpled.

"They conducted forensics on Paul's devices. His work devices. Personal ones in the Georgetown place. All of them." I tapped the printed email with my index finger.

Her bottom lip trembled. She looked as though she wanted to say something but then thought better of it.

"You lied to me. I know about the affair, Charlotte. There's a paper trail. Emails, phone calls, receipts. I know that's why your husband left you."

"I don't . . . how?" she stuttered. Her eyes searched the paper beneath my finger. She wanted a closer look. To read exactly what it said. But I kept it at arm's length from her on purpose.

"Bank card receipts. They place Paul physically in Raleigh at times Gray believed him to be traveling on business. To Canada, funny enough."

Still only wide-eyed silence from Charlotte.

Clasping my hands together, I leaned forward. "Do you know what that means?"

Shivering, she managed to shake her head. *A damn good actress.*

"It means that in addition to you also being at Ruby's the night Paul was murdered, you were his mistress. How do you think that looks?"

She rubbed the back of her neck, maybe to stifle the tic she'd begun showing.

I glared at her now. "Tensions ran sky-high that night. An intoxicated Gray? Paul flying into a jealous rage over her and Jacob? Tell me, did you fly into a fit over Paul's jealousy towards your sister?"

She shook her head. "No," she answered, hardly above a whisper.

Rubbing my palms together, I softened my expression. "If you did, I can understand why."

"What?" She met my eyes. "Why?"

"After everything that's happened to you. You and Gray both," I replied. "I don't only know about you and Paul. I know about Gray and Matthew. Your sister told me, and my aunt confirmed her account. If Matthew had . . . a thing . . . for children, then . . ."

"No," Charlotte said sharply. She clenched her fists atop the table. "Matthew never touched me."

I sat back in my seat, folding my arms. "You were so young, Charlotte. There's nothing you could have done. You were left alone and defenceless with a dangerous man. A predator. Something like that messes up a kid. They grow up with skewed ideas of right and wrong. Maybe they don't even know there's such a thing as right and wrong."

"I said Matthew never touched me!" Her fists shook.

Charlotte's eyes bolted from one side of the tiny room to the other, like a cornered animal just waiting for the walls to close in. The trap to spring shut with a metallic whine.

"I get Paul. I get why you blew up at him. Seemed like a real asshole when he was alive. But why Gray? Why torture your own sister? This Annie business, it's . . . sadistic."

Charlotte muttered. Nothing coherent, her act unraveling in front of me.

I pressed, "And the cat? You need help, Charlotte. Serious help."

"I love . . ."

"I can get you help. But you have to start by talking to me. You have to tell me the truth, or I can't help you."

"I'm not Annie." As she spoke, a tear cut a path down her right cheek. "I love Gray." She cast her eyes down as though ashamed to cry in front of me. Or maybe . . . ashamed of what she had done? Was she still acting?

"If you love her, why hurt her? Why twist the knife?" I asked, leaning into the table.

"I said I'm not Annie! And I never wanted to hurt Gray." She reached for the tissue box sitting flush against the wall. "Paul pressed so hard. It's almost like he wore me down. The worse things became between me and Will, the better Paul looked." Her shoulders shook as sadness swept over her. "Paul loved Gray. He really did. But she's just so . . . she's got problems. More than once he called me her name by mistake."

Dabbing her cheeks, she coughed and continued, "The first time, I figured it was because we look so much alike. But then I realized he was with me *because* of our looks. I was the version of Gray he wanted. Put together. Well-adjusted. I don't even care for wine."

Sincere pain marked her words, and hurt hid behind her eyes. She appeared to love her sister while harboring feelings for the woman's husband. The situation she'd found herself in must've been impossible. But impossible enough to kill? Paul's stabbing had been a crime of passion. And passion poured out of this woman now.

Launching into a second coughing fit, she shredded the tissue in her hands.

I narrowed my eyes. "And that night? What happened on Paul Revere Highway?"

Her eyes locked onto mine again. She spoke with steely determination. "I was never on Paul Revere Highway with them. I told you that from the start. I left the bar early. It was Christmas Eve, and I wanted to kiss my kids goodnight. Paul called *me* from the highway."

My mind switched tracks to Matthew. To the sexual abuse. "And what about Matthew? You knew what he'd done to your sister as a child?"

She glanced at the ceiling and back at me. "Of course, I did. I was young, but Gray and I were thick as thieves back then. She told me in her own way before she told Mamma. We've spoken of it a handful of times since, but delicately. Carefully."

"He never touched you?" I strained to hide the incredulity in my voice.

"No. It makes me sick to say it this way, but . . ." Her next words appeared to genuinely pain her. "He only had eyes for Gray."

"Did you know your mother had Gray tested for sexually transmitted infections?"

Charlotte sneered, eyeing the strips of tissue on the table before her. "It doesn't surprise me. If she did, it's one of the few good decisions she made regarding that whole situation."

Leaning in a second time, I added, "I believe she had Gray's samples labeled as my Auntie Tilda's so there'd be no record of it. Did you know anything about that?"

She shook her head. "I didn't, but that's not shocking, either. You've met Mamma, haven't you?"

"Who was the family doctor? The one who ran the tests?"

She glowered. "Dr. Conner. Mary-Ann Conner. She has a practice on Main Street but she used to make house calls."

I scratched a checkmark next to the name Mary-Ann Conner in my notepad. Two people now put her at Piper Point on the night in question. Confronting her was my next stop.

Pushing the pile of tissue to one side, Charlotte pressed on. "I've told you what happened. I've told you what I know. I've confessed to sleeping with Paul for Christ's sake. Do you know what it's like? To grieve in silence? To be Gray's shoulder to cry on while hiding my own tears? I've lost someone, too. I might've been a stand-in for Gray, a sober replacement, but I did care for him, Nina. There's a part of me—a significant part—that felt something for Paul. I still do."

I searched Charlotte's face for something to hang on to. Every crease, every wrinkle, every freckle. Something to let me know she was telling the truth. Or lying. It didn't matter which so long as it was the right answer.

"Can I go, Nina? Do you want anything else from me?" The bags beneath her eyes had grown heavier since we'd begun the interview. "Am I under fucking arrest?"

Rubbing my temples, I sighed. "Don't leave town, do you hear me?"

She nodded.

"Say it aloud," I instructed, my own head whirling. "Say you understand what I told you."

She sniffed. "I won't leave town."

* * *

I exhaled shakily as Gray's sister vanished through the station's front door. I turned on my heels and headed back to Sammie.

"Interview with Charlotte's done," I announced, stepping into his cubicle. "First one, anyways. She confirmed the family doctor, but otherwise stuck to her story. Wiretaps catch anything?"

"Mother hasn't made any unusual calls. Neither has Charlotte—before the interview, at least. Certainly no calls from Annie. But . . ."

"But?"

Sammie threw an edge into his voice. "Andrew—your pal from Security Solutions—took a call from Gray."

"What about?" I asked, crossing my arms.

"She was looking for Annie's identity. Thought Mr. Huang might have gleaned something during his own investigation." Sammie continued, "He drew a connection between Charlotte and Annie."

40

Gray

My eyes burned. My jaw tightened. My ribs could barely contain the swelling fire in my chest. Uncut, unadulterated rage.

The quiet serenity of it frightened me. Silent anger. The closest I'd ever been to such a wrath had been witnessing it from Paul. Christmas Eve at Ruby's, for example. Even shit-faced, I saw how much he seethed that night. I could practically taste it in the air.

And now I saturated the room with it, too. It spilled out from my eyes. Leached from beneath my fingernails. Slipped through the cracks of my grinding teeth. And it rushed towards Charlotte. My sister.

After I hung up with Andrew Huang, I walked into the salon where I took a seat on the couch facing the foyer. My eyes froze on the front door. I'm not sure how many minutes passed. The grandfather clock wasn't in my field of view, and if it chimed, I didn't count the number. Finally, the gravel outside crunched beneath Charlotte's rental. A car door slammed. Slow steps up the front porch. Keys jingled.

"Gray," she said, closing the front door. "You scared me half to death. What are you doing sitting here alone?"

I said nothing, felt only coldness as my fingertips tingled.

"Gray? Did you not hear me? Are you okay?" She paced towards me. I sat on the couch like petrified wood. Ancient and angry.

"Did you have a nice time with Nina?" I whispered.

She knotted her brow, halting her steps. "A nice time? Why would I . . ."

An uneasy silence passed between us. Her eyes grew wide as she pieced together what was happening. She knew I knew. She knew I'd learned the truth about her and Paul. Her and my husband. Judging by her wary face, she wasn't sure how I'd learned. Undoubtedly Nina had been asking her about it, too. Fatigue stained her eyes a pale yellow. I could tell she was tired of answering for it.

I didn't give a shit how tired she was.

"Gray." Her voice caught in her throat. "Gray, let me explain."

"How long?" I asked.

"What?"

A sudden rush of fire burst through me. The rest of my body remained still as I screamed, "How long have you been fucking my husband?"

Charlotte shook, losing her balance at my outburst. She fell back onto the couch opposite me. She began to cry. "Gray, please. It's not like that . . . he loves you . . . he loved you. He just couldn't . . ." Her crying turned to sobbing, and heaves chopped up her words into bits and pieces. Dismembered them.

Reaching into the pocket of my slacks, I retrieved my phone. My shaking thumbs danced across the screen, opening the images from annie@shadowmail.com.

"You sent these to me." I threw my phone at her. I intended to strike her face, but it hit her wrist when she raised her arm.

"No!" she sobbed. "No, I didn't! I'd never!"

I stood slowly. "The phone calls. The pictures. The fucking cat."

"Gray, please. You have to believe me."

Laughter rose from somewhere inside me. "Cirilo's? You put up such a fight over lending me your car. Such a fucking fight. You knew all along what would happen. You knew I'd drink. That's what you wanted."

"That's not true!" Charlotte stood now, too.

"Did you kill him, too? Did you kill Paul?" My eyes bulged in their sockets. My ears rang so loudly, I expected blood to trickle out from burst drums. "Did you murder my husband?"

She held the back of her hand to her mouth as though she felt sick. "What makes you think I'd be capable of—"

I shoved her shoulder hard. "Capable? What *aren't* you capable of?" I screamed, pushing her a second time.

She fell back onto the couch, rubbing her arm. "How could you even think that?"

As I closed in, she drew her legs onto the cushion. She felt threatened. *Good.*

My fists trembled at my side. Charlotte's eyes locked onto them. 'What the hell am I supposed to think? You're my sister, and you've been sleeping with my husband! My *dead* husband!" I laughed a second time, shaking my head. "The pictures? The disgusting pictures!"

When I lunged at her, she leapt over the back of the couch, stumbling towards the front door. I followed her, keeping pace.

"Gray, what are you doing? You know I didn't kill Paul. You have to know!" Tears soaked her splotched cheeks. Her chest heaved as she tried to catch her breath.

"You murdered him." My voice lowered as the silent anger returned. Quiet, but I still trembled. "You fucked Paul. Then you killed Paul."

As I said the words aloud, I wondered what Charlotte must be thinking. Why I hadn't already called the police. If I thought she was Annie, if I thought she murdered Paul, and didn't call them, it must terrify her to wonder why not.

Nina could handle all of this. But not the way I wanted it handled. Not the *right* way.

Reaching the front door, Charlotte shook her head. The fear scrawled across her face told me she'd wondered the same thing. Hesitating for a brief moment, she turned and bolted outside. I started to chase after her but froze in the open doorway. A surprising feeling washed over me. An entirely unexpected emotion.

Relief.

Not relief because Charlotte was frantically getting into her car or because I'd run her off. A different, truly horrifying sense of relief.

I hadn't killed her.

The invisible band around my head squeezed, and my entire body shook. I rummaged through a junk drawer in the kitchen, wet hands slipping from rubber bands to thumb tacks to—what I was hunting for—a screw driver. The wine cabinet was locked, and I planned to disassemble it. If I couldn't remove the lock, well, I just might break it. I'd do whatever the hell I had to at this point.

*　*　*

I stood in the dining room, my memory snipped and re-stitched with pieces missing. I didn't recall walking here. I'd lost time before, but I was excruciatingly sober now. The liquor cabinet doors, one part-ways off its hinge, swung open. On the table, a drink sat poured. A martini.

As an image of Charlotte fumbling with her car keys replayed in my mind—setting the alarm off twice before she managed to get inside—I reached for the drink. A sudden vibration caught my attention. My phone rang against the hardwood planks feet away in the salon. I guess it landed there from when I'd thrown it at Charlotte. Next to a hammer. But I'd grabbed a screwdriver from the kitchen, didn't I?

A voicemail.

"Hello, Hummingbird, it's me. Annie."

When the hell had Charlotte called me again? While she barreled down the highway? The voice needled me, pricking me like a voodoo doll.

"I'm sure by now you've learned I wasn't the only other woman in Paul's life. Your sister fucked him, too. Oh yes, that's right. Me and Charlotte both. You see, my name really is Annie. There's no mystery to it. No pseudonym. No hidden identity.

"But on the note of what a sad sack of shit Paul was, I'm sure we both agree he deserved what he got. He deserved to die. You should've seen the look on his face when I did it. When the knife slid into his neck, his eyes bulged like they might explode. That look—the shock. The realization he'd been bested. Utterly blind-sided. Come to think of it, his eyes looked the same as they did when he'd cum. Just saying it out loud now is making me wet.

"But enough about that. I've got my work cut out for me, Hummingbird. See you soon."

41

Nina

Mary-Ann Conner's practice sat downtown on a corner in a black-shuttered single-story building painted pink. A wooden sign swung from a post out front, reading PALMETTO STATE INTERNAL MEDICINE. Dr. Conner's name, second from the top.

I left my phone in the car so Burton couldn't reach me. Matthew had called him, and Jim's voicemail had been blistering.

"*You're done, Nina,*" he'd bellowed. I could picture the beet-red splotches across his cheek and brow. "*You're off. Goddamnit, you are fucking off this case!*" I'd hung up then. He was right. Completely right. But I decided to maintain deniability for one last interview before passing it off to someone whose judgment wouldn't be clouded—along with the tidbit about Joanna calling the police that night.

Entering the waiting room, the citrus scent of mopped linoleum replaced the rain-soaked pine from outside. A heavy-set woman at reception swiveled in her chair as I approached.

"Sign your name on the sheet and indicate which doctor you're here for." She tapped a clipboard with her pen. "If you're a new patient, there'll be additional paperwork."

I reached into my pocket and produced my badge. "Detective Nina Palmer. I need to speak with Mary-Ann Conner, please."

My badge rendered the woman speechless. She'd likely never seen one this close before. Seeming to gather her thoughts, she replied, "Dr. Conner's with a patient now. Can I set you up in her office?"

"That'd be perfect."

I followed her through a side door and down a narrow hall. As the receptionist closed the office door behind me, I took a seat in one of two deep leather chairs before Dr. Connor's desk.

Moments later, the office door opened, and I turned around.

"Good afternoon, Detective Palmer," A silver-haired woman said in a voice like sweet tea. "I'm Mary-Ann Conner." The enormous diamond on her ring finger contrasted with the green costume jewelry around her neck.

"Thanks for taking the time, Dr. Conner," I replied, brushing my thighs with my palms. She removed her white coat and hung it with the others. Taking a seat behind her desk, she adjusted thick-rimmed glasses—the sort that might be fashionable if you squinted.

"Certainly. I'm not sure what I can possibly help you with, but I'll do my best," she said, smiling.

"I appreciate that," I said, pausing for a moment. "If I'm not mistaken, you've been the King's family doctor for decades. I'm here to talk with you about the family. I have serious concerns."

Mary-Ann appeared to freeze. I'd never seen someone go so pale so quickly. Except perhaps Charlotte.

"Gray King Godfrey, specifically," I added, prodding for a reaction.

Her silence grew uncomfortably long. Finally, she shifted in her chair and spoke up, voice catching at first. "I'm afraid I can't discuss any patients of mine." She drew a deep breath, "Not from any point in time."

I leaned forward. "I'm aware of patient-doctor confidentiality. I'm also aware that when the well-being of a child is at stake, the confidentiality contract becomes void. In fact, you're legally obligated to report what you know."

"Mrs. Godfrey isn't a child."

"She was at the time you were her doctor."

Dr. Conner's face went from shocked to irritated. "I've served the King family for quite some time. They trust me because I respect their privacy. Now, you're clearly here without Mrs. Godfrey's consent. She may have been a minor when I saw her, but she isn't anymore. If she needs information about the care I've provided, she can request it."

I brushed her response aside. "Let me try this another way. When medical disclosure is in the public's interest, you're also compelled to relay that information to authorities."

She arched an eyebrow. "Public interest?"

"If there's a sexual predator—a pedophile—at large, for example."

The woman swallowed loudly.

Training my eyes onto hers, I continued, "Gray has made some allegations to me privately. Disconcerting allegations regarding her cousin, Matthew. She claims he sexually assaulted her when she was nine."

"That doesn't involve me."

I sharpened my tone "Except it does, doctor. As I'm sure you're aware, my Auntie Tilda was caretaker—among other things—to Gray and Charlotte. It turns out she made some allegations of her own. When she discovered what had occurred—multiple times, mind you—she went straight to Seamus and Joanna."

Dr. Conner's chest began to rise and fall more rapidly. Her reaction dashed any doubt that she hadn't known the truth about Auntie's samples.

I went on. "Mr. and Mrs. King had their own concerns. Seamus was readying a presidential bid. Beginnings are important, and the attention from a story like that would've sunk his chances. Especially at a fragile time." I folded my hands across my lap. "That's not to say they wanted to sweep the whole thing under the rug without at least some thought for Gray's well-being. According to Auntie, they barred Matthew from Piper Point. Seamus threatened to blow the boy's brains out if he ever came near Gray again."

Dr. Conner's voice trembled, "I still don't know what this—"

"Charlotte Barfield confirmed you were in the habit of making house calls for the Kings," I interrupted. "And Auntie told me you made one the night it all came out. You tested Gray for sexually transmitted infections, didn't you, Dr. Conner? You tested a nine-year-old girl for STIs, and you didn't report it."

The woman's face hardened. "That's not true. There are records. I tested Matilda Palmer, not Gray. Your Aunt asked for the exam herself."

Imploring me to check records? This woman knew. She knew exactly whose samples she'd run.

I shook my head. "Drop it, Mary-Ann. You labeled Gray's samples with my Aunt's name, but Joanna knew the results would be her daughter's. I'm sure you all breathed a heavy sigh of relief when they came back clean."

Dr. Conner stood. "I have to ask you to leave now. I don't want to talk to you any longer. You're welcome to speak with Joanna yourself, but—"

"I'm not going anywhere. Not without answers from you. You broke the law. You endangered a child. Because of your inaction, who knows who else Matthew assaulted. How many little girls he's hurt. You know he's got a daughter, himself? She's about the age Gray was when all this happened. Name's Susannah."

Dr. Connor rested her hands on her desk as though to steady herself. Veins in her brow grew engorged. "Stop it."

"Did you know Gray can't go a day without a drink? That she nearly killed herself in a car wreck down the street from this office earlier this week? Then there's the sister, Charlotte. Trust me, doctor, you don't even want to know what she's become."

"I said stop it." Her whole body quaked, knuckles white on the edge of her desk.

I kept my eyes locked onto hers. "Look at the damage you've caused by staying quiet. Auntie, also. She even took checks from Joanna for her silence. If I was a betting woman, I'd wager you have, too."

"You need to leave this office."

I leaned back, arms crossed, shaking my head. "At least Auntie didn't let things go. She took matters into her own hands and made sure the world knew exactly what sort of folks the Kings were. But you? You were in a position to change everything, and you did nothing."

"Goddamnit!" Mary-Ann shouted, slamming her fists on her desk once, twice.

The outburst knocked several photographs onto the floor, breaking their frames.

"I made sure Gray was okay. I made sure there wasn't anything physically wrong with her."

I couldn't believe her excuses. Her reaction suggested she didn't believe them herself. "Physically wrong? What about psychologically?"

Dr. Conner said nothing. She released a heavy breath, regained her composure.

I got up from my chair, straightening my back. "You need to tell me what you know, Dr. Conner. You've known her since she was very young. Through the ordeal with Matthew, through everything. Did you know about her alcoholism, too?"

Wiping her brow, she stooped to pick up the pictures she'd knocked over, then muttered, "Alcoholism? That's hardly all of it."

"All of what?"

"Gray's problems." Dr. Conner's unsteady hands dropped one of the frames a second time.

I knelt down to give her hand. This woman knew something. Something I didn't. The back of my skull tingled "What are you trying to say?"

"What happened to that girl was terrible. No doubt about it." She hesitated for a moment. "But it changed her."

"Something like that changes a person, Dr. Conner. I'm not sure—"

She spoke slowly, "Changed her in ways I couldn't quite put my finger on, at first. It's almost like Matthew—" another long pause. "Like what he did blackened her soul."

An interesting turn of phrase. *I saw the Devil.* I knotted my brow. "Blackened her soul?"

"She became given to all sorts of outbursts and behaviors. She lied, too. That girl became the most destructive liar."

"What sorts of things would she lie about?"

Dr. Conner brushed the front of her floral skirt and returned to her chair, broken frames now piled at the edge of her desk. "Absurd things. Some small, others not so much so."

"Like what?"

"Oh, I don't know." She paused, said, "Like those cats for instance. A litter of kittens went missing one by one that year at Piper Point. Gray suddenly had scratches all up her arms, and when Joanna questioned her, she lied about where they came from. Every damn cat disappeared except the one Gray had taken a liking to."

Hattie.

"Now I don't know if she really had anything to do with the kittens disappearing, but that wouldn't be her most absurd lie. Once, when she was sixteen, she stood in this very office and lied about her name. About who she was."

I reclaimed my own seat. "I don't follow—"

Dr. Conner seemed to grow tired, perhaps even frustrated. "She told me, *tried* to convince me rather, that she wasn't Gray King, but another little girl. An *alter*, she called it. She insisted she had a particular dissociative disorder. Dissociative identity disorder, it's termed. And that Gray wasn't who I was speaking with."

"That sounds a bit far-fetched." An understatement, but something stirred in my mind, the inklings of something new. Something frightening.

"I couldn't agree more. DID is exceedingly rare and pervasively exploited." Dr. Conner tapped her nail to her bottom lip. "After the media popularized the notion in the eighties, everyone seemed to have it all of a sudden. Everyone uncovered traumatic memories, buried deep."

I finished her thought. "And used them as defenses in criminal cases."

"Correct. But I'm not inclined to believe it. I'm not a psychiatrist, of course, but the chances that Gray had more than one personality were too cosmically small to consider. But Gray, she simply would not drop it. She's a liar, but to go to such lengths?

To keep up a charade for years? As she aged, Gray's lying became pathological."

The wheels in my brain began to turn faster. Pieces started to click into place, or at least drew closer to where they fit. If Gray was a liar, pathological, as the doctor suggested, then everything she'd ever said to me would be in question.

"You mentioned trauma," I said. "Trauma that catalyzes a disorder like that. Liar or not, her account of abuse has been confirmed by others."

"Detective," Dr. Conner leaned in, lowered her voice, "you said yourself folks use dissociative disorders and buried pasts in criminal defenses. I don't need to remind you that what you're dealing with here in Elizabeth, with Paul Godfrey, it's criminal."

A sense of dread took hold, its claws squeezing my heart. As a question bubbled up in my mind, the walls of Dr. Conner's office darkened and closed in. The ground swayed and swooned as though a fierce undertow had taken hold. Was it me who'd walked into a trap? A realization come far too late as it sprang shut?

"The *alter* . . . the person Gray pretended to be in your office . . . What was her name?"

Lips pursed, Dr. Conner paused for a moment, appearing to think.

"She called herself Annie."

42

Nina

I slammed my hands against my steering wheel two, three times. How could I have been so stupid? How could I have overlooked Gray? But then again, how could I have known this? In what universe would I even have suspected it?

She'd been too drunk to do or remember anything on Christmas Eve. Everyone said so. Charlotte. Jacob. Jonas Hatfield. She'd admitted it herself right off the bat. But had I underestimated her tolerance? After all, she'd been unbelievably intoxicated after leaving Cirilo's and yet still able to somewhat operate a vehicle.

Of course, Annie never showed up at the fucking restaurant.

Different rivers of thought—each flowing separately since Christmas—began to merge. Auntie's checks from Joanna. Paul's disappearance and murder. Annie. Matthew's history of sexual assault. They were all one narrative. The story of one, single person: Gray.

As I reached to start my car, my cell phone vibrated on the passenger seat cushion.

My racing heart stopped. Nineteen missed calls. One from

Burton and the rest from Sammie. I dialed Sammie back, not bothering with the messages.

He answered on the first ring. "Nina!" His voice was loud, loud and desperate. I started to reply—to tell him what I'd uncovered—but he wouldn't let me speak.

"The IMSI-catcher," he exclaimed. "The device we used to tap the cell phones at Piper Point . . ."

I held my breath.

"Annie called Gray again," he said. "Annie used Gray's own cell phone to do it. How'd she—"

"Gray *is* Annie."

Silence on his end.

"Dr. Conner claims Gray used to call herself Annie. When she was little."

"Nina, this is too far. Burton's on the war path. He's taking you off—"

"Sammie, listen to me! Annie called from Gray's phone—"

"Forget the phone for a second. How the hell would anyone prosecute something like this? And Matthew . . . He rang up Burton, ya know—"

Matthew. What had he said when I'd confronted him at the club? I'd brushed the comment aside, too focused on little Susannah King.

"In fact, Gray called me earlier today. Said she wants to catch up."

Nothing about the woman I'd sat beside in her hospital room suggested a desire to see the man who'd molested her. But the woman who'd stabbed her jealous husband in the neck . . . *that woman* would want to catch up with Matthew. That woman would want nothing more.

"I hate this." Sammie swallowed. "This kills me, but Burton took you out. And—"

Don't say it, Sam.

"I agree with his call."

"Sammie, I fucked up. I will answer for all that. I promise. But we need to move fast. Right now. Please listen to me." I steadied my voice. "Gray isn't finished. We need to get tabs on Charlotte and Joanna. Maybe Dr. Conner. And get Matthew on the phone. Tell him to stay put."

"What the hell's going on?" Sammie asked, stunned.

"Get uniformed officers to King, Floyd, and Powers. Then get in your car. Meet me at Piper Point. I'll explain when you're on your way."

"I'll get it done, Nina, but this is it," he replied. "This is the last one."

"That's on me, Sam." My engine cranked with a smoky, coughing fit. "Right now, get to Piper Point. And bring backup."

43

Annie

The legs of the Queen Anne chair scraped against the foyer's planked floor. My broken shoulder popped, and electric pain crackled down my arm. Wincing, I pushed through.

Matthew might wake any moment.

I didn't bother precisely calculating Joanna's Valium, but I wasn't careless, either. I'd read the drug was mostly safe in large doses. Safe and alcohol-soluble. Gray had assumed her mother removed the pills from the medicine cabinet, but in fact I'd needed something to make Matthew compliant. Or at least dead weight.

Matthew arrived just after Charlotte took off. Right on schedule and long before Joanna's planned return. With everything going on, he was unable to resist a drink and a peace offering. Unable to resist *me*. On a table in the salon sat the half-empty martini I made for him. Complete with a single speared olive. Joanna might've locked the liquor cabinet, but the piece was a flimsy antique.

I'd taken a hammer to it.

Matthew stirred as I dragged the chair toward the staircase. Like the liquor cabinet and everything else in this house, Joanna's hearth chair was outdated. But it served my purpose: strong enough to contain a grown man, but weak enough to tip when he inevitably struggled.

I placed the chair at the bottom of the staircase and turned it to face the front door. I wanted the possibility of escape, of safety, to remain in his mind. Hope would make his final moments the most excruciating of his life. Perhaps more than the physical pain I'd planned. My heart fluttered. The prospect of watching him slowly come to, piecing together what happened to him—*who* happened to him—filled me with almost unbearable joy.

"Hello, Matthew." I smiled, welcoming him back to the waking world.

In an instant, any residual grogginess from the drugs evaporated. His eyes opened, bulging as though they might pop—just like Paul's. A tingle ran up the inside of my thigh. His eyes and the protruding vein crossing his forehead gave him a savage appearance. Savagely frightened.

A thump-thud followed frantic breathing through flared nostrils. Matthew began to rock in the chair, fighting against countless layers of duct tape around his legs and wrists, encircling his chest, across his mouth. He shook violently, and the chair tipped over. He moaned as his left temple struck the floor.

People were quite predictable.

"This is the moment I tell you not to struggle. That fighting is useless." I spoke with deliberate flippancy. "But to be honest, I'd prefer that you do."

Using my weight as a fulcrum, I hoisted the chair back on all four legs, angling it towards the front door once more. A second snapping arc of pain shot down my shoulder.

His cheeks puffed as he exhaled in heaving breaths through

his nose. Beads of perspiration collected on his brow. His breathing grew more regular as the initial shock of his circumstances melded into what must've been a duller, sustained panic. I'd get that erratic breathing back soon.

I smelled his adrenaline-soaked sweat as I leaned down to his ear. Flicking my tongue inside it, I whispered, "I want you to struggle hard, Matthew. I want you to struggle because I want this to last for a long, long time."

I willed my warm breath to send shivers through him as I dug into the pocket of my jeans and fished for the knife's black rubber handle. I held it in front of his eyes and watched them widen cartoonishly.

The paring knife was subtle, delicate. Stained rust-red in places with Paul's dried blood. Dulled a bit from what I'd done to him and the cat, but still plenty sharp.

I thrust it into Matthew's thigh.

He howled. As I tore it loose from the muscle, his sharp cry became an anguished baying, like an animal struck and left for dead by a reckless car.

"Why, you sound like you have something to say, cousin." I fisted a handful of his dark locks and jerked his head back, chin to the ceiling. He trembled. I slid the knife between his right cheek and the silver tape. In a single movement, I cut upwards, slashing a shallow cut beneath his eye as the gag split in two, still stuck to the sides of his face.

"Fuck!" Mouth freed, he wasted no time. "You stabbed me! What the fuck are you doing, Gray? I'm bleeding!" A spoonful of spit ran down his chin as he screamed. The disbelief on his face was exquisite. "You stabbed me!"

I'd let him think I was Gray all the way to the end. No reason to complicate the story for him since he had only a short time to hear it. I stepped in front of him, standing a few paces away. Time for him to plead his own case for once.

His twisted lips fell flat, a passing silence as he gathered his thoughts.

"Gray," he choked. "What are you doing?"

"What am I doing?" I lowered my voice, training my eyes onto his. "It was sick enough feeling your wet hands slipping in and out of me, but you decided to do it in front of a mirror, didn't you? I had to feel it, and smell it, and hear it, and *see* it. I had to watch it."

"Gray—" He coughed and a moist sound bubbled up. His face flushed with hot blood, spittle still on his lower lip. "This isn't the way to handle it. Tying me up, stabbing me? You won't solve anything. You've said your peace, and now this can end. I can make what you've done here go away. It never happened."

"Never happened?"

I plunged the knife into his other thigh. Gag-less, he wailed. The empty home echoed with his stuttering sobs.

"We were both kids!" he screamed.

My face shook. "You were seventeen! I'm goddamn family!" He clenched his eyes shut as I shouted.

"Are you going to kill me?" The distilled fear in his eyes when he opened them was real. I saw that much. The only thing he ever truly cared about—himself—was in mortal danger.

I turned up the corners of my mouth. Spreading blood soaked into his tan dress slacks from both quaking thighs. I scraped the stubble atop his Adam's apple with the dull edge of the blade and traveled down his Oxford, picking at each button with the knife's tip.

I stopped at his crotch and pressed the weapon's flattened side deep into his zipper.

"I'm going to carve you up in all the worst ways."

"Please!" Matthew screeched. He unraveled into something primal. The whites of his eyes stained red from broken blood vessels. "Stop this fucking madness!"

The chair stuttered twice, three times against the floor.

"It'll stop when I'm ready for it to stop!"

"What the hell do you think is going to happen next? You think that through at all?"

I hesitated, losing focus for a flash. "This is going to be—"

"Nothing good. This is going to be nothing good for you. My blood's on the ground, on the knife, on you. You've got one move, Gray. Let me go. Go back to D.C., and we forget this happened."

"You don't know a goddamn—"

"Either we both make it or neither of us do. You kill me, it's fucking over for you."

My knuckles whitened around the knife's hilt. He was right—this was messy. I didn't want it to go this way so soon. Between Paul's schemes and the drunken shit Gray pulled at the bar, planning went out the window. I wanted to be more careful. I was pushed.

"Let me go," he said, almost a whisper. His voice was unnervingly steady as though he was regaining his senses. He wanted me to think he was controlling his fear.

Something reflective glimmered over Matthew's shoulder. The mirror on the stair landing. Someone had brought it out from the cellar, set it back into the wall. My cheeks warmed and the tips of my ears began to burn.

"That mirror," I started, my head pounding. "Who put the fucking mirror back?"

Matthew fell silent, craned his head, "I don't know what you're asking."

A vice in my chest cranked. Numbness crawled down my arms and legs. I couldn't stop looking at the mirror now that'd I'd seen it.

"Who put it back?" I screamed.

My ears ringing, I felt control draining away like a tide. I couldn't lose control. Not now. Not—

"Gray, untie me. Let—"

44

Gray

"—me go."

Pinewood planks groaned under my shifting weight. I stood inside Piper Point. The foyer, specifically.

I must've blacked out again.

But I've had nothing to drink.

My heart beat against my sternum with each pulse, my right hand throbbed. I clung to a small knife so tightly my fingers cramped. Drops of fresh, oily blood dotted the blade. Why was I holding a knife?

A man's voice cried out. "Gray, we won't ever talk about this again."

Matthew?

I turned, facing my cousin, and my thumping heart stilled. He'd been tied to a chair in front of the staircase. What the hell was happening?

"Please," he repeated between broken breaths. "We were children. Just go home. Leave me. Leave Elizabeth. No one will hear about any of this."

Was he bleeding? Nausea swept over me, and I stumbled backwards, catching my weight with one leg before I fell.

Steadying myself, I noted my surroundings—the house, the staircase, Matthew's injuries. A sensation of detachment edged into my mind. Everything became abstract. Surreal and blurred around the edges.

Except for one thing, vivid and magnetic: the landing mirror.

Matthew's pleading barely registered as I walked towards the mirror. One foot in front of the other, I started up the creaking, sagging steps. The knife remained firmly in my right hand.

As I inched closer to the landing, my reflection materialized on the enormous glass surface. The top of my head first, auburn hair tied back yet disheveled. Then my face. Only I didn't recognize it. It looked like me. Our eyes were the same color. Our cheekbones and faint freckles and lashes, all the same. An identical scar from a childhood tumble, nearly invisible, cut a centimeter across the left brow. But I didn't recognize the woman staring back. She was someone else.

"This has been a long time coming, hasn't it Gray?" The woman's voice was my own, yet lowered by an octave. And darker.

"I don't know who you are," I told her.

The woman's lips—exactly like mine—cracked an unsettling smile. "Of course you do, Hummingbird."

Silent, I stepped closer to the mirror. Long shadows formed beneath the woman's eyes as she lowered her head, gaze tightly focused on mine.

"You've known me for a very, very long time." She glanced from one side to the other. "Why, this is where we first met. Right here in this mirror."

"I don't understand." Was I hallucinating from alcohol withdrawal? A severe hallucination of talking to my own reflection?

The woman on the other side seemed to find this humorous.

"Of course, you don't understand. You don't understand much of anything. But I should be thankful for that."

"Who are you?" Holding my breath, I braced for her answer.

The humor disappeared from her face. "You really are that stupid, aren't you?"

Another step.

"After all I've done for you, I'd expect some gratitude, but that's never been your strong suit."

I froze. How was this even possible? My throat turned to sandpaper, and I swallowed a scratchy lump.

"Who the hell are you talking to?" Matthew's piercing voice broke through, mirroring my own thoughts. "Your fucking reflection?"

I directed my attention back to the woman who stood before me in the glass. I choked, drew in a staccato breath. "You're Annie. I—I'm—"

She smiled, wryly. "I'm Paul's Annie. I'm Matthew's Annie. But most of all, Hummingbird. I'm *your* Annie."

Her words unwrapped snippets of memory. Unspooled them like Christmas ribbon. "You called. Asked me to meet you at Cirilo's. Emailed me the photos. Killed—"

The smile fell from her face. "I had to kill Paul. To save myself. To save both of us. But that's always been my job, hasn't it? To save us. He was going to kill you—and me," she replied.

I remembered that night, after the dance floor at Ruby's. Somehow, I knew she—*I*—spoke the truth.

The rain had grown into a downpour while we'd been inside the bar. It lashed against our car as we sped through winding darkness. Forehead pressed against the passenger window, I watched droplets streak by like tiny comets.

The car abruptly pulling over and braking caused me to

bump my head against the glass. My door opened, but instead of tumbling out, I was caught by someone. *Paul.* He hoisted me out of the car, stood me upright, and then jerked me—violently—into the woods.

That's why I'd been so sore Christmas morning. Because Paul had been ruthless. Because he'd meant for me to die anyway. He hadn't been concerned with causing pain or the memory of it.

She did it. She really killed him. *I killed him.*

Matthew seemed to hear the same thing I did. "You murdered your husband, Gray? *You* killed Paul?" A pause, and his chair bounced up and down with renewed desperation.

"Help!" He screamed into the empty foyer. "Help me!"

Annie wasn't done reminiscing. "Charlotte didn't dress you for bed that night. Paul sure as hell didn't—he'd gone cold by then"

I hesitated, "You dressed me for bed."

"A nightie. Silk. Got rid of your soiled clothes." Annie went on, ignoring Matthew's struggle behind us. "You're a drunk, but you're the best sort of drunk. A rich one. Paul thought so, too. Bet you didn't know that."

"What do you mean? It was about money?" It didn't make sense for Paul to go through such trouble for funds that were already his.

"Not *just* about money. You're many things, but most of all, you're a liability. To everyone in your life. To Joanna. To Charlotte. Shit, even to me. But to Paul? Such a capable young man? As dapper as he was politically astute? You were a ticking time bomb."

I spoke slowly. "He thought I'd ruin everything, didn't he? The run for office. Everything."

"Somebody help me!" Matthew again.

Annie replied, "That's right, Gray. You want to know the exact moment he decided the risk outweighed any benefit you might provide?"

I knew the answer to her question. "When he came home from Toronto. When I threatened him if he didn't buy me a bottle of wine."

"Correct. That's when he decided you had to go. But killing you happened to have an enormous silver lining. An irresistible bonus that swept divorce off the table."

"Daddy's trust," I whispered.

A peal of laughter flew from her mouth. "And his money problems? The ones you've been ignoring all these years?" She raised her left hand, snapping her fingers. "Gone."

"Jesus Christ!" Matthew screeched behind me.

Annie shook her head. "No doubt, he'd originally planned to be diligent about it. There's a million and one ways for an alcoholic to die without anyone batting an eyelash. You could have taken a tumble. Washed down ten too many Xanax with your ninth glass of wine—"

"I could have drowned in a marsh . . ."

". . . after you took off running into the rainy night. Too upset and distraught and confused to know where you'd stumbled till it was too late. And after the stunt you pulled with Jacob, I knew it was coming. He pulled over on the highway shoulder. He marched our drunk ass right down to the water's edge."

My teeth began to chatter. The only way someone like me could be a better wife was to be a dead one.

Behind me, Matthew's chair scraped against hardwood again. "Please, Gray," he cried. "You've gone off the fucking deep end!"

But I only stared deeper into the mirror as Annie went on.

"I'd come prepared, though. I had a feeling things were coming to a head even before the bar. Paul was far too eager to leave D.C. Getting away with murder isn't easy—I'd know—but it's a tad easier in Elizabeth."

My hand grew sorer. I clenched the knife handle so tightly, my arm shook.

"You're so weak, Gray. When Matthew first touched us, you couldn't face the truth of what happened. What kept happening. Every time he cornered us, it was me who took it. I took the pain so you wouldn't have to. But I'm sick of your fragility. The way you were around Paul. Your spinelessness made me retch. I couldn't take it anymore."

I'm Annie. I've lost my fucking mind. Maybe it splintered years ago, but now—confronting myself—it finally broke. My knuckles whitened around the knife. It grew difficult to hold my hand back. I wanted to kill her. I wanted to kill myself.

"You were easy to break. A handful of phone messages and some nasty pictures of Paul." Annie spit. "One dead cat. You were already so close to the edge. Pushing you over it was simple."

"You're fucking insane!" Matthew shouted again, bouncing the back legs against the floor harder. A popping sound as one of the legs began to crack. It would break any moment. "Someone help me!"

"What are you going to do?" My shaking intensified.

"I'll be killing that noisy fucker behind you for starters. Then it's your turn, Gray. You're going into the dark, and you're never coming out again." She sneered, hate swirling in both eyes. "You don't deserve life. Every privilege has been extended your way, and you've done nothing but squander them. You're a damned ingrate. That's all you are."

My fist trembled.

"You are a weak, ungrateful bitch."

Her words struck me like a lead pipe. Her face, her twisted smile.

My fist flew into the landing mirror. A spider web of fractured glass splintered across its surface. In an instant, my reflection shattered into hundreds of pieces. Searing heat shot up my arm from the shards buried deep inside my hand. Where there had been a single Annie, there now stood countless more. Each laughing wildly. Fiery eyes multiplied across jagged edges.

"You can't destroy me," each Annie laughed in unison. "I'm not inside this damned mirror. I'm inside you."

45

Nina

My engines revved as I floored the gas, rocketing down Paul Revere Highway. The place we'd first found the abandoned rental car whirled by. The turn for Atalaya Drive came up, and my weight shifted as I cut into it too fast. Tires squealing.

Piper Point stood on the distant bluff. Ominous. Almost evil against the serene backdrop of the inlet marsh. A sprawling, rotten house.

Screeching to a halt before the looming, pillared porch, a bolt of adrenaline shot through me. The front door stood wide open. Another car had parked out front. One I didn't recognize. A Porsche so yellow it almost looked neon beneath the pink evening sun.

A vanity plate read M KING. My stomach knotted. I might be too late.

Sliding my keys out of the ignition, I hesitated. *I should wait for Sammie. I should wait for the uniforms.* I had no idea what to expect, what scene I might stumble on inside Piper Point. But one thing was certain—danger lurked in that house. Gray or Annie or both were inside. Likely alongside the object of their shared hate. One spark and everything might erupt in flames.

I should wait for backup. That's protocol. It's for my own safety.

A noise escaped from somewhere deep inside the house. A moaning that sent a shiver down my back. Someone was in pain. Someone needed help now.

I grabbed the receiver. "I've got a probable location on Matthew King. Send a bus. I'm going to enter the home."

"Hold off, Nina," Sammie answered from his own car before the dispatcher confirmed my message was received. "I'm minutes away."

"Possible injury. I'm entering."

Another message crackled over. *Burton.* "Nina, just what in the goddamn hell do you think you're—" I closed the car door behind me. Heart on fire, I drew my weapon and steadied my arms as I followed the tip of my gun up the porch steps.

The moaning grew louder through the open front door. A baying, long and low, that sounded almost . . . wet. The porch planks whined under my boots. My heart pounded its way up my throat. I entered.

White with terror, Matthew quaked in a chair he'd been bound to. He appeared to be alone. Someone had wounded him, but his blood-soaked clothes made it impossible to gauge how badly. He wasn't gagged any longer, but from his trembling, he was plainly in shock.

"Help me!"

I nodded in the affirmative.

Both feet now in the foyer, I turned to my left and right. The salon—empty. The library—empty. What I could see of the dining room—empty, too.

A moaning trickled from Matthew's lips like a dripping faucet. I cringed at the sound. No matter who he was or what he'd done, a sudden compassion swept over me. I fought back a primal urge to put him out of his misery. Instead, I focused on survival. Matthew might be the only person I saw, but we weren't alone. *She* was here, too.

"Gray?" I called out to the house. No point in keeping quiet. She must've heard my car pull up. From nearly any window, she'd have seen me driving for a mile. "Gray, are you here? It's Nina."

No answer.

Matthew ceased moaning. Hearing Gray's name seemed to silence him.

"Gray, I know you're here." I cast another glance Matthew's way. The blood appeared to be coming from injuries on both thighs and a cut to the cheek. "We need to talk."

A sudden noise rang out behind me. My shoulders jumped, and I turned. The grandfather clock chimed for the quarter-hour. I exhaled and breathed deeply. "Gray, please talk to me."

Nearly to the stairs, I froze. A thought crossed my mind, and my stomach tightened. *Perhaps Gray isn't here.*

As fear inched up my spine, I did my best to call out clearly. "Annie?"

The ceiling creaked, suggesting footsteps in the room above me. If I remembered correctly, Gray's room. The steps traveled to the top of the staircase.

The landing mirror halfway up the stairs had been smashed. Shards lay strewn around its base, leaving only sharp pieces jutting from its frame. A pair of legs reflected in its jagged teeth as they came down the stairs one slow step at a time.

Her face came next. Her knuckles bled.

"Annie?" I asked once more as Gray—*no, Annie*—paced closer towards me. Her hands appeared to be empty, but I trained my gun on her.

"You found me." She caressed Matthew's shoulder as she brushed by him.

Her touch thawed his shock. Voice cracking, he shouted, "She's got a knife!"

I squeezed my gun's grip tighter. "Then it's you? It's Annie?" Time was the one thing I desperately needed. I'd stall for as much as I could get. Liar or not, playing along with Gray was my best bet.

"It is." Her voice assumed an altogether different tone. If Gray was acting, she was damn good. "Who spilled the beans? Mary-Ann? She's the only one I've ever spoken to. But that was when I was younger. Before I knew better. Before I had a plan."

"That's not true," I countered. She paused mid-step. "The pictures you sent to yourself . . . to Gray. You've spoken to Paul. Been intimate with him."

She cracked a grin. It turned my stomach. "Mary-Ann was the only one who ever *knew* she was speaking to me," she corrected. "Paul thought he'd lucked out in the bedroom. That quiet, demure Gray was secretly a woman of fetish." Her eyes glowed like lit candles. "I guess he figured she owed him at least that much. Drunk in the streets, freak in the sheets."

A lump rose in my throat. She took another step closer. I took aim squarely at her chest.

"Stop there," I ordered. "Don't move." Halfway between myself and Matthew, she halted.

"No, Paul never knew about me." She shook her head, that grin still plastered across her darkened face. "Not even at the end. He needed to think Gray did it. To know Gray had killed him. Hurt more that way." She tensed her jaw.

A single car braked outside. Then the clamor of doors opening and shutting. Frantic voices. Joanna asking why the front door was open. The housekeeper, too. The women walked into the foyer together. Cora unleashed a horrid scream.

My eyes focused on Annie, I steadied my voice. "Go back outside, Joanna. Take Cora. Go back outside, and let me speak with your daughter."

"Gray? What in Jesus' name? What's happened?" Joanna cried. "Charlotte called frightened to death. She met us in town and grabbed those boys. On her way back to Raleigh by now." She gasped, likely spying a bound Matthew over my shoulder. "What in . . . ?"

"Aunt Joanna," Matthew hollered. "Talk to her! Talk to Gray!"

"Go," I shouted. "Ambulance is on the way."

Cora turned and leapt down the porch steps. Joanna remained in the foyer. I cursed under my breath. Why didn't she ever listen?

"Gray," Joanna spoke softly, standing shoulder to shoulder next to me. "Gray, listen to Nina. I don't know what's happened here, but—"

"Really?" Annie scoffed. "You can't for the life of you piece it together? Any of it?" She looked wildly at Matthew, drenched in his own blood, then back at her mother.

Joanna choked. "I can." Her composure buckled. "I can, Hummingbird . . . and I'm . . . I'm so sorry."

"Sorry?" Annie laughed. "You're sorry? You're fucking *sorry*?"

Joanna's trembling shoulder brushed mine as she took a step closer. "Hummingbird, please understand. I've made a mistake. I know I have, but—"

Gray whipped a knife out from her pocket. I jolted but stopped short of pulling my trigger. She staggered backwards to Matthew.

"Put down the knife, Annie!" I shouted as she brought it to Matthew's throat.

"Please, Gray," he moaned. "Please don't."

Joanna turned to me. "Annie? Why did you call her . . ." Her eyes widened and her bottom lip shook like the rest of her body. Casting grieved eyes back to her daughter, disbelief poured into her words. "Gray? You're . . . *you're* Annie?"

"That's what happens when you don't get your own daughter help, Joanna," Annie called back. "That's what fucking happens when you cover it up, when you lie. When you bury it!"

"It festers, Joanna," Annie continued. "It festers and rots and it never goes away." She pressed the sharp edge of her knife deeper into Matthew's throat. A tiny crimson droplet fell to his collar. "It only gets worse. It gets . . . infected."

"Don't do it, Annie. Don't make me shoot you," I pleaded.

"Tell them, Matthew," Annie ordered. "Tell them what you did."

As he mumbled, saliva bubbled from between his trembling lips.

"Tell them how you betrayed Gray!" Annie screamed, rattling the room.

"I . . . I touched her," he whimpered. The knife pressed deeper into his throat. "I *raped* Gray. When we were younger, and I'm . . . I'm sorry . . ."

The fury on Annie's face evolved into something else. Something like amusement. "You know, Matthew," she started, eyes still locked on mine. "If I recall correctly, Gray wasn't the only one down in that cellar." Her voice hardened, cemented in hate. "Gray wasn't the only one who saw the Devil that day."

I narrowed my eyes. "You saw the Devil, too, didn't you, Matthew?" Annie asked, knife still pressed against the swollen artery inside his neck. "Did you see the Devil? Did you look him in the eyes?"

Matthew shuddered, mouth hung halfway open.

"Did you see him?"

"Yeah . . . yes," he coughed.

"Tell me!"

"I—I saw the Devil."

"Then what does that make you? What does that make you, Matthew?"

"It makes me—It makes me a . . ." His voice dwindled to a whisper. "A bad . . ."

"Tell everyone what it makes you," Annie hissed. "Tell us all what seeing the Devil makes you. Tell everyone what you made me say! What are you, cousin?"

"I'm a . . . I'm a bad girl."

"Louder!"

"I'm a bad girl," Matthew screamed. His head fell limp, rolled downwards. He began to cry. To heave.

Joanna unraveled next to me. "I'll get you help, Gray. I know you need it. I'll get you the help we should've gotten you decades ago." She sobbed uncontrollably now, too. Despite everything, her tears shocked me. "If I could take it back, I would. I regret it every day. Please believe me. No matter what happens, I'll die knowing I've failed you." She drew in a stuttered breath, clasped her hands together as if in prayer. Shaking them at her daughter, she begged, "I'll die knowing I'm a failed mother, Gray."

"I'm not fucking *Gray*," Annie spat. Her eyes returned to mine. The contempt in them said time was running out. It wouldn't be long before she put an end to it.

I swallowed a lump in my throat and tensed. Maybe Gray wasn't the shameless liar Mary-Ann thought.

"This was always a suicide mission, wasn't it?" I asked her, balancing my voice. "This was always your plan. Take down Paul, Matthew, then Gray."

Her eyes danced around the room. I sensed the pressure building inside her. The frantic search for a next move. But there weren't any more moves. She held a knife. I held a gun. But Annie could still win. She could take them both down. Matthew with a swift stab to the throat, prompting me to shoot her. Suicide by cop.

If I had to kill Annie, I'd kill Gray, too.

Silence swallowed the room. Pounding hearts and heaving breaths, the only sounds.

Annie raised the knife, lunged. Joanna screamed.

I fired.

* * *

The gunshot would've rang out across the marsh. Echoing through the tree line, bouncing from trunk to trunk. Sending flocks of birds scuttling into the air.

As I emerged from Piper Point's darkness, I squinted at the setting sun. Police sirens wailed from the front yard. Red and blue lights flashed. Car doors opened and shut. Gun drawn by his side, Sammie's eyes searched mine for an answer. I couldn't give him one. A distant ambulance made its way down Atalaya Drive, followed by a fire truck. Uniformed officers rushed past me.

Sheriff Burton slammed his car door, bringing up the rear of the line. When he spotted me, he ran my way instead, yanking his sunglasses from his red face. "Nina, you are fucking finished in this town—"

"You knew."

He stopped in his tracks, breathing heavy from the jog. "What the hell are you talking about?"

I spoke coolly, almost detached. "You knew about Matthew. And you sat on it because you were told to."

Eyes narrowed, he stood in silence. He seemed afraid, too. For a flash, I wondered if he'd appeared the same way before Seamus King decades ago. He ran his hand over his face, as if to refocus himself. Then he made for the front door. The conversation was left unfinished. For now.

Behind where Burton had stood, a gaggle of sandpipers, the sort of bird the property was named for, perched motionless in the crabgrass a dozen yards or so from the commotion.

Countless pairs of beady, black eyes glowered at me.

Funny, I thought to myself. I'd discharged a weapon, and they hadn't been startled off. Instead, they scowled at me— fearlessly—as though I was an intruder.

Unwelcome in their world.

Epilogue

Nina

Two months later

This particular March day was a hot one, even for South Carolina. Haze wafted off the asphalt, mocking the whole idea of four seasons. Wiping sweat from my brow, I turned the air conditioner higher. A vain attempt—it broke a couple weeks back—but I still fiddled with it out of habit.

What a day to wear black.

I drove somewhere in the middle of the convoy as it rolled through downtown Elizabeth. I hadn't felt compelled to get closer to the front. I let everyone else fight over those coveted spots.

We drove by all the familiar sights. The sheriff's office on Marion Avenue. The Dairy Queen—filled to capacity with folks fresh from Sunday sermons. The steepled church on Main Street, Blessed Lamb Baptist. Joanna King's church.

We'd driven in a long line from the funeral home on the east side of town. The Elizabeth County Cemetery, our destination.

Before long, we reached the spiked iron gates that cordoned off the graveyard from the rest of Elizabeth, where the living still dwelled. Two motorcycle officers had dutifully escorted us. Now they waved the line of vehicles onto the grounds, flashers strobing in silence.

Pulling round the canvassed open grave, I parked and exited the car. Tugging at the hem of my dress, I drank in the crowd of mourners already gathered. Joanna King stood to one side in head-to-toe black. The parts of her face her wide-brimmed hat didn't mask were obscured by enormous sunglasses.

Halfway to the graveside, I paused. I took a deep breath and then puffed out my cheeks. It was time.

Joanna glanced my way as I approached, then cast her covered eyes back to the gravestone. I followed her gaze to it. It looked better than I expected. Cleaner. Crisper. I read the name etched across it.

Matilda Beverly Palmer.

"Join me now in song," Auntie's pastor announced as the last attendees climbed the tiny slope to her casket. "'Bridge Over Troubled Water.' One of Tilda's favorites."

The pastor began to sing. Others joined him. Parting my lips, I whispered the lyrics to myself. As I sang, I thought of Auntie. Of her long life, of her cotton robe. The one I'd carefully tucked into a box at the top of my closet. Auntie smelled like home. Like love and warmth and perseverance. I'd treasure her scent on the cloth for as long as it lasted. Like hugs that were otherwise now impossible.

"I'm so sorry, Nina," Joanna said, startling me. She'd slipped over as the funeral ended, and now stood next to me beside Auntie's grave. The only other time we'd stood so close had been that day in Piper Point's foyer.

"Thank you," I replied, eyes straight ahead.

"She meant so much to the family, too," she added.

"Did she?" I asked in a biting tone.

Joanna fell silent. Focused squarely on the casket, I sought to squash any anger towards her. Auntie's funeral wasn't the place for ill feelings. "How's Gray doing?" I asked instead.

"The wound on her leg from . . . from the incident . . . is healing nicely. She's on crutches now. No more wheeling about." She lowered her voice to a near-whisper. "The doctors at the Charleston hospital seem to have found a combination of drugs that shows promise. There's been no . . . you know."

Joanna seemed to readily buy into the idea Gray and Annie really were two different people. But, it was too convenient for me. Still, I wasn't privy to Gray's psychiatrists' conclusions and Joanna likely was. It certainly gave the Kings the deniability they craved.

"That's good to hear. I plan to visit her in the next couple days."

"She'll really like that, I think." Joanna smiled. "To be honest, we're both anxious for the trial to begin. I've never been patient, but I know we have to get her better before any of that."

"She won't go to prison," I replied. "She'll stay in a hospital." The irony of my words struck me. Here I stood at Auntie's funeral, assuring Joanna *her* daughter would be okay. Maybe Gray wasn't a liar, or maybe she was, but the truth was she'd never see the inside of a cell.

"Speaking of prison," Joanna said, "are you close to charging Matthew? I understand Mary-Ann Conner agreed to testify."

"Between that, the statement from Auntie, and, well, everything with Gray, there's a case. A small one, but it's there. Most importantly, his wife Ellen took Susannah with her to her parent's home in Atlanta." I hesitated. "I've also lodged a formal complaint against Sheriff Burton. You'll get a call asking what you told the police that night years ago. And what your husband told Burton next. I'd appreciate honesty this time."

Visibly relieved, Joanna exhaled. A pang of anger shot through me. The woman didn't deserve relief. Not a single ounce.

"You've done something terrible, Joanna." I said, evenly. "There's no statute of limitations on child endangerment, either. If anyone else deserves to go to prison, it's you."

She drew in a deep breath, turned her head my way. Behind her sunglasses, I knew her eyes were tightly focused on mine. "Build your case, Detective Palmer. Then do as you see fit."

I couldn't tell if her remark was meant as a challenge or an actual invitation. I wondered if a part of her agreed with me. Knew she had crimes to pay for.

But then Joanna did what Joanna King always did best. She brushed past the uncomfortable—the unpleasant. She buried it deep beneath her Charleston drawl. "In the meantime, do me a favor, would you? I've made a banana pudding. It's always been Gray's favorite. You mind taking it to her when you visit?"

* * *

I rolled down my window as I crossed Charleston Harbor. The sea breeze stilled my mind. Gave me a sense of peace. The silver cables of the Arthur Ravenel Jr. Bridge whisked by on both sides. The bridge was immense. One of the longest cable-stayed bridges in the Western Hemisphere, I'd read somewhere. A monument to modernity in a city frozen in time. A jarring contrast against a skyline unchanged since the nineteenth century. Like everything else in South Carolina, the scene came off as appropriately incongruous. A place that truly had no idea what it wanted to be.

Its namesake, Mr. Ravenel, had been a prominent politician, first in the state senate and then Congress, like Seamus King. A part of me wondered if the bridge might've born his name had things turned out differently for him. For Auntie Tilda. For Gray.

When I arrived at the university hospital downtown, an escort promptly ushered me to a secluded ward.

"Would you mind waiting for Mrs. Godfrey in here?" He asked.

"Of course," I replied, gauging the space. Sparse, which I'd expected. A handful of cushioned chairs. Walls painted a soothing green. A large window overlooked the harbor and the colonial estates, all painted rainbow colors, that crowded around it. I sat Joanna's casserole dish of banana pudding on the chair next to me.

Five minutes passed. Then ten. Then twenty. Finally, the room's only door opened, and Gray hobbled in, leaning on one crutch. The tiniest of smiles crossed her face.

Standing, I shook her free hand. "It's great to see you, Gray. You look better. Much better."

It wasn't a polite lie; she did look much better. She wore comfortable sweats, and her hair was tied back into the same ponytail she always kept. But the bags under her eyes had vanished. The dark circles, paled. Her skin glowed—hydrated fully in the absence of alcohol.

"Should we sit?" she asked, motioning to the chairs.

I moved the casserole dish to the other side of me and helped her limp into a seat. She leaned her crutch against the armrest. "Banana pudding courtesy of your mother," I announced. "Your favorite, I think."

"No," she answered. "Not really. But it's a nice thought."

"So," I began, brushing my thighs nervously. "You're getting well?"

"You mean to ask if Annie has disappeared?" She chuckled, and I wondered if she saw doubt in my eyes. The doubt I held that Annie even existed. "I'm on about six or seven different medications. The irony of which isn't lost on me. There's a mood-stabilizer. An antidepressant. Something for anxiety. Something to get me to sleep. Another to wake me up . . ." She laughed.

All things considered, it relieved me to see her laugh. From what I understood, recovery was inextricably linked to one's frame of mind. Their outlook. And regardless of the truth—the truth *only* Gray knew—I did want her to be better. After Matthew, after what she'd alleged Paul had planned, my heart hurt for her. She could've grown into an entirely different woman if she'd had the love and protection family was meant to afford. Maybe she still could be that woman.

"They tell me to take it one day at a time." Gray sighed. "Which is what I'm doing."

"And how about the counseling? Has that been helpful?"

She rubbed her fingers against her palms. "At first it wasn't easy, but I'm getting the hang of it. Talking things out, that is. I've got a wonderful therapist. She reminds me of . . ." she hesitated. "Of my sister. I've told her as much, and we're determined to address me and Charlotte's estrangement when I'm healthy enough."

I cast my eyes down until the uncomfortable mention of Charlotte passed, and Gray spoke again. "But, I haven't had a drop to drink in over a month. Longest I've gone in years. Funny how sharp my mind's been these days, even with all the medication."

"You're going to get healthy, Gray," I told her warmly. "I know you are."

She smiled. "Denial's a way of saving yourself from some awful truth. Something so terrible, so categorically horrible, you believe acknowledging it might break you. I know now the breaking of a person isn't the worst that can happen."

"What do you mean?" I asked, though I already knew.

She seemed to grow tired as she answered. Her glowing cheeks flushed with fatigue. "When a person breaks, it's a frightening thing. Not because of what's undone, but because of what might be unleashed." She met my eyes. "The very rotten thing that might be unleashed. But that's the thing I must accept. I have to take responsibility for what I've done and turn the rot into something new. Become a different woman than I was before."

A hospital orderly rapped on the door and peeked inside. "Mrs. Godfrey, we'll have to be getting back now. Lunch time." He tapped a leather wristwatch.

"King. Ms. King," she corrected him. "And I know. Every calorie counts. Doctor's orders."

"That's right," he said, beaming. "I'll be back to collect that dish, too. When the desk checked it over, they said they'd never smelled such a yummy pudding." With that, he left to let us finish the visit in private.

I stood and helped Gray to her feet, tucking her crutch under her arm. I held the door open as she hobbled towards it. The orderly had vanished somewhere down the hall. I reckoned Gray knew where to go from here.

"One last thing, Nina." She stopped and turned to another door just outside the room. "Do you mind helping me wash my hands for lunch?"

"Certainly," I answered. The second door opened into a single toilet bathroom. I stood in the doorway, propping it open as she lathered and rinsed her hands. I passed her a paper towel to dry them.

"Banana pudding. I said it's not my favorite," she stated, toweling her hands dry. She cast her eyes into the tiny mirror hanging above the faucet. They met mine in the reflection. "It's Gray's."

Acknowledgments

I wrote *The End*, and then the work began.

A tremendous debt of gratitude is owed to the entire team at Crooked Lane Books, but most of all, my editor: Chelsey Emmelhainz. Thank you for your unending patience, bottomless well of wisdom and encouragement, and breathing life into this story. It couldn't have found a fiercer advocate. Likewise, I owe my agent, Chris Bucci of CookeMcDermid, enormous thanks for his invaluable insight and support. I'm in over my head without you.

A very special thank you is owed to Beth Phelan and the writers, agents, and editors who organize and participate in #DVpit. The #DVpit mission is powerful and cannot be overstated.

I'm so fortunate to have family and friends whose thoughtful questioning and candid support elevated this work beyond anything I alone could do. April, Christa, Chris M., Craig, Daniel, Dee, Jodi, Justin, Kathy, Katie, Kristen, Lise, Liz, Paul, Renée, Rhiannon, Swati, and many others: Thank you.

My parents, Mark and Mary. Thank you for stoking my zeal

for life. I'd never believe I should if you'd never taught me that I could.

Finally, Barry. Your faith and love has carried me over the finish line.